The Arsonist

The Arsonist

Children of Strife
The Arsonist

Tyler Kirk

Illustrated by Hank Cunnington

The Arsonist

Copyright © 2023 by Tyler Kirk

All rights reserved.

No part of this publication may be reproduced, distributed, or transmitted in any form or by any means, including photocopying, recording, or other electronic or mechanical methods, without the prior written permission of the publisher, except as permitted by U.S. copyright law. For permission requests, contact Tyler Kirk.

The story, all names, characters, and incidents portrayed in this production are fictitious. No identification with actual persons (living or deceased), places, buildings, and products is intended or should be inferred.

Book Cover and Illustrations by Hank Cunnington

2nd edition © 2025

ISBN 9798280947023

Tyler Kirk

The Arsonist

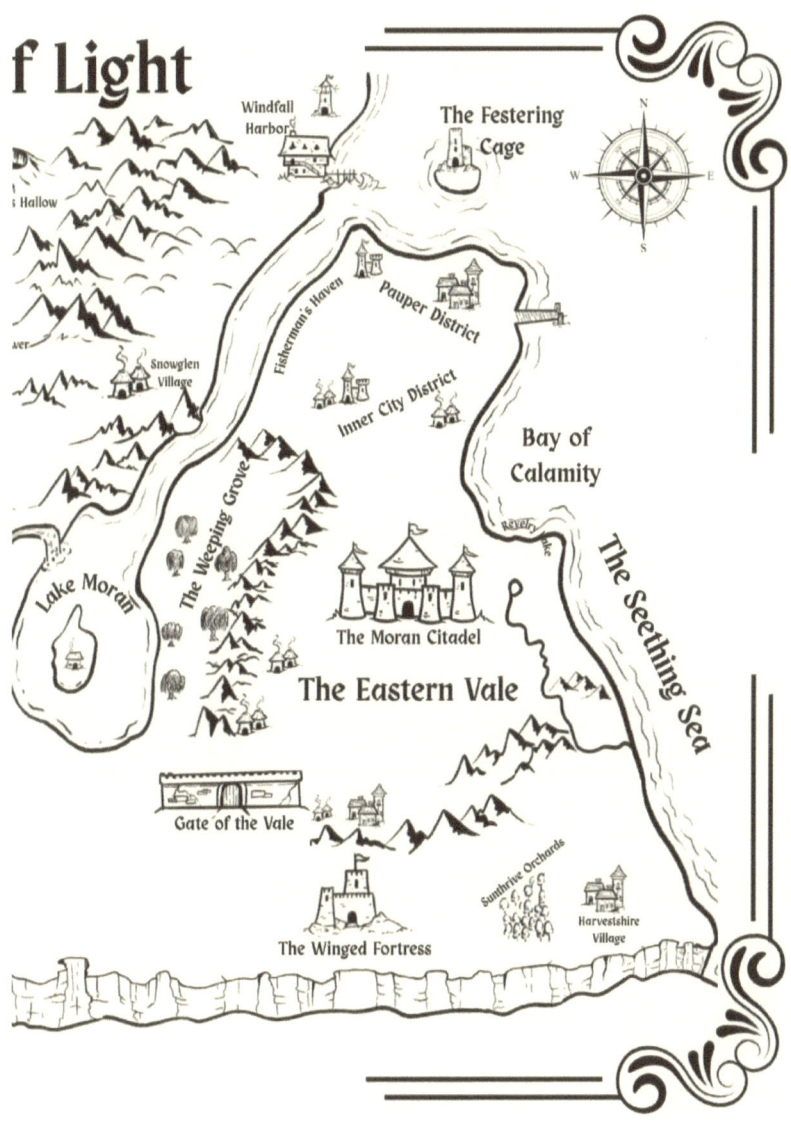

The Arsonist

Prologue

    The porcelain mask he wore bore no mouth or nose, just eye slits adorned with red wings coming out of the corners. It concealed his faintly glowing red eyes and foggy breath. He was a regular stranger in this town, always keeping a low profile. A dark cloth hood helped draw less attention to him on the crowded streets of Yokelshire as he led his horse Xenos by his bridle.
    A cool breeze blew through the autumn trees, causing their frost-touched leaves to sound off in a scratchy melody. The bleak backdrop that was the grey sky above showed promise of afternoon rain. The masked man stopped in front of the Rusted Pitchfork Inn; he contemplated going inside, for unlike the streets he carefully walked, the inn appeared quite vacant. It did not have a good reputation for it rarely saw travelers.

The Arsonist

The lantern post on the street outside had collected crisscrossed spider webs that glistened like crystal dream catchers. The cool breeze returned and pushed through the buttonholes of the man's long coat. He decided not to enter the inn; it was too risky. He was looking for a bounty he could complete for coin while doing his best to avoid anyone who might recognize the one for his head. He pulled his horse down the street to where the help-wanted task board made of wood resided. As he approached it, he shook his head in disgust before ripping off a wanted poster and stuffing it into his coat's pocket. It read, *Wanted: The Arsonist* in black ink. The man smirked behind his mask as he read the price tag on it.

"If I can't find a bounty by nightfall, I may have to turn myself in so I can afford to buy us some food, Xenos," he said. While gently patting his horse, he noticed a very tan-skinned man in a straw hat approaching the task board. His wet green eyes and shivering body told a story of fear and desperation. The dusty and muddy clothing he wore was poor, and it revealed to the masked man that he was likely to be one of the many local farmers in Yokelshire. He led his horse by its bridle as he neared the masked man.

"Are you posting work or looking for it?" the farmer asked.

"I'm not interested in agriculture if that's what you need help with," the masked man replied. He felt confident that the man in the straw hat was not looking for farmland help, but he wanted to be sure.

The farmer shook his head miserably. "They grabbed my farmhand, Billy, and I knew I couldn't save him. Their claws and fangs were already dug deep into him before I could even react, so I sealed the barn behind me before making my way to Yokelshire to find help."

"What did they look like?"

"Well, he was about this tall," the farmer lifted his hand to the bottom of his chin to show how tall Billy might have been.

"Not the farmhand, the people that grabbed him," he said as he stepped closer to the farmer.

"They were those creatures I keep hearing about, just like in the stories they were pale and red-eyed," he said.

The masked man attempted to look down behind his mask to help conceal his faintly glowing red eyes while listening to the farmer.

"So, are you looking for work? It's not every day that a traveler comes through Yokelshire seeking food and lodging."

"I am looking for work, but I request half the payment upfront and the other half when the job is complete," he said as his red eyes gazed into the worried eyes of the farmer in the straw hat. A chill shot down the spine of the farmer. He was too desperate and scared to question the masked man's glowing eyes.

"Alright, I'll agree to your terms and pay you upfront, but we need to leave town and head back to my land right away," he said. The masked man nodded as he mounted his horse. The farmer mounted his horse, and together with the man in the mask, they made haste out of the town and into the nearby forest.

Chapter One

The sound of two galloping horses echoed through the Amberwood forest, shaking the silence off the trees and frightening the chirping birds away. The riders brought their horses to a halt as they entered the glade. One, who was wearing a straw hat, looked over to the dark hooded rider and nodded at him to confirm that they had arrived.

"We should dismount here. I don't want to risk getting bucked off my horse when it hears the shrieking," the farmer said.

"Mine is used to the shrieking, but I will continue on foot with you if that is what you wish," the dark hooded rider replied. He maintained control of his horse as he slid down the side and descended to the ground. His cavalier boots immediately sank into the muddy pasture below.

"Damnit," he said. His dimly lit red eyes narrowed behind his porcelain mask he wore as he looked down at his boots that were now caked in mud. The mask he wore bore no mouth or nose, just eye slits adorned with red wings coming out of the corners.

"What is it?" The farmer asked. His worried scrawny green eyes gazed at the dark rider as he tried to pull up his brown pauper pants with his left palm.

"Nothing. Let's keep moving," the dark hooded rider replied.

Both men trudged their way through the mud while paying no attention to the rain clouds that sat high in the sky, ready to unleash a downpour at any given moment. When their boots finally made contact with the grass that stretched out before them like an ocean of emeralds, the man in the straw hat moved his right arm in front of the dark hooded man to prevent him from taking one step further.

"Like I said back at the tavern, that barn over there by my farmhouse is where I found them, the terrible noises that they make seem to be gone so maybe they're dead now, but—,"

"They're not dead, they just haven't noticed us yet."

"Well, when they grabbed my farmhand Billy, I knew I couldn't save him, their claws and fangs were already dug deep into him before I could react and so I ran for my life and sealed the barn behind me before making my way to Yokelshire to find help."

"I remember you telling me this just moments before we departed the tavern."

"I'm sorry, I just still can't believe this happened. I mean, I heard the stories about those infected with the black blood, but I just never thought I'd actually see them, especially so close to my home of all places." The farmer's skin was weather-beaten by long hours in the sun. His dark hooded companion had his attention fixed on the distant, looming barn. His eyes glowed a soft red, the porcelain mask they sunk behind did nothing to hinder his view of the structure and the surrounding auburn-colored trees.

"Alright, now that we have arrived at our destination, and I have had a chance to assess the situation, I think it's time we get down to business," the dark hooded man said.

The farmer clenched his teeth together nervously as he removed the straw hat off his head—it had previously cast a shadow dark enough to conceal the worried look that painted his face during the ride over from Yokelshire. He scratched the bald spot on his head nervously before reaching deep into his pocket for a sack of coins.

"Right, you mentioned that you liked to receive half of the pay for the job upfront and the other half after it's complete," the farmer said. The dark hooded man reached out to snatch the sack of coins from his hands, revealing a metal gauntlet. Before the hand could reach the sack of coins, the farmer pulled away.

"I never got your name; you said that you would tell me what it was when we got here, and you knew that you could trust me. I think if you're accepting my pay then that means you must trust me," he said.

"Very well, if my name is that important to you then I will tell you, I suppose it is only fair and polite, after all." The dark hooded man rolled up the sleeves of his long coat to reveal strange fingerless gauntlets with very thin tubes connected to them that ran all the way up his forearm and disappeared into where his coat sleeves were rolled up to.

"I am the Arsonist," he said.

"How?" the farmer asked.

"I'm sorry?"

"How can you be the Arsonist? He is a criminal, and criminals don't help people, especially us Yokel folk." As the farmer went to put his straw hat back on his head, he felt the Arsonist swiftly snatch the sack of coins from his hand.

"I'm not a criminal, you've been reading too many wanted posters," the Arsonist said.

"I can't read," the farmer replied.

The Arsonist tucked the sack of coins into his pocket and adjusted the tall collar of his coat that was flipped up around the back and sides of his hood. The sound of a terrifying screech erupted from the barn and sent a shiver down the farmer's spine. The Arsonist made haste towards the barn entrance as the screech returned, this time it was joined by another, and then another, until the barn shook with howls of terror. The Arsonist arrived a few meters outside the barn and could tell that whatever was inside knew his presence was near. The shrieks inside the barn went silent as the Arsonist approached the wooden door latch that kept them sealed within. Out of the corner of his left eye he could see the farmer darting into the nearby farmhouse only to let the door slam shut behind him, leaving the Arsonist outside and alone standing before the looming barn.

    The Arsonist wasn't afraid of what awaited him behind the barn door, for he had dealt with this menace many times before. He didn't fear death, for it was all he knew in the nineteen years of his life. He was raised by his father, alone with no siblings or mother, and dealing with the infected that crept up from the Southern Wastes was the only thing that he knew he was good at. He did fear pain, though, and knew that if he made a mistake with that which lurked within the barn, he would suffer very painful consequences.

    "Are you going to stand there staring at the barn door all day or are you going to open it?" The farmer's voice called. The Arsonist turned away from the barn door to see the farmer standing with crossed arms in the open window of the nearby farmhouse.

    The outburst of piercing howls from the barn returned, providing an opportunity the Arsonist knew he wouldn't get again. He lifted the latch to the barn door to unlock it and then sprinted a few meters away before twirling back to face it. The doors to the barn slowly opened out towards the Arsonist. As the screeches escaping the barn grew sharper and louder, the Arsonist held his hands outward along each side of his body while ignoring the scent of blood that had escaped the barn and found its way into his nose. Glowing red eyes, pale flesh, and frothing fanged mouths could be seen charging out from the darkness and towards the Arsonist.

    The Arsonist thrust his gauntlets outward from his body and applied pressure to the tiny lever inside the palm of each gauntlet with his fingertips. As he pressed down, the pressure released a fuel line allowing the flammable liquid material to pour from the concealed reservoir under his coat into a nozzle that ignited a jet of fire from the barrel vent of the gauntlet. Fire spewed out of the top of the gauntlet away from the Arsonist's shielded hands. With full force he shoved his hands forward and released a cone of incinerating fire into the charging pack of pale skinned fiends. The fire emitting from the gauntlets made its way to the barn gate, as well as the grass, quickly setting them both ablaze. The fiends released one final howl of terror before bursting into ash.

A haze of blood, smoke, and dust surrounded the Arsonist. The concealed reservoir underneath his coat had run out of fuel for his gauntlets. The flames that were being emitted from them had died out and they were releasing a faint sizzling sound. The heat of the gauntlets and the fear of the pain that the creatures could have inflicted upon his flesh had left the Arsonist's masked face drenched in sweat. He could feel cold rain drops hitting his covered head and he could see the steam coming off his gauntlets as rain drops hit them.

"My barn," the farmer cried. He was now standing outside the farmhouse looking out at the flames as they climbed up from the scorched grass and up the barn walls towards the roof.

"Hopefully the rain will prevent it from spreading to the forest," the Arsonist said. He reached into his inner coat pocket to pull out a vial of yellow liquid to refuel his gauntlets. The farmer ran back inside the farmhouse before quickly returning outside with a small wooden bucket full of water.

"I don't think that's going to do much," the Arsonist said.

"I lost my farmhand, livestock, and now my barn," the farmer said. "If I lose my farmhouse too, I'll be done for."

The Arsonist finished refueling his gauntlets and made his way towards the farmer who had just finished chucking a bucket of water at the burning barn. He unrolled his sleeves and pulled them back down over his gauntlets to cover them and protect them from the rain.

"I believe you owe me the other half of my payment," he said.

"Are you crazy? Look at what you did to my barn!" The farmer trembled as his scrawny eyes made contact with the Arsonist, whose red eyes blazed murderously behind his porcelain mask.

"You're one of them, aren't you? You're one of those things. I was trying to understand how your eyes could be that way before, but now it all makes sense," the farmer said.

"Don't be a fool, if I was one of those things I wouldn't have helped you, I would have killed you and taken your money the moment we departed Yokelshire," the Arsonist replied. The farmer dropped the bucket into the grass and ran for the nearby farmhouse. The Arsonist shook his head in disappointment and then chucked the empty fuel vial at the burning barn.

"I'm sure the rangers will compensate you for your loss if you explain to them that you lost your farmhand, livestock, and barn to the infected," the Arsonist called after him. He lifted his mask up above his chapped lips and placed two of his fingers into his mouth to produce a sharp whistle. His dark brown horse came darting out of the nearby forest in response to his signal. Before he could prepare to mount his horse, he noticed the farmer coming back towards him slowly.

"The rangers? You think they'll do that for me?" the farmer asked.

"They're supposed to compensate the farmers for any losses made as a result of a war crime," the Arsonist replied.

"A war crime?"

"Aye, a war crime."

"Who are you, stranger? You're obviously not a criminal, so why're you called an arsonist?" The farmer asked.

"It's my reminder for why I do these things, and my motivation to keep doing them, there are a lot of people that I have to prove wrong, and now you are no longer one of them," the Arsonist replied. He mounted his horse and leaned down towards the farmer as he held a sack of coins out towards the Arsonist.

"Thank you," the Arsonist said.

"If you're not one of them then why cover your face? Your eyes are not natural," the farmer replied. He took his drenched straw hat off his balding head and pressed it against his soaked chest with both hands. The Arsonist's hesitation to answer the farmer's question was concealed by his mask.

"Stay safe," the Arsonist said. He faced his horse east and then rode off into the woods.

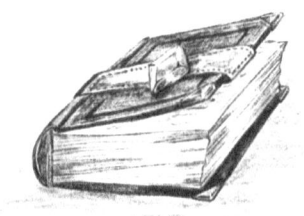

Chapter Two

His grey-colored eyes snapped open; his heart was pounding as he looked around the bedroom. He was paranoid, thinking the horrors he dreamt of had followed him from the nightmare to his home. He got up out of bed cautiously and stumbled over to the front door window to see the sunlight that was piercing through the glass. The light washed away the vestiges of the horrors that had haunted his sleep. The warmth from the sunlight touching his skin reminded him that he was awake and that he was alive. He noticed a shadow creeping up behind him and jumped back towards the window.

"Good morning, Rhys," an old man said.

Rhys clenched his shirt with his shaking hands as if hoping that he could reach inside his chest and calm his pounding heart.

"Uncle," he said, "you scared me."

"Bad dream again?" the old man asked.

"Yes," Rhys replied. Rhys walked away from the old man to grab the wooden bowl on his desk so that he could take a sip of water.

"Did this one have the masked figure again as well?" the old man asked.

Rhys nodded at the old man as he set the bowl back down on the desk. He began pulling clothes out from a nearby basket and smelling them to check if they were clean or not.

"I didn't do laundry this week yet," the old man said.

"I did," Rhys replied.

The old man made his way into the only separate room within the tiny house. He closed the door behind and undressed himself down to a fully nude state before beginning to do the same thing as Rhys, pulling clothes out of a basket onto the floor and smelling them to see if they were clean or not. His nose winced at the foul smell that was being emitted from the pair of trousers that he was holding up to his face. He quickly cracked open the door and stuck his head out.

"Rhys, do you by chance have any clean pairs of pants that you could lend your uncle?" The old man asked. An embarrassed smile slid out from the old man's bushy beard as he stood there naked behind the door with his head peeking out. His eyes were brown and the hair on his head and face was completely snow white. A slight bald spot had formed on top of his aged head.

"Oh no, not this time uncle. Do you remember what you did to the last pair of trousers I lent you?" Rhys replied.

Rhys had already quickly gotten dressed and was placing his foot on the wooden edge of his bed as he tied his leather pointed shoe. His long silvery hair was pulled half-up on top while the bottom layers rested on his shoulders. His skinny neck was squeezed tightly by the red linen tunic that he wore over a pair of brown trousers.

"I have apologized for what happened to those trousers too many times, when will I ever hear the end of it? Can't you just help your uncle Farbris out?" he said.

"You stretched out the waistband so much that I could wear them as a kilt, not that I would want to since you defecated in them while we were walking back from our hike through The Northern Headlands," Rhys replied.

"I told you before that I don't know how that happened, I think I that divided the poorer district of the village that he lived in from the cleaner and wealthier parts.

As he came down the other side of the hill into the town square of Prosperwood, a familiar beauty caught his eye in the distance underneath the town square clock tower. It was Natalia Winter. Rhys knew it was her because she was the only woman in all of Prosperwood that constantly had a flock of men following her around attempting to gain her favor. Her dark hair and blue eyes playfully lured men underneath the stone clock tower every afternoon. She would fish for compliments in the crowd that surrounded her, asking the men that drooled at her feet if they liked her outfit or not.

Rhys' grey eyes were lost in the torrent of yellow that swirled behind Natalia as she walked through the opening archways of the central clock tower. His trance was broken when he noticed her begin to wave in his direction. Rhys quickly looked behind him to see nobody else around him at the base of the hill. He looked back at Natalia to notice her laughing at him as she swayed back and forth in her yellow dress. Despite Rhys feeling embarrassed, he managed to muster up enough courage to walk over to her and say hello.

A trail of sweat began to droop from his neck down his back and he knew it could be seen through his red tunic, so he uncovered the compendium he was holding and put his brown twill jacket on over his tunic. It wasn't just that he was nervous to speak to an attractive woman that was highly sought after, it was also the fact that he had not spoken to Natalia since they were children.

The men crowding behind Natalia began to scowl at Rhys like the aggressive little dogs that they were.

"So, you did see me wave at you?" Natalia asked.

"Yes, yes I did," Rhys replied.

She smiled. "What are you up to today on this lovely fall morning?"

"I was just heading to the schoolhouse over on Keyhole Street."

"Oh? What might take you there?" she asked. "A child I assume?"

"Children, actually, lots of little tykes," He replied.

"All yours?" she gasped. "My goodness, you have been busy since we were kids!"

"Oh no, they're not mine," Rhys said, his face burning scarlet.

Rhys started counting back from nineteen in his head. He knew that Natalia was a year older than him and that he was ten years old the last time they spoke, which would have made her eleven. Rhys began to realize that for him to have had multiple children over the age of six at that age would have been almost impossible. He was nineteen years old now and she was twenty.

"So, are you their teacher then?" Natalia asked.

Rhys finished doing the chronological math in his head and then got lost in Natalia's eyes. They were like tiny sapphires embedded within a perfectly round sheet of snow. Her nose was not too small, and it was not too big either, at least not in Rhys' opinion.

"Rhys? Are you alright?" Natalia asked.

"What's that? Hmm? I'm sorry?" Rhys replied.

"Is this twig in a tunic bothering you Lady Winter?" a young man's voice said from beside Rhys.

"No, Dorian, this is an old friend from my childhood that has come from out of town to teach the little kids down the street, please mind your manners if you are going to grace us with your presence," Natalia replied.

Dorian made his way towards Natalia's left side and stood next to her. He looked up and down at Rhys to examine his physical stature. He was a tall and slender man with long black hair pulled back into a ponytail. He had white skin, green eyes, and a pair of chapped lips that looked as if they could conceal a forked tongue. In his left hand he held a sealed violin case. He had pointed, black leather boots with purple-colored trousers tucked into them. Both the collar and the cuffs of his white shirt were puffy. He wore a burgundy-colored jacket that was embroidered with intricate golden threaded designs, the finest coat you could buy in The Eastern Vale at the time.

"Hello there, friend," Rhys said.

Rhys extended his hand out to shake Dorian's, but Dorian looked at it and did not move a muscle.

"Friend is such an interesting title to give to someone that you just met, don't you think?" Dorian replied.

Natalia kicked Dorian in the shin with her slippers. They were the same shade of yellow as her dress. Dorian smirked and extended his hand out to Rhys.

"Ah yes, where are my manners, please forgive me..." Dorian leaned forward and moved his hand about as if hoping Rhys would reveal his name.

"The name is Rhys, and Natalia, I am not from out of town. I have been living over the slump of a hill that's behind me over there for pretty much my entire life," Rhys replied.

"Rhys, please call me Lady Winter," Natalia said.

Rhys squinted at her and turned his head to the side slightly.

"I had no idea you were in town Dorian; I thought you had left us for the east for good this time," she said.

Dorian sat his violin case on the ground and grabbed Natalia by her left hand with both of his by placing his left hand in hers and his right hand on top. He leaned forward and kissed the top of her wrist.

"I could never stay gone for long knowing that such a beauty resides here in the west, Lady Winter," Dorian replied.

Rhys looked up into the clear sky in hopes that a bolt of lightning would magically appear and strike Dorian down.

"I am flattered as always, but I can't help but feel that there is more that you have to come to tell me," Natalia said.

The men that buzzed around Natalia previously had now grown bored and began to disperse away into the town's streets.

"I have come to tell you that I will be in town for the next few months to help train and rehearse the symphony, at your father's request of course. And would you look here, his ears must have been burning," Dorian said.

Natalia's father Henry made his way towards the three young people with a glimmer of joy in each eye. He wore a similar outfit to Dorian, but it looked more washed out, and the color of the jacket he wore was a shade of dark blue.

"There he is, the man that will bring the Light of Deliverance to our ears," Henry said.

"Ah, Mayor Winter, how do you do?" Dorian replied.

Dorian let go of Natalia's hand so that he and Henry could embrace one another with a hug. Natalia smiled at Rhys, who was looking around anxiously and clicking his jaw.

"You still do that thing," Natalia said.

"What thing?" Rhys replied.

"The jaw thing," she replied. Natalia touched the jawbone of her face with her now free left hand.

"That has to be bad for your teeth," Dorian said.

"Who is this?" Henry asked.

Rhys and Natalia's eye contact was quickly broken at the disruption of her father's question.

"Father, this is Rhys, a boy from my childhood," she replied.

Henry looked up and down at Rhys, clearly unimpressed by his appearance.

"How does a young man like yourself have hair whiter than mine?" Henry asked.

"Daddy, that was rude," Natalia said.

Dorian couldn't help but laugh as he picked up his violin case. Rhys continued to click his jaw while using every bit of strength he had to withhold any sarcastic or angry language.

"I need to get to the theatre so I can get acquainted with the musicians I'll be working with," Dorian said.

"Will you be playing or only instructing?" Natalia asked.

"Well, the fall season is nearly over but your father has informed me that there will be a winter season symphony, which is why I have returned," Dorian replied.

"Yes, it is true. I have decided to have our first annual winter symphony. I thought we could have everyone bundle up in their fancy furs and we could congregate at the theatre and listen to Dorian and several others produce magic with their Violins and Cellos," Henry replied.

Dorian, Henry, and Natalia started to discuss the winter symphony details but were interrupted by a loud shout from atop the hill behind Rhys. It was Farbris bellowing Rhys' name at the top of his lungs.

"Rhys, you said you were running late and now you're gawking at the mayor's daughter instead of teaching those poor tykes how to sew a pair of mittens together!" Farbris hollered.

Rhys' light skinned face became overwhelmingly red with embarrassment as his eyes widened in disbelief.

"Do you know that drunkard?" Henry asked.

"Is he talking to me? I think he is trying to talk to someone else," Rhys replied

"I think he said the name Rhys. That is your name, is it not?" Dorian replied.

Rhys clenched his fists and began to make his way down the street to the west that led to the schoolhouse.

"Farewell Natalia, it was nice to see you after so long, but I must be going now," Rhys said.

"Her name is Lady Winter," Dorian said.

Natalia was too distracted with her father pulling on her dress and scolding her for wearing such a low-cut torso piece to hear Rhys' departing words.

"Right," Rhys replied.

Farbris began to make his way down the hill to pursue Rhys while whistling in an attempt to get his attention. Rhys began to furiously mutter words quietly under his breath to himself as he walked down the winding cobblestone path.

"Stupid violin. Stupid jaw. I guess I'll just disappear and not see her for another nine years so that she can notice me again," Rhys said.

"Rhys my boy, please wait up, don't make your old uncle run and chase you down half a city block," Farbris said.

Farbris bent down and grabbed his knees while trying to catch his breath. Rhys turned around to see him and wanted to burst into anger, but he withheld himself.

"I'm sorry Uncle," he said. "I'm already running extremely late."

"I'm sorry for embarrassing you my boy," Farbris wheezed. "I just wanted to rescue you; I hate to see you getting wrapped up in some vanity drowned girl who doesn't even know you exist."

"I can't help it; she was the only kid that was nice to me growing up. Everybody else made fun of my grey eyes and hair constantly," Rhys replied.

"Silver hair and silver eyes with flecks of blue," Farbris corrected.

Rhys rolled his eyes and pulled the heavy book close to his chest with both arms as he continued down the cobblestone path. Farbris put his arm around Rhys as he followed him down the path to the schoolhouse.

Chapter Three

"You there, boy," an enthusiastic voice said.

Bregan Moran's green eyes which were nearly concealed by his curly locks of blonde hair squinted as if they were refocusing themselves.

"Are you deaf, boy? Don't tell me the only cook here is one of the lame," the enthusiastic voice said. Bregan turned away from a black pot of boiling water that was filled to the brim with various vegetables to give his attention to the man that demanded it.

"Sorry sir, I must have been daydreaming," Bregan said.

"Can't say I don't blame you there, watching water boil is about as exciting as watching paint on the hull of a ship dry," the man said.

Bregan smiled and started to walk over to the table where the man was seated.

"Hold it, I was trying to get your attention earlier because I would like some more vinegar to go with my crab here," the man said.

Bregan stopped as his sixteen-year-old face went flush with embarrassment. He quickly grabbed a bottle of vinegar off the wooden shelf above the stove and carried it over to the man at the table. "Here you go sir, this is all the vinegar we have but please use as much as your heart desires," Bregan said.

The man snorted as he laughed so hard he almost fell backward out of his chair.

Bregan looked at him with visible confusion. "I don't understand, is there something wrong?" he asked.

The man snickered and snorted as he tried to regain his composure. "Boy, how old are you?" he asked.

"I'm sixteen years old," he said.

The man's laughter came to a swift halt as his brown eyes widened with amazement. "I'll be damned, you are a young one," he said. He reached out his hand to Bregan who looked down at it with the same visible confusion he had earlier. "It's not going to shake itself, boy," he said.

Bregan reached forward and shook the man's hand despite the reluctance he was feeling. "What's your name, boy?" the man asked.

"Bregan M-, my name is Bregan," he said. He caught himself from saying his surname and repeated his first name. It was as if he could hear the voice of his father Farbris reminding him to never tell anyone his true surname.

"Nice to meet you, Bregan. My name is Viti," he said. He reached his hands inside his coat and pulled out a lemon and began cutting it in half with his dinner knife.

"What is that?" Bregan asked.

"This? It's a lemon," Viti replied.

"A lemon? Like one of those yellow fruits from down south?" he replied.

"Aye, a lemon from down south. I can't say I'm surprised you've never seen one of these before being a northerner and all but how did you know it was from the south?" he asked.

"My father visited the south once, he used to tell me all about the food he once had down there when I was a boy," he replied.

Viti held his hand out flat to Bregan revealing a sliced lemon wedge. "Give it a try, I know you're curious," Viti said.

"Oh, I probably shouldn't sir. I really should get back to work," Bregan replied.

"Come on, you're the only one working here and I'm your only patron tonight. Don't you want to know what your old man was always fussing about?" he asked.

Bregan gulped and undid the knot of the apron he was wearing before taking it off and setting it on the table.

"Take a seat, relax, and enjoy some lemon. It's great on crab with a little vinegar," Viti said.

Bregan took a seat and smiled. He took the lemon wedge from Viti's hand and took a bite out of it.

"You're not supposed to eat the peel, idjit," Viti said.

Bregan spit it out into his hands and turned away from the table with a puckered face and spat onto the floor behind him.

Viti laughed as he squirted a lemon wedge over his crab legs.

"That was awful, how can you eat those?" Bregan asked.

"I don't eat them, I squirt them," Viti replied.

Bregan studied how Viti dressed his food with lemon, salt, and vinegar. He was always raised to believe that staring at people while they ate was rude but this time it felt okay to him. "So, you're a Southerner then?" Bregan asked.

"Did the brown skin on my face give that away or did it really take me pulling out a lemon for you to figure that one out?" Viti asked.

Bregan began to feel anxious as a small pool of sweat began to develop on his lower back.

Viti snickered with a mouthful of crab as he reached out to pat Bregan on his shoulder. "Relax, I'm just messing with you, there's no need to be so nervous and tense," Viti said.

Bregan wanted so hard to believe that Viti was harmless and that it was okay to let his guard down, but he just couldn't help but feel uneasy around him at the table.

"So, what brings you up this far north to Windfall Harbor?" Bregan asked.

"Well, you seem harmless, so I suppose I could tell you," Viti replied.

Before Viti could continue, he was startled by the sight of water and produce boiling over the pot behind the counter and onto the burning logs below it. Steam filled the atmosphere of the kitchen as Bregan rushed in to try and pull the dangling pot off its hook carefully without spilling any of the boiling water all over his feet.

"I'll take the blame for that and pay you for whatever that was you were boiling," Viti said.

Bregan hung his head low and sighed loudly. He was annoyed with the situation and disappointed in himself. "This was supposed to be dinner for my mother and I tonight when I got home, it was supposed to be a surprise. She hasn't had much to eat besides bread ever since she had to quit her job at the casino," Bregan said.

Viti put his hand on Bregan's shoulder but before he could think of words of comfort to give him, they both jumped at the sound of the door to the shack being kicked open. A handful of pale skinned men with white hair, red eyes, and wicked grins charged in as the one that kicked down the door and now stood in front pointed at Viti and Bregan.

"There's that smuggler son of a bitch," a raspy voice said.

"Run," Viti said.

He unsheathed a small, curved sword from his waistband before dodging a mallet that one of the pale skinned men lunged at him with. With a quick but effortless strike, Viti sliced the pale-skinned man's head off. Black blood oozed from the severed head of the man as it went flying across the kitchen toward the panicking Bregan. Viti unlocked the backdoor that led out from the kitchen and toward an alley outside. He motioned Bregan to follow him out as more armed pale-skinned men began to crowd the kitchen after them.

As Viti took off running down the alleyway toward the crowded streets outside, Bregan slipped on the ice behind him and fell to the ground. Viti reached the end of the alleyway and turned to see Bregan lying on the ground. Before he could act it was too late, the pale-skinned men had grabbed him, and a few others were closing in on Viti.

"I'm sorry Bregan," Viti said. He took off and vanished into the

"This bow is not to be taken lightly my son. I have wielded its power for decades now and yet I still lack the ability to fully comprehend its capabilities."

Thaniel held the bowstring back into his anchor point, which was a point on the right side of his face, a common anchor point for most rangers in the west. Normally Thaniel would've had to release the arrow by now, for a normal ranger's longbow pulls back a draw weight of a hundred and twenty pounds; however, Arrowguard was different. Its ethereal body made it as light as a feather and its arrows that it generated were weightless. Thaniel could pull back the bowstring and hold it for as long as he wished. Due to this bow generating its own mysterious arrows that were made of pure light, it didn't require a quiver. This allowed Thaniel to be even more concealed under his cloak when moving with stealth through the forests.

"You can feel it can't you?" Renson asked.

"Yes, I can hear it as well," Thaniel replied.

"Do not worry, that vibration you feel and hear will eventually become as familiar to your body as your own heartbeat," Renson Said.

"I look forward to not noticing it anymore."

The arrows that the bow generated made a strange humming sound and sent out a slight vibrating pulse through the wielder. Thaniel could feel it in the bones of his forearms despite the skin being concealed by armguard bracers.

"Try not to take one of the courtyard's columns out," Renson said.

"I got it."

"Loose."

Thaniel released the light arrow at Renson's command. The arrow flew with intense speed that could not be caught by the naked eyes of Thaniel or Renson, nor the rangers that surrounded the opening ways to the courtyard. The target that Thaniel was aiming at had ceased to exist. It was as if it had spontaneously combusted before his blinking eyes.

"I'm proud of you son, you didn't even hesitate this time. If only your mother was here t-," Renson said.

"Sir, I need to speak with you," A tall, hooded ranger said.

"What news?" Renson asked.

"We had another fire incident near the southern hemisphere of

the glades," The ranger replied.
"We must investigate then. How many dead?" Renson replied.
"None, sir," the ranger said.
"Good, this is better than last time then," Renson replied. He placed his right hand upon the left shoulder of Thaniel.
"Well, it looks like you have your first task ahead of you," Renson said.
"My first task?" Thaniel asked.
"I mean, unless you're not ready of course," Renson replied.

He began to walk up the short steps of the courtyard and into the northern passage that entered the Cyanakin Hold. Thaniel quickly followed behind him while holding the bow in his left hand.

"I am ready, I just wasn't expecting this time to come so soon," Thaniel said.

"That's how it works my boy, the birds never know when it is their time to leave the nest, it is their mother that pushes them out and makes them fly," Renson replied.

A somber look cast a shadow of grief upon Thaniel's young face. He had lost his mother when he was nine years old. He was twenty years old now, but the memory of her ravaged body on the Glade Belt Road still haunted him.

"I'm…I'm sorry son…I should have said that their father pushes them out and makes them fly but I…I didn't want to confuse you with how nature works," Renson said.

"I'm fine," Thaniel replied.

Renson walked into what appeared to be his study at the Cyanakin hold. He took a seat in front of a shining black instrument that looked like the sky on a cool summer night. Renson's blue eyes lit up with teeming possibilities as he looked down upon its white and black keys that rested beneath his fingers.

"I just had it delivered from the Eastern Vale last week and haven't had the time to sit down and tinker with it," Renson said.

"Is it an instrument?" Thaniel asked.

"Yes," Renson replied.

Thaniel looked around at all of his father's hunting triumphs that lined the walls and even part of the ceiling. A plain wooden table stood in front of the only window, a large one that was reinforced with steel bars on the outside. Sitting in between the table and the window was a plain wooden chair. The table was empty except for a map of the Realms of Light. A single chair was pushed into its sitting area and had accumulated a noticeable amount of dust.

"You haven't been using your study very much lately have you?" Thaniel asked.

Renson seemed lost in the melodic sound as his fingers flew over the keys like birds darting into the ocean to catch a fish.

"They call it a piano," Renson said.

Thaniel stood in the doorway as he watched his father passionately strike the keys. "Have you played one before?" Thaniel asked.

"Yes, your mother taught me how to play one when I met her in the Inner City District of the Eastern Vale while traveling on official triumvirate business" Renson replied. "This was, of course, before they decided to call it a piano," he added.

"Why do you still call it that? Thaniel asked.

"Call what still, the piano?" Renson asked.

"The triumvirate."

"Because it is in fact a triumvirate."

"A triumvirate is a coalition of three people who hold equal share of authoritative power," Thaniel said.

"Yes, and that is what it is," Renson replied.

"Then why are there only two of you that I know of?"

"Your uncle Nielas is such a big-headed handful sometimes that we needed the third slot to carry his enormous ego and brain," Renson explained with a smirk.

"Was there ever a third?" Thaniel asked.

"Yes, but that was long ago," Renson replied. He stopped playing abruptly after striking a sharp sound that interrupted his melodic focus. He sighed.

"What happened to them?" Thaniel asked.

"They died years ago."

"How?" Thaniel asked.

"That is a gut-wrenching story for another time. I believe you have work to do now," Renson replied.

Renson pointed to the door space that Thaniel had come to occupy during the asking of so many questions.

"Right, I am going to head down to the armory and gather some supplies," Thaniel said.

"Son, I want you to take Garrick and Hyde with you," Renson replied.

"Am I not to go alone on this mission?" Thaniel asked.

"No, you are ready for this task, but I do not wish for you to go about this business alone," Renson replied.

A moment of awkward silence came between Renson and Thaniel as their blue eyes met one another from across the space of the study. A tension between the piano space and the doorway to the study had quickly appeared and it was so thick that either of the two men could cut it with a knife.

"Why do I have to bring Garrick? He is repulsive," Thaniel asked.

"Because I said so," Renson replied.

Renson turned his attention back down to the keys of the piano, thus breaking eye contact with his son.

"Very well," Thaniel replied.

As Thaniel turned to exit the study and leave his father to his new instrument, he was greeted by Hyde awaiting him at the doorway at the end of the hall leading to the courtyard space.

Chapter Five

A line of men and women wearing frayed brown robes stood at attention before one angry sounding individual. Surrounding them was a large grove of willow trees. The people of the realms referred to them as Salix trees, and this grove was the only known location of their existence in the world. Their light green leaves were typically elongated with serrated edges. The buds of the tree were covered by a single leaf-like scale. The Salix tree was known throughout the Realms of Light for its simple, gloomy look, which is why the dark-skinned druids that preserved and tended to them nicknamed the place The Weeping Grove.

Eight men and three women stood in a straight-line facing Lake Moran, which was covered by the branches and leaves of many Salix trees. A tall and lean looking man in a frayed blue robe named Crane paced back and forth from each end of the line of men and women.

"There are many of you here that have been told that you are special or that you are gifted. This is a false narrative given to you by your loved ones in an effort to preserve what little self-respect and confidence you may have. I will not lie to you here; you may have been accepted to trial as a new druid recruit, but you are still outsiders to me. This is my grove, and I will give my life to defend it from outsiders, so until you prove yourself worthy to me you are nothing more than another village dwelling imbecile that lives over those mountains behind you" Crane said.

The recruits standing in a horizontal line before Crane were silent.

"Today you will be introduced to the elder druids that reside in the larger Salix trees above you, they are the ones that guard the Monolith Sanctum. You should be grateful for this opportunity, especially if you are a woman. Never before has the Weeping Grove been desperate enough to accept female outsiders as recruits," Crane said.

Lylah, a young eighteen-year-old girl with blonde hair and grey eyes, took a barefoot step forward from the line of men and women that stood before Crane. Her skin was fair beneath her frayed brown robe and although she continued to stand at attention, she was now standing ahead and apart from her ten other peers.

"Were the first elder druids not women? The Evenfall Tribe that resided in the southeastern valley and saved the Moran family line has been historically noted for their connection to a group of old druids that lived in the trees of what they called the Weeping Grove. These old druids were historically documented as being only female," Lylah said

Crane's green eyes lit up as if they were ready to turn red. With the stomping of his footsteps, he charged his way towards Lylah.

"Mind your tongue girl, you may be a Proditore, but I am still your superior as a master ranked druid," Crane replied.

"If you say so," Lylah replied.

Crane put his face directly in front of hers and began to raise his voice in an effort to make Lylah falter. Her grey eyes remained still while unflinching at the roaring voice that left Crane's mouth.

"Do you want to be sent home? At the snap of my fingers, I could have you taken out of this grove and sent back to your snowy little tower," Crane said.

"No, I think I'll stay here just so I can see the look in your eyes when I quickly climb the chain and outrank your sorry self," Lylah replied.

As Crane raised his hand to backhand Lylah down into the earth, he was stopped by the shouting of an elderly man's voice.

"Enough," the elderly man boomed.

A very short man with dark brown skin and light brown eyes approached both Lylah and Crane. He had a long pointy grey beard that neared his kneecaps in length. His head was bald and shiny beneath the overcast sky that the sun struggled to peer out from. His robe was frayed like Lylah and Crane's, but it was a dark purple color. Crane adjusted his frayed blue robe while feeling embarrassed. His bald light skinned head was also shining beneath the overcast sky. Lylah stood quiet and still with her eyes fixed on the trees whose leafy branches concealed Lake Moran from her vision.

"Lylah Proditore, is it?" The elderly man said.

"Yes, elder one," Lylah replied.

"My name is Juspen. It is nice to meet you," the elderly man replied.

Lylah grabbed the frayed ends of her robe with each hand and took a curtsy fashioned bow before Juspen in a very polite and ladylike fashion.

"I can take it from here, master Crane," Juspen said.

Crane stormed off away from Juspen and the recruits while looking back every now and then to glare at Lylah.

"Please fall back in line Ms. Proditore," Juspen said.

"Yes, elder one," Lylah replied.

Lylah returned back to the formation with her fellow druid recruits.

"Master Crane may have already explained to you the important role a druid has in this grove but let me take this time to remind you of something. You are druid potentials, but you are not druids yet. I see eleven of you standing before me but only four of you will qualify to become druid apprentices of the grove. Two of those four will become novices," Juspen said.

Juspen began to dig his toes into the grass beneath his feet, revealing clumps of dirt in between each of his toes that came up with them.

"Follow me to the Monolith Sanctum please, this way," Juspen said.

The concealed sun's light finally began to bleed through the clouds and into the ocean blue sky as it started to set. The eleven recruits followed behind the slow and fragile Juspen as he took them north through the Weeping Grove.

"Psst! Hey Lylah, that was pretty impressive and brave of you," a young girl's voice said.

Lylah looked behind her to see a brown girl's face whose dark almond shaped eyes glimmered like they were catching a glare of sunlight as it fell across the nearby lake. She was one of the only three female recruits and she followed right behind Lylah in the straight line that proceeded to follow Juspen. A smile erupted across Lylah's face that looked like it could shatter her cheekbones. As their

eyes met each other in the silence of awkward happiness, Lylah decided to reciprocate the kindness.
"I like your hair braids," she said.
After a few moments of marching behind Juspen the eleven recruits now stood before a large silvery metallic pillar that stuck out of the ground. It appeared to be a strange metallic obelisk that glowed brightly at the top during the hours of sundown. When the sky was just dark enough but dimly lit by the setting sun it appeared as if the obelisk was absorbing or emitting its own form of sunlight. The elder druids had always called it the Monolith and it had been safely guarded for over two hundred years of recorded history.
"This is your new home," Juspen said.
Juspen waved both his hands around him as he slowly spun around in the open space that the Monolith resided in. The old man began to walk away towards a group of similar looking older men to brief them on the instructions that were about to be given. The eleven recruits broke out of their formation and began exploring the Monolithic space. They noticed large Salix trees that towered above them. At the top of each Salix tree was a small cloth-like tent structure that appeared to be the home of each elder. When the breeze caught the tops of the Salix trees it sounded like a thousand hands giving applause within a small room. The leaves blew back and forth against the sky like a lazy coat of ruffled bird feathers. Lylah felt a tranquil sensation wash over her as she approached the strange silver obelisk structure.
"Oh wow," a young girl's voice said.
Lylah walked around to the other side of the large obelisk to see the girl from earlier touching the obelisk with both her hands. "I could stand here and do this all day," she said.
"What in Deliverance's name are you doing?" Lylah asked.
The girl quickly brought both her hands to her side as if she were a child that just got caught touching something that they shouldn't.
"Nothing," she said.
"I don't think we should be touching the Monolith," Lylah replied.
"I saw a few others do it, and none of the elders seemed to care," the young girl replied.
Lylah turned her attention from the young tan skinned girl to the Monolith, she desperately wanted to give into her curiosity and reach out and touch its smooth metal surface.
"My name is Celosia by the way," Celosia said.

Lylah turned away from the Monolith and looked back at Celosia. "Nice to meet you Celosia, my name is Lylah," she said.

"I know, I heard you get addressed earlier," Celosia replied.

"Oh, that's right," Lylah said, a touch embarrassed.

Lylah quickly looked back at the Monolith and then back at Celosia.

"Just touch it already," Celosia said.

Lylah, feeling somewhat embarrassed, decided to give in to her curiosity and finally reach out to touch the Monolith. She pressed both her hands against the metal surface and felt a cool sensation along her palms. It soothed and relaxed her hands as a slight pulse of vibrating energy entered her body through her forearms. Although she did not appear to be shaking, she felt as if she was due to the strange sensation that engulfed her whole body from head to toe.

"I can see why the elder women stayed and guarded this place for so long," Lylah said.

"I know, like I said, I could stand here and touch this thing all day," Celosia replied.

"I think if I had one of these back home, I would never go outside," Lylah replied.

"It sure does feel good, I wonder if elder Juspen has ever—," Celosia stopped.

"Having a bit of fun, are we?" Juspen asked.

Lylah quickly brought both her hands to her side just like Celosia did when she caught her touching the Monolith. Both the girls nervously looked around to see that the nine other recruits were standing clustered together with a few of the elders. The whole group of men stared at the two young girls with confusing looks on their faces. The one other young girl recruit stood alongside the men with her arms crossed. The girls could tell that the dark-haired young lady was not quite fond of them.

"I guess we got a bit distracted," Celosia said.

"I am so sorry my elder one," Lylah said.

"It's quite alright girls; it is quite easy to get lost in such a beautiful place filled with such strange energy. I understand what you must be experiencing" Juspen said.

Juspen winked at the girls as he turned away from them and motioned them to follow him. The two girls both slightly smirked as they proceeded to follow Juspen towards the group of other elders and recruits.

Chapter Six

Alongside the wooden cellar door attached to the back side of the Forlorn Cathedral lay a wolf. The wolf had a thick brown and grey coat with white hair on top of his tail, along his nose, and on his forehead. The hairs along his back formed a broad grey stripe, with black hair tips on the shoulders, upper chest, and rear of the body. The sides of his body, tail, and outer limbs were a dirty brown color, while the inner sides of his limbs, belly, and groin were grey. The wolf was roughly six or seven years old, and he lay down next to the cellar door flat on his belly with his eyes shut. A battered, empty bucket sat nearby in the dirt, its contents long since evaporated under the sun.

The sound of the front gate to the cathedral space being creaked open could be heard by the raising ears of the wolf. His yellow eyes popped open as he quickly arose from his lazy nap in the sun. From around the corner came the Arsonist and the dark horse that he led behind him.

"Good afternoon, Glacier, having a lovely nap in the sun, are we?" The Arsonist said.

Glacier sniffed the Arsonist's muddy boots while running

around him in circles.

"You best enjoy it while you can before the winter rain falls upon us," The Arsonist said.

Glacier sat next to the cellar door with his tongue hanging out as he panted. Other than to chase the occasional rabbit, he had not run much, and he was quite thirsty. He frequently shut his mouth so that he could whine at the cellar door as if trying to motion the Arsonist to open it.

"You must be thirsty. I will open the door and meet you down there in a minute. I am sorry this trip took so long, had I known that it was going to take me almost two days to locate and complete a bounty I would have just taken you with me. You know how I feel about taking you into town around other villagers, they are frightened of your kind and wouldn't understand," he said.

Glacier let out a howl at the sky as if trying to desperately tell the Arsonist to open the cellar. The Arsonist finally stopped trying to tie the horse to a nearby tree and walked over to the cellar door. He pulled out a ring of keys and opened the cathedral's cellar which allowed Glacier to dart in faster than a loose arrow. The wolf quickly found his bucket of water and buried his snout in it as he gulped the water in with his tongue. The Arsonist slowly followed Glacier down the stairs into the cellar.

"Not so fast buddy. You're going to make yourself sick again," the Arsonist said.

Before the wolf could hear the plea from his master, he started spewing the excessive water he had consumed.
"Oh, not in here again, damnit Glacier, if you do that one more time, I'm putting your bucket outside, and you can quickly remember why you grow a thick coat during the winter," the Arsonist said.

Glacier licked up the water that he spewed onto the stone-cold floor as the Arsonist gently patted him on the back.

"I have to go back up and tie Xenos to a tree so he doesn't wander off into the cemetery again," The Arsonist said.

As the Arsonist began to walk towards the steps that led out of the damp cellar, he remembered that he was still wearing his white and red porcelain mask. He reached into the back of his hood with both hands and untied the mask from his face before removing it completely. He pulled his hood back to free his mane of hair that was blacker than the nighttime sky. The removal of his mask revealed his faintly glowing red eyes that contributed to his pale complexion. He caught his reflection in a broken piece of glass hanging from an old rusty mirror that was once upstairs in the cathedral. He felt a familiar self-loathing enter his mind as he looked down at his hands to see the mask that he was holding. The white mask was decorative and appeared to be almost ceremonial in design with an elegant red wing like paint that curved out from the corner of the only holes in the mask. It had been given to the Arsonist by his father long ago.

"I assume you already ate supper?" The Arsonist asked.

Glacier lay next to his tin bucket of water happily, with his tongue hanging out the side of his soaking wet mouth. The Arsonist exited the cellar to see his horse companion Xenos already starting to wander off into the amber colored forest.

"Where are you going, Xenos?" The Arsonist said.

He quickly grabbed onto the reins of Xenos and led him back to a tree that shaded the entry point of the cathedral's cellar. The Arsonist glanced around, his sharp eyes scanning the woods that stretched beyond the dark iron fence separating the cathedral grounds from the glade, ensuring no unseen watchers lurked among the trees. Satisfied, he tied Xenos to the tree with a length of rope, enough to let the horse wander and graze within the shaded area, but not so much that he could stray to the front of the cathedral, where he might catch the eye of patrolling rangers or, worse, the feral, pale-skinned fiends that roamed the wilds. With Xenos secured, the Arsonist made his way down to the cellar below. He locked the cellar doors behind him, just as he had done with the gates to the cathedral space that lay south of the cellar. Once inside, he began to undress, peeling off his gear down to his linen shirt and trousers, carefully removing his flamethrower gauntlets. He sat his muddy boots near the steps of the cellar to avoid tracking dirt into the space.

The small cellar had been somewhat renovated to accommodate the living quarters of someone at one time. The Arsonist's father had once told him when they first moved into this cellar together that it was where both his mother and father once lived. His father used to say that this was the room where the bishops would allow the bell ringer boy to sleep at night the day before their worship service so that he could awake on time without having to travel through the woods at sunrise. The cellar had a small wooden bed with a few cloth sheets tossed over the wooden planks that made up the bed. A small tough pillow lay at one end of the bed and at the foot of the bed were noticeable pieces of dog hair that had come off Glacier during his slumber.

A small space for a fire was created along one of the walls that could be used to boil a bucket of water. The Arsonist would often use this as a method of making various soups from the herbs and small animals that he found within the surrounding forests. It was hard for him to do without opening the cellar doors and he did not feel like opening them again. He believed that it was best to keep the cellar doors shut when the sun went down for, although the cathedral was surrounded by a tall steel pike wall that was aligned with sharp points at the top making it impossible to climb over, it could still easily be seen through and it had a space in between each pike that was wide enough to reach an arm or head through. Not quite wide enough for a human being to climb through, but it still prevented the Arsonist from feeling comfortable with revealing his location at night.

As the Arsonist sat on his bed drinking water from a small wooden cup he could feel his stomach growling. Glacier lay at the foot of the bed and had already begun to snore. The Arsonist looked over at his gauntlet that lay on a table next to his dark cloth cloak and remembered that he was down to one last fuel vial. It became clear to him at that moment that it was time for him to pay another visit to the Niedereach brothers. As he lay down on his back in his wooden bed, he made sure to carefully place his left foot in front of Glacier while placing his right foot behind Glacier thus not to wake the snoring wolf. He lay his head down on the flat rough pillow and placed his hands on his chest as he stared at the damp dark ceiling. The sounds of a snoring wolf, growling stomach, and occasional drop of water from the ceiling hitting the stone floor was a familiar music to his ears. The Arsonist knew he was home, and he was anxiously excited for the next day to start so that he and Glacier could pay his old, inventive friends a visit.

*

The next morning the Arsonist awoke to Glacier clawing and whining at the cellar door in an effort to get out so that he could go out into the woods to stretch his legs and relieve himself. The Arsonist crawled out of bed onto the floor before standing up to let Glacier out of the cellar.

When he opened the wooden doors, he was immediately overwhelmed by the bright glaring sunlight that shined down upon him. He brought a bucket of water out from the cellar that he had been saving for Glacier and set it down in front of Xenos so that he may drink.

"Good morning Xenos, drink up, we have a long day ahead of us," the Arsonist said.

Glacier stretched his back and his legs as he slowly made his way into a nearby forested area that lay behind the gated premises of the cathedral space. The Arsonist stretched his back and arms too before relieving himself on the tree that Xenos was tied to. Xenos turned its head away from the Arsonist as if disgusted by what was taking place in front of him.

"Don't make this weird Xenos. It's natural and you do it too," the Arsonist said.

The Arsonist made his way back inside and quickly donned his mask and cloak before carefully placing his gauntlets around each hand and strapping them on tightly to his bracers. He placed his muddy worn boots on before closing the cellar behind and locking it.

"Alright, who is ready to go on a trip with me?" the Arsonist asked.

Glacier sat next to Xenos' back legs while sniffing a pile of manure he had left behind after relieving himself. The Arsonist pulled his hood over his head and began to untie Xenos from the tree.

"That smells awful Xenos," the Arsonist said.

The Arsonist mounted Xenos and began petting him slowly. Glacier sat on the ground looking up at the Arsonist while wagging his tail while his tongue hung outside the left side of his mouth.

"Are you ready to go boy?" the Arsonist asked.

Glacier jumped up onto all four legs and let out a bark with excitement that he could barely maintain as his whole body shook from left to right.

"Who's a good boy?" the Arsonist asked.

Glacier let out another bark of excitement as he attempted to jump up on his hind legs to touch the Arsonist's legs with his front legs. The jumping up of Glacier had Xenos rearing in terror which nearly threw the Arsonist off. The Arsonist quickly grabbed a hold of the reins as if his life depended on it and tried to calm Xenos down.

"It's okay, it's okay," The Arsonist said.

Glacier cowered away from Xenos to avoid being trampled as the Arsonist finally got Xenos to stop rearing out of control. Glacier began barking at Xenos as he sensed danger for his friend and master the Arsonist.

"I'm alright, Glacier," the Arsonist said.

The Arsonist whistled at Glacier and motioned him to follow as he had Xenos slowly make his way towards the front side of the cathedral. The cathedral was quite grand looking even after all these years, despite its ominous feeling that it gave off to those who observed its beautiful architecture from outside. The cathedral never quite felt right to the arsonist when he looked upon it. It seemed as if a permanent rain cloud hung over the cathedrals pointed roof at all times, even during the brightest days of summer. When the Arsonist was young, he recalled being so curious about it that he wanted to enter its domain and explore what treasure he thought could be found inside. That warm childish nostalgia was always snuffed out by the memory of how his father forbade him from going inside the cathedral or anywhere near its locked doors.

    Xenos came to a halt after finally bringing the Arsonist to the front gate of the Forlorn Cathedral space. Glacier wagged his tail as he followed behind the mounted horse. The Arsonist pulled out the ring of keys and opened the gate again before closing and locking it behind him. He motioned Xenos forward, and they were off. The dark steed and its rider rode into the Amberwood once again, but this time they brought another companion. Glacier swiftly trailed behind them as they headed north of the Forlorn Cathedral and into the Glade Belt.

Chapter Seven

A fierce knock on the door was all it took to wake the sleeping Farbris who lay on Rhys' bed with a book covering his face from the glaring sunlight that pierced through the windows. Farbris ignored the fierce knocking the first eight times, but the ninth one was accompanied by an angry yet familiar female voice.

"Farbris, I know you're in there," she said.

"I'll be right there, dear," Farbris replied.

As the fierce knocking and yelling from outside continued, Farbris looked around for the trousers he had borrowed from Rhys the day before. After getting himself properly dressed he approached and opened the door to the small house.

"Ah, I always knew that you would come crawling back to me, Faelina," Farbris said.

Faelina struck his face with a swift slap. "I have not come here because of you. I have come here because of our son," she said.

She had long grey hair that was pulled back into a ponytail. Her pale face was aged like Farbris' and her small green eyes sunk back behind her tiny, pointed nose. Farbris rubbed his now sore bearded face as he welcomed her inside his filthy home. Faelina's pointed nose was held up so high away from the riddled with filth living space that it looked like she was raising a dagger into the air with her mouth.

"Some things never change," Faelina said.

"You could say that again," Farbris replied.

Farbris offered Faelina a cup of water, but she shooed him away with her left hand as she pinched her nose with her right.

"Why are you here Faelina? What is it that you want?" Farbris asked.

Faelina unplugged her nose and acted as if she was holding her breath.

"Oh, for Deliverance's sake, stop being so dramatic," Farbris said.

Faelina finally gave in after her pale face began to turn red. She was disgusted with the living conditions of the small house that Farbris and Rhys lived in.

"I have come on behalf of our son," Faelina said.

Farbris' eyes lit up eagerly as both his eyebrows raised above his wrinkled brow.

"How is he?" Farbris asked.

"He is—," Faelina said.

Faelina quickly started looking around for a box of tissues to reach for as tears came pouring down her cheeks. Farbris handed her an old piece of brown cloth he had in his trouser pockets that he used to wipe butter off his shirt with the night before. Faelina held it up in front of her face as her nose began pointing upward again in disgust. She gave in and convinced herself that the butter scented cloth would suffice.

"He is in prison, Farbris," she said.

"Prison? Like, the Festering Cage prison?" Farbris replied.

"Yes, they took him a few nights ago and I was notified by one of the Windfall Harbor town criers," Faelina replied.

"What happened? What did he do?" Farbris asked.

"Apparently he did something at one of those damned casinos," Faelina said.

Farbris stood up in disbelief, for he had no idea what he was going to do. He shook his head as he leaned against a nearby wall for support of his legs that suddenly grew weak.

"My Bregan, my boy, my son..." Farbris said.

The two wept together as Faelina walked over to Farbris and embraced him in her arms.

"Farbris, you must bring our son back, you must," Faelina said.

"That prison is beyond my power, you know how limited I am

now," Farbris replied.

"Our son will not last a month there," Faelina replied.

"What would you have me do, woman?" Farbris asked.

"You come from royal blood, venture to the east and ask the nobles or whoever is in charge these days to release him. You could probably get a pardon or something if you used the same damn charm you used to lure me into your bed all those years ago," Faelina replied.

Farbris dried his tears in silence as he looked over Faelina's head towards the full bookshelf that towered over Rhys' bed. He knew exactly how long it would take to reach the Eastern Vale on foot, but he knew very little of what powers governed the east now since the Severance event occurred.

"Please Farbris, you were incapable of accomplishing many things during our short-lived life together, but I know that this is something you can fix," Faelina said.

Farbris knew of the dangers that had spread from the Southern Abyss across the Brooding Bridge and into the Northern Reach. He knew of what terrors awaited him should he choose to leave Prosperwood. The fear of the creatures that lurked outside the palisade walls of Prosperwood did not compare to the sorrow he felt drowning his heavy heart. He feared what lurked in the dark borders of the Western Glades, but he feared losing his son more. As Faelina buried her crying face into his right shoulder, he knew what must be done.

"I will go and bring our son back," Farbris said.

Faelina pulled her face away from his shoulder to reveal a snotty nose and tear drenched face.

"You promise?" she asked.

"I promise," Farbris replied.

Faelina dried her nose and face as she hugged Farbris tightly. It was the first time in a long time that Farbris had been able to hold Faelina this way.

"I know I have a history of not keeping promises to you," Farbris said.

Before he could continue, she grabbed his face and kissed him on his right cheek leaving behind a smudge of light red lipstick. Farbris touched the familiar sensation he felt on his cheek.

"I will be staying with an old friend of mine over on the upper part of town near the symphony hall on Livinworth Street," Faelina said.

"Oh no, you're staying with Sabrina again, aren't you?" Farbris said.

"You know she has been one of my best friends since I was a little girl, she helped me a lot when we split up, you know," Faelina replied.

Farbris rolled his eyes as he poured more water from a canister into his wooden cup.

"Oh right, how could I forget?" Farbris said.

"I expect you to leave as soon as you can and not come back unless you have our son with you," Faelina replied.

"I will be leaving tonight but first I must run a quick errand; do you know what time it is?" Farbris said.

"It is one o'clock in the afternoon, my goodness Farbris, were you sleeping when I showed up here?" Faelina replied.

"I really need to invest in one of those pocket watches I always hear Rhys babbling about," Farbris said.

"Rhys? That boy still lives with you?" Faelina asked.

"Yes, of course he does Faelina, he is my nephew for light's sake," Farbris replied.

Farbris began to pull out a large trunk from underneath his bed as he looked around on the floor for where the key might be.

"I know. I just assumed he had grown up and moved on with his life by now," Faelina said.

"He is my responsibility regardless of how old he is," Farbris replied.

"You never talked about Bregan that way," Faelina replied.

"Bregan is different, he is strong like his old man and witty like his mother," Farbris replied.

Farbris's eyes lit up as he picked up a pile of clothes on the ground that was hiding the bronze key's location. The sunlight coming through the window above Farbris' bed hit the key and revealed itself to his sight.

"Besides, our son is a Moran, he has the blood of kings within him, I am sure that he is using his father's charm to make some resourceful allies in that dreadful place," Farbris said.

"Just bring him back to me, Farbris," Faelina said. Faelina opened the door and walked out of the house before slamming the door behind her.

"Don't you mean bring him back to us?" Farbris asked.

Farbris opened the trunk with the bronze key and pulled out a book that was caked in dust. Farbris blew the dust off the book and let out a loud sneeze. It was a book of spiritual incantations that was gifted to the scholars of the Mekaner Tower of Spiritual Enlightenment when they graduated. Holding the book in his hands after over a decade brought many memories to Farbris' mind. Inside the trunk he also found his old scholar robes that were still in pretty good condition. The scholar robes were dark grey in color, but they were threaded together by a fine red silk only found in the Southern Wastes. The robe came with a red hooded cloak that was made from the same red silk. Attached to the cloak was a brooch; a tiny obelisk with wings that was made of solid gold. The brooch of a qualified scholar that had finished at the top of his class while attending the Mekaner Tower of Spiritual Enlightenment. Farbris grabbed his old briar wood pipe off the windowsill above his bed and packed it tight with the leftover tobacco he had in a small satchel tucked away under his pillow.

As Farbris stepped outside the front door of the house, he struck a match and began to light his pipe bowl. He puffed on the long wooden stem attached to the bowl of the pipe as the tobacco burned inside the bowl.

Farbris had begun to make his way towards the schoolhouse for youngsters, for that was where Rhys was during this time.

*

Rhys was continuing his history lesson with the children that he had started a day prior.

"Has anyone here ever seen or held a living weapon before?" Rhys asked.

The fifteen children sitting at tiny wooden desks in front of him within a dimly lit schoolhouse classroom remained silent.

"I figured as much," Rhys continued. He held the book open in front of him with both his hands behind it.

"According to Lord Proditore, there are only three living weapons that exist in this world and all of them have been accounted for by the northern council. They discovered these three weapons while on an expedition down into the Light's Hollow crater," Rhys said.

The children were holding their heavy-eyed faces up with their palms as they drifted off into boredom while listening to Rhys talk about the living weapons. Before Rhys could finish his point about the strange feeling one has when wielding such a weapon, the class was disrupted by Farbris barging in unannounced.

"Farbris, what in light's name are you doing here?" Rhys asked.

"I have come to bring you home, something important has come up and I need you to come with me at once," Farbris replied.

Rhys noticed something different in Fabris' demeanor. He could tell he was not drunk, and he could tell something was very wrong with his uncle.

"Yes, right away then," Rhys said.

Rhys rang the school bell outside his classroom door which signaled the parents to come by and pick up their children outside. Rhys gathered his belongings and locked the door as he bid the young tykes farewell. Farbris quickly put out his pipe as he led Rhys into the home that they both shared. Farbris began to explain to Rhys what was going on while trying to stop himself from talking too fast.

"It's your cousin Bregan, he has been taken to the Festering Cage off the northeastern coast," Farbris said.

"Oh no, what could have led to such a terrible fate?" Rhys asked.

"That remains to be unknown to me, but I must go to him, and I cannot afford to leave you here alone. You must come with me to the Eastern Vale where we can seek out aid from the nobles that reside there," Farbris replied.

"I can't just get up and leave, what about the children? They need me here, uncle," Rhys replied.

"Oh, and I suppose that you're going to also tell me that Natalia needs you too?" Farbris replied.

"She might," Rhys replied.

"Come on Rhys, you know damn well that this life brings you no joy," Farbris replied.

"It is the hand I was dealt so I make the best of it," Rhys replied.

"Your cousin has been dealt an even worse hand and if we do not go to his aid then we will be leaving him to die alone in a rotting light forsaken dungeon," Farbris replied.

"Why can't you just go alone?" Rhys asked.

"Because I don't fit the role that is required, not anymore, anyway," Farbris replied.

"What do you mean?" Rhys asked.

Farbris walked into his room and grabbed his old scholar garments that he had set down on his bed. He turned to the doorway of his room to see Rhys standing there, confused.

"I have not been completely honest with you my dear nephew,"

Farbris said. He held up the old grey robes and red silk cloak in front of him to show Rhys.

"I used to be a scholar of the south," Farbris said.

Rhys' eyes squinted and then opened wide when he realized what his uncle was trying to say.

"How is this even possible? You're not a man of the south, you are a fair skinned hermit from the east," Rhys said.

"Let's just say that I come from a very important family and I never quite told you the history of our blood that we share," Farbris replied.

"Well, maybe you should start talking then," Rhys replied.

"There is no time," Farbris replied.

"Make time, then," Rhys snapped.

Farbris handed the scholar garments to his nephew and went back to collect the book of incantations that he had also set on his bed. Rhys held the garments up in front of him and was surprised by how soft and light they felt.

"What is all this stuff?" Rhys asked.

"That is your new outfit for the next few days," Farbris replied.

"And why do I have to wear this particular set of clothes?" Rhys asked.

"These once belonged to me, but they no longer fit," Farbris replied.

Farbris lifted up his brown colored tunic to reveal his large gut that hung over his belt loops.

"I see," Rhys said.

"Don't worry, I didn't defecate in those robes," Farbris replied.

"So, you did defecate in those trousers I lent you?" Rhys asked.

Farbris winked at Rhys as he started to pack up supplies and pour the fresh water they had from a glass vase into two leather flasks.

"That outfit is extremely comfortable, I envy your ability to wear it for I wish it was me that could still be wearing it," Farbris said.

"It feels comfortable," Rhys said.

Rhys put the cloak to his nose so that he could smell it. He was surprised by how it had almost no odor of any kind. The cloak smelled as if it had a slight hint of metal but that must have been due to the trunk that it had been stored in for the last decade and a half.

"At least explain to me why this outfit is so important, though," Rhys said.

The Arsonist

"I need someone who looks like a scholar to get into the Noble Quarter of the Eastern Vale cities. I cannot possibly gain access if I look the way I normally do," Farbris said.

"So, you want me to pretend to be a scholar even though I have no prior training or knowledge in that field of study," Rhys replied.

"Yes, precisely," Farbris replied.

Farbris had nearly finished packing two cloth bags worth of supplies for them both to take on the road, but he was missing one last thing.

"I will explain more along the way," Farbris said.

Rhys closed the door to Farbris' room so that he could undress and change into the scholar outfit.

"When are we leaving?" Rhys asked.

"Tonight," Farbris replied.

Rhys was surprised at how hasty his uncle was being, but he understood the circumstances enough to be okay with it.

"The robes fit kind of big but I think it works," Rhys said.

Farbris opened the door to his bedroom to see Rhys standing at the doorway fully clothed in the scholar outfit with the brooch holding the red hooded cloak to the robes.

"My goodness, you are a twig," Farbris said.

Rhys had a lot of extra space in the robes due to his extremely thin figure. Farbris hugged Rhys and asked him to follow him to run a quick errand on their way out of town.

"So, where are we going, uncle?" Rhys asked.

"The Yokel Exchange near the entrance to town," Farbris replied.

"I don't think I have been there since I was a boy," Rhys replied.

"You'll always be a boy to me," Farbris replied.

"You know what I meant," Rhys replied.

Rhys' white hair was pulled back less than usual so that the mane of his hair could be more easily concealed within the red silk hood of his robes. He followed his uncle through the Yokel Exchange shop door with an anxious feeling wrestling inside his nervous head. A man with a curled mustache and tricorn styled hat stood at the counter. He noticed Farbris immediately as he walked in with Rhys.

"Right this way Farbris," the man said.

"Why don't you wait here, and I'll be right back," Farbris said.

"Alright," Rhys replied.

Farbris followed the man at the counter back into a room behind the counter. He was only gone for a few moments before he returned to Rhys with an old bag that was once used to carry tomatoes and potatoes in Yokelshire.

"Food for the trip?" Rhys asked.

"Food, yes, but not for us," Farbris replied.

Rhys squinted in confusion at his uncle as they exited the shop.

"It is going to be a long journey on foot my boy, and I do not like to stop for any reason during the night," Farbris said.

"Understood," Rhys replied.

"This means that you need to relieve yourself before we leave because we will not be stopping until sunrise," Farbris replied.

"Alright, well, let's get on with it then," Rhys replied.

"Very well," Farbris replied.

Both Rhys and Farbris exited Propserwood Village that evening on foot heading southeast of the village towards the glade belt which separated the Amberwood Cemetery glade from the Argentwald Manor and Brooding Bridge glade. Farbris tossed the Yokelshire produce bag over his left shoulder with his bag of supplies from home tied around his back. Rhys continued to stare at the Yokelshire produce bag that his uncle carried, hoping that he could figure out what it was without openly guessing. He carried the same-sized bag of supplies tied to his back that Farbris had tied to his back. As they both disappeared from the lantern lights that hung above the Prosperwood Village gates, a feeling of dread entered both their minds that neither would admit to one another.

Chapter Eight

Deep in the dungeons of the Festering Cage, Bregan was mercilessly whipped and left to weep over a hard hunk of bread and a small wooden bowl of water. The Festering Cage was always a scary story prescribed to children who didn't obey their parents. Bregan had finally come to know why that was.

"You there, rat boy, get up, it's time for daily exercise," a guard's voice said. She was a [insert description here]

Bregan wore a dark blue jumpsuit that he buttoned up in the front from his waist to his collar. He was barefoot and the bottoms of his feet were black as coal as a result. His body ached and yet he knew it had not even been a week yet.

Every morning at sunrise he was woken up by this same guard that seemed to watch over the cage area that he and several other men shared. She escorted him and several other men to a sandy part of the island where they were chained to a series of large rocks that poked out from around the prison and into the ocean. It was there where they were allowed to speak quietly amongst one another while they waited in line to bathe in the freezing cold ocean waters. Most men refused to step foot in the water for if they suffered any ailment from the waters, they would not receive any medical treatment.

After waiting in line to bathe, they were then given the option to stay on the beach in the cold where they would work on large wooden ships for hours. Choosing the option to work on the ships meant they were working non-stop until sunset, and then off to their cages without food.

The other option was to go back inside the prison and be greeted by Bal the Warden who would whip their back into a bloody pulp before sending them to the chow hall for food. They were given ten minutes to eat before they were allowed to return to their cage. Bregan quickly learned that if he continued to choose the second option to be whipped and then fed that his back would never heal, and he could risk infection, which is also why he had yet entered the ocean to bathe.

Miserable was a word that did not do the Festering Cage justice.

Bregan waited in line as the men chained to the rocks in front of him entered the freezing cold ocean waters. He noticed that the men that stepped out of the ocean had feet as blue as their soaking wet jumpsuits, and that the shackles around their ankles were rubbing the skin there raw.

"Get in the water or make your choice, rat boy," the guard said.

"I think I'll work on the ships today," Bregan said.

"Feeling bold today, are we?" she replied.

Bregan was moved over to the shipyard on the east side of the island where he was given a hammer and a bucket of nails to work with. Multiple guards with crossbows circled the prisoners as they relentlessly worked on the wooden boat that was being constructed.

As Bregan entered the work site and was unshackled, his usual guard stepped up. "If you try to run and swim away, I'll shoot you with my crossbow. If that doesn't kill you, well. You'll wish it had. These waters are infesting with Seething Sharks, and they can smell blood from roughly twenty miles away."

Suddenly, a large round shadow appeared over Bregan's small body as the guard released him from his shackles.

"Looks like I found myself a young little lady," a very deep voiced man said.

"Play nice, you two," the guard said.

At first, Bregan thought the large prisoner that he turned around to see was talking about the guard. He quickly realized that the man

The Arsonist

was talking about him.

"Come here and give Hobart a kiss," Hobart said. The large round prisoner with a very deep voice picked up the tiny Bregan and pulled him into his chest.

"You're so small I could unbutton my blue fester suit, stick you inside of it, and take you back to my cage for later," Hobart said.

Bregan remained silent, for in his mind he thought that if he was perfectly quiet and still that perhaps Hobart would get bored of him and let him go.

"Quiet, huh? That's alright, ask any of the boys from my cage and they'll tell you that I can make any little pig squeal," said Hobart.

Bregan couldn't take the advances of Hobart anymore and began to scream for help.

"Shut your damn mouth before I cut your lips off and feed them to you," Hobart said. He reached into the unbuttoned top of his blue jumpsuit and pulled out a long, thin piece of wood that had been sharpened into a knife-like fashion. It appeared to be the same texture as the boat wood planks that surrounded them on the sandy beach.

"Let him go, Hobart, or I'll knock out your other front tooth," a man said.

"Damn you Alarick, you will pay for standing between a man and his lady friend," Hobart replied.

Bregan was released by the choking grasp of Hobarts very large arms and quickly crawled away from Hobart in fear. Hobart tucked his wooden knife back into his blue jumpsuit and stomped away into the boat construction site. The prison guards stood in the distance behind Bregan mocking his scream for help with laughter. Bregan was confused as to why they refused to help him.

"Why didn't you guys shoot that bastard?" Bregan asked. Bregan's usual guard pointed her crossbow at him and let loose a bolt at his feet that barely missed his right foot. Tears began to flow down both of Bregan's cheeks as he turned around to see Alarick standing before him in a rugged blue jumpsuit.

"Are you alright, son?" Alarick asked.

"Never been better," Bregan said miserably.

"Come on, we've got to get to work before they cuff us and send us to Bal for a good whipping," Alarick said.

"I would rather take my chances with the sharks and be rid of this place," Bregan said.

"You don't want to do that, trust me," Alarick replied.

"Death can't be worse than the life I have left here," Bregan replied.

"This is only temporary, boy. I promise you," Alarick replied.

"I was given a life sentence, though," Bregan replied.

"We all were, they don't send you here unless it's for life," Alarick replied.

"Well, then there is no point in living anymore, my life is forfeit," Bregan replied.

"Don't be such a morbid young man, for this too shall pass," Alarick replied.

"You are way too optimistic for this place, how long have you been here?" Bregan replied.

"Long enough to know that if you don't start hammering those nails into a piece of wood here on this boat, you're going to get thrown in a cage with Hobart." Alarick said.

"Why are you here?" Bregan asked.

"Because I want to be." Alarick replied.

Alarick walked away and left Bregan with the most confused look on his face.

The two worked for hours together inside the hollow shell of the wooden boat that the prisoners were constructing. Every now and then, Bal the Warden would grace them with his presence to remind them that his whip was always willing to show them that they were here and that they were alive if they needed it. Bal was a tall man with short white hair and red eyes. He had light skin and a light-haired mustache that concealed his thin upper lip.

"I never caught your name, boy," Alarick said.

"The name is Bregan," he said.

"Bregan? I have a brother whose son's name is Bregan," Alarick replied.

"Oh yeah?" Bregan replied.

"Yeah, he lives somewhere in the Western Glades," Alarick replied.

Bregan suddenly stopped hammering and looked up at Alarick, who was a few inches taller than him.

"What is your brother's name?" Bregan asked.

"Farbris," Alarick replied.

Bregan suddenly felt excited for the first time in over a week.

"Farbris Moran?" Bregan asked.

"Yeah, don't tell me you know him," Alarick replied.

The Arsonist

"That's my father," Bregan replied.

Alarick froze. "How in light's name did you end up here?" he asked.

"I got grabbed by some men with fangs while I was working at a fish shack back in Windfall Harbor," Bregan replied. "Why were you working in Windfall Harbor and not with your father?" Alarick replied..

"He and I don't really get along, so I moved to the harbor with my mother," Bregan replied.

"What a shame," Alarick replied.

Bregan noticed his guard skulking about inside the ship's walls and so he picked up his hammer to resume nailing a nearby plank to another piece of wood.

"The time is very late, you little rats," she said.

Multiple guards started to enter the ship building sight while shouting and shooting their crossbows at the feet of the prisoners. Hobart stood outside the hull of the ship's construction, glaring at Alarick and Bregan. The guards rallied the prisoners up and placed them in a single file line to march back into the Festering Cage.

"Don't worry Bregan. There is still hope for us," Alarick said.

"If you say so," Bregan replied.

The two were placed in shackles and were separated into different lines of prisoners. Each line of prisoners marched into the prison one at a time and placed into their respective cages. As Bregan entered the prison, he could hear the screaming of a man coming from a nearby cage that was accompanied by a deep laugh that sounded eerily similar to that of Hobart's.

"Looks like Hobart found a new lady friend this evening," his guard said.

A lump sank through Bregan's throat as he was placed into a large cage with six other dirty looking cellmates. He crawled into a ball on the floor in one of the vacant corners of the cage just like the night before. Before he could completely drift into the void of sleep, he was awoken by the shouting of the guard. Bregan was confused because he had not fallen asleep yet and he knew it was not sunrise. "Looks like we've got another fresh face for the cages," she said.

Bregan sat up in the corner against the metal bars of the cage and saw the guard dragging a new prisoner down the hall by a chain. She opened the door to Bregan's cage and unshackled the new prisoner before throwing him in. The prisoner nearly landed on his face as the large woman tossed him into the cage before closing the door behind him.

"Hello mates, what does a fellow criminal have to do to get a drink around here?" the new prisoner asked.

"Viti? Is that you?" Bregan asked.

"Bregan?" Viti blanched.

The new prisoner was none other than Viti, the pirate lowlife that sold the sharp metal counterfeit deck to Bregan.

"What happened? Why are you here?" Bregan asked.

"They caught me selling illegally smuggled goods down by the docks, and instead of a slap on the wrist, they gave me a life sentence for being a pirate," Viti replied.

"Well, as horrible as that is, I sure am glad to see a friendly face around here."

"Yeah, I bet." Viti replied. "Too bad I don't plan to be here for too long."

Bregan tried to laugh but his throat was too dry, and his chest hurt. "Are you going to try to swim past all the sharks out there?" he asked.

"I actually thought I might bribe the female guard," Viti said with a smirk.

"Bribe her for what?" Bregan asked.

"Keys to the Festering Cage prison of course," Viti replied. The two bundled up in their blue jumpsuits next to each other in the previously vacant corner.

"How do you plan to bribe her?" Bregan asked.

"Why, with the best night in bed she could ever dream of having with the most handsome pirate in all the Realms of Light," Viti replied with a wink.

Bregan quietly chuckled as Viti roared with laughter.

"Good luck with that, Viti. I don't think she likes boys very much," Bregan said.

Viti started looking around at the other six cell mates that he shared this cage with. They were all asleep except for one that quietly cried alone in the direct opposite corner.

"If I was a woman and I had to stare at these sorry men all day, I probably wouldn't like them either," Viti said.

"If you're planning to choose labor over food tomorrow like me, you better get some rest, my friend," Bregan replied.

"I might have to choose the whipping option once or twice because I don't know how long I can go without food before the captain arrives," Viti replied.

"Captain?" Bregan asked.
"Aye, Captain Saesh," Viti replied.
"Who is that?" Bregan replied.
"I've said too much as it is. Look kid, I like you, like I like you a lot, but consider these lips of mine sealed shut from this point on," Viti replied. S

Bregan couldn't quite make sense of it all, but he knew that every pirate crew had a captain. He closed his eyes as he lay on the damp cold dungeon floor that reeked of fowl ocean spray. As he lay there gripping his hungry aching stomach he began to wonder if this so-called 'Captain Sesh' was planning to break Viti out of prison.

Chapter Nine

Garrick crouched down beside the mud that surrounded the entryway to the burnt barn. He reached down to touch the large boot print left in the mud and then he stuck his fingertip into his mouth before spitting it out onto the grass.
"Yup, it's definitely a man's foot, alright," Garrick said. Hyde leaned against a nearby tree that had not suffered the wrath of fire. His dark brown hair was short and wavy, and his eyes were green. Pressed between both his chapped lips was a short briarwood pipe that he puffed on as he laughed at Garrick's actions.
"We already knew that Garrick," Thaniel said.
An angry tanned man in a straw hat began to yell at the men from the porch of his half burnt down farmhouse.
"Alright, alright, alright already," Hyde said.
"Please start over from the beginning again, sir," Thaniel said.
The man in the straw hat pulled his pants up as he let out a long, drawn-out sigh. "As I said before, a dark hooded man in a creepy looking mask came riding in here with me on a dark horse and claimed to be the Arsonist."
Thaniel looked over to Hyde and both their eyes quickly met and pierced through one another as the man continued. "He took care of my problem, and he took my money, but he also burnt my land

down in the process, so now I need reimbursement from the rangers for uh, an uh, war crime" the man in the straw hat rambled.

"Right, well I can't promise you compensation, but I can promise you that we will find the man who did this," Thaniel said.

"That's not good enough, damnit," the man in the straw hat snapped.

"Are we going to have trouble, sir?" Garrick asked. He towered over the tan skinned farmer and his straw hat. It was almost as if he was blocking out the sun as a six-foot-three human eclipse.

"N-n-no Mr. Ranger sir, we have no trouble here," the man in the straw hat replied.

Hyde put out his pipe before tucking it into his waist band as he approached Thaniel. "So, what do you think?" he asked.

"I think this is the work of the same pyromaniac that burnt down the Amberwood Village schoolhouse a few years ago," Thaniel replied.

"Garrick, let's go," Hyde said.

"Do you have his trail?" Garrick asked.

"No, perhaps you could eat more mud and find it for us," Thaniel replied.

"Not funny," Garrick replied.

Both Hyde and Thaniel broke out into laughter as they mounted their grey horses. Garrick mounted his and eventually caught up to them as they rode off into the amber colored forest. Thaniel followed the horse tracks that the Arsonist had left behind and both Hyde and Garrick followed closely behind him as they all three rode east of the Yokel Ranch glade.

"Stop," Hyde said.

Both Garrick and Thaniel came to a halt and turned to see Hyde dismounting his horse.

"Not another one..." Hyde said.

"What is it?" Thaniel asked.

Hyde knelt beside a deer corpse that had been completely disemboweled and shredded into multiple chunks. The only way Hyde could identify it was by its broken antlers that were no longer attached to its missing head. Thaniel began to feel sick to his stomach as he looked upon the maggot infested wounds of the discovered deer. They were similar wounds to those that were inflicted upon his deceased mother. As Hyde examined the body, he looked away and rubbed his eyes as if he could wipe the image away from his mind and escape from the past to return to the present.

"Looks like a deer," Garrick said.

"What's left of one anyway," Hyde replied.

"It was probably just the remains of a glade wolf's feast," Thaniel replied.

"I have never seen wolves tear an animal apart like this," Hyde replied. He flicked his reins and trotted off in the opposite direction, away from the desecrated remains.

"What kind of beast can cause such damage to an animal?" Garrick replied.

"Whatever it was, it sure was hungry," Hyde replied. He mounted his horse and prepared to continue following Thaniel, who was now far ahead of them. Garrick rode fast and swiftly caught up to them. Thaniel was trying hard to stay focused on the mission and follow along the Arsonist's horse hoof prints.

"We aren't going to create a proper burial for it?" Garrick asked.

"We don't have time for such rituals, Garrick," Thaniel replied.

"Why are you in such a hurry? He's probably going to just get away again," Garrick asked.

Thaniel came to a sudden stop with his horse in front of Garrick's. He turned around and pointed directly at Garrick as their eyes met.

"You were one of the rangers that was supposed to catch him in the first place," Thaniel replied. He lowered his pointing hand and adjusted his horse's reins as he continued. "I was not there at the time, but had I been, then this mad man's head might be stuck in a pike somewhere outside Cyanakin Hold."

"That's not fair, you have no idea what we're up against," Garrick replied.

"I think we better find a place to camp out, it will be dark soon, and it will be difficult to follow his tracks in the dark without using light and, I don't know about you two, but I don't want what happened to that deer over there, to happen to me," Hyde said.

"You're right, we should return to Cyanakin Hold and come back first thing in the morning," Thaniel replied.

"The Forlorn Cathedral is only a couple miles ahead, we could always camp out there to save time," Garrick suggested.

"That glade is forbidden," Hyde said.

Thaniel nodded gravely. "I was always told by my father that the Forlorn Cathedral is an accursed place."

The Arsonist

"It's the last place a creature of evil would want to be near," Garrick argued.

"And how would you even know that?" Hyde asked.

Before the two could start to bicker, Thaniel intervened and overpowered their voices with a loud shout thus breaking up their dispute. "We will follow these tracks until the sun disappears from our sight and then we will rest at the Forlorn Cathedral."

Both Garrick and Hyde nodded in compliance with Thaniel's order and within seconds, the three were off again following the hoof prints left behind by the dark horse of the Arsonist. As the sun disappeared from the sky and left behind a dark blanket of white stars, the three men arrived at the grassy field that lay before the iron gates to the cathedral space.

"The hoof prints are going all over the place in multiple directions, but it appears that they go into the glade and past the cathedral courtyard gate," Thaniel said.

"Maybe the Arsonist has been hiding out in the cathedral all along," Hyde replied.

"Should we go knock on the door and see who's home?" Garrick asked.

Thaniel dismounted from his grey horse and approached the gate. "It's locked, and the walls are too dangerous to climb," he said.

"I wonder how he got ahold of the keys," Garrick said.

"Why don't you use that new bow of yours and blow the lock off with it?" Hyde suggested.

Thaniel raised his eyebrows in amazement. "I didn't even think about that, I am still not used to possessing such a powerful weapon," he admitted.

Hyde rolled his eyes as he began to dismount from his grey horse.

"So, why did your father give you his legendary bow, anyway?" Garrick asked.

"I'm not sure to be honest. I have been asking myself that for a few days now," Thaniel replied. He pulled the bow off his back where it was holstered and took aim on the lock of the gate. He let loose a bolt, knocking the lock of the gate clean off and searing the two iron bars that lay behind it in half. "Well, isn't that just impressive," he murmured. He pulled back another arrow as he kicked the loose gate open.

"So much for the subtle approach of rangers," Garrick said.

"I'm sure he knows we're here already, we weren't being

particularly quiet," Hyde replied.

"Yes, but now we have him trapped if he is still here. The entire cathedral is surrounded by this tall, sharp metal fence," Thaniel replied.

"Well, it was my idea to blow open the gate, so if he gets away this time you can blame it on me," Hyde said.

"He won't get away," Thaniel promised.

Both Garrick and Hyde drew their bows and readied an arrow on the string in case the Arsonist appeared in their sights. They slowly approached the front doors to the cathedral but noticed that the hoof prints along with footprints and paw prints all trailed off to the back of the cathedral.

"Do you think he went inside this way?" Hyde whispered.

"It doesn't look like this cathedral has been opened in years," Thaniel hissed back.

The three men readied their bows again as they followed the trail of prints that led to the cellar doors that lay in the back of the cathedral.

"He has got to be in there," Hyde said.

Garrick looked at Hyde and nodded in agreement as Thaniel let loose an arrow on the cellar door lock, blowing the wooded doors apart. Garrick charged down into the cellar first to find the damp and dark cellar completely abandoned. A lantern lay abandoned next to a makeshift, wooden bed. The dust on the glass surface was smudged clean where a hand seemed the have opened it.

"He isn't here," Garrick said, "but he was."

Each of the three rangers had a similar look of defeat on their faces as they searched the cellar for any clues of the Arsonist's whereabouts.

"It is forbidden to step foot on such holy grounds," a woman's voice said.

The three men looked over at the cellar doors once to see where the voice was coming from. They turned back to the entrance as a hooded ranger walked down the steps into the space.

"Mavis, is that you?" Hyde asked.

"Hello, Hyde," Mavis replied.

Mavis had light brown hair, green eyes, and brown skin. She stood in the entryway to the cellar with the same ranger attire as the three ranger men. A long dark grey cloak with a hood, brown vest, and a set of matching brown and tough woven pants. Her cloth gloves were fingerless at the tips. In her left hand she held a shiny red apple, and in her right, a long wooden bow. Two long daggers were sheathed on the sides of her waist, attached to a belt that hung down lower than the men's belts did.

"What are you doing here, Mavis?" Garrick asked.

"I came to ask you three the same thing," Mavis replied.

"We asked you first," Garrick replied.

"Enough, Garrick." Thaniel said. "Mavis, we are here on official business."

"Official business that involves breaking into an abandoned yet sacred place?" Mavis asked.

"We are searching for the Arsonist at Lord Cadere's request," Hyde interjected.

"The Arsonist?" Mavis asked, incredulous.

"Yes, isn't he the reason why you're here?" Hyde asked.

"No, and what makes you so sure that it's a he?" "Because Mavis, what kind of sick bastard burns down a schoolhouse full of men and women? Only a mad man would do that, women don't commit such crimes," Garrick said.

"If you say so," Mavis replied. The shadow cast over Mavis' face by her hood slightly concealed her smirk as she took another bite of her apple.

"If you're not here for the Arsonist, then why are you here, Mavis?" Thaniel asked.

"I was charged with protecting this cathedral space," Mavis replied.

"Well, you haven't done a very good job of that."

"This place was sealed tight and abandoned until you showed up!"

"No, it was not."

"The Arsonist has been living here under your nose this whole time, Mavis," Garrick added.

"How did you not see him coming and going as he pleased?" Thaniel demanded.

Hyde tapped his chin thoughtfully. "Or maybe she did know, and she just didn't want to report it."

"Have you three lost your minds?" Mavis waved her apple around in front of their faces as if to bring them back to reality. "I had no idea he was here, and I just got assigned this place yesterday as a result of Lord Cadere pulling more rangers away from Fort Quiver."

"Why would he do that?" Thaniel asked.

Mavis frowned. "He's your father, I was hoping you could tell me." "I heard that Lord Cadere was pulling rangers away from Fort Quiver so that he could cover more ground in the Western Glades," Garrick offered. "He didn't like having a whole army clumped up there."

"That doesn't make any sense—Fort Quiver is our only defense against the south and east, if it is not reinforced or well protected and it falls, we will lose almost the entire Amberwood forest along with all of its villages," Thaniel replied.

Garrick shrugged. "Maybe it's because of whatever had ravaged that deer we saw earlier."

"Doubtful," said Hyde.

Thaniel stroked his chin. "I must go and see my father at once," he said. The chance of Garrick being correct about anything were slim, but the fact that Mavis heard something similar about the movement of troops in Fort Quiver was concerning.

"I'm coming with you," Mavis said.

"Why?" Hyde asked. "Don't you have a duty here to protect this place?"

"Yes," Mavis replied, "but no thanks to you, that duty has now been nullified."

The four rangers stepped up out of the cellar to see the star lit night sky above them. They strapped their bows to their backs and prepared to leave for Cyanakin hold. Garrick stopped patting his horse when he noticed a pile of horse droppings near the tree that cast a shadow over the cellar door. He approached it curiously and kneeled beside it to touch it with his fingertips to taste it like the mud from the Yokel Ranch barn glade.

"What is it that you found there, Garrick?" Hyde asked.

Garrick placed his fingertips on his tongue before spitting out the vile substance in disgust.

"Garrick? What is it?" Mavis asked.

Garrick cleared his throat. "Horse shit," he said decidedly.

Hyde scrunched up his nose in disgust. "I told you to stop doing that, it's not civilized."

Garrick stood up and looked at Thaniel, who was now mounted on his grey horse and approaching slowly. "This did not come from any of our horses," Garrick said.

"How do you know that?" Thaniel asked.

"It's fresh, but it's not that fresh," Garrick explained.

Mavis and Hyde burst out into laughter as they both mounted their horses. Garrick scowled at both of them as Thaniel sighed. "Its dry texture and mild taste means that it is less than two days old," Garrick said.

"You're sure of this?" Thaniel asked at length. Was Garrick ever sure of anything?

"How did you manage to gather that much information from a pile of shit?" Hyde asked.

"Because," Garrick retorted, "unlike you, I actually paid attention during the academy exercises."

"I saw a trail of hoof and paw prints outside the gate to the perimeter, they were heading east towards the Amberwood cemetery, so maybe he has gone to bury someone?" Mavis asked.

"Maybe," Garrick replied.

"If you actually paid attention in the academy, you would know that you can figure out the same information without tasting the animal feces," Hyde said.

Garrick put his hand on the sword that hung from his waist as he approached Hyde on his horse. "One more word out of you and I'll cut out your tongue."

Hyde pretended to act scared as he laughed at Garrick.

"Stop, no more fighting you two," Thaniel interjected.

"So, what's the plan?" Mavis asked, pointedly ignoring the others.

"The Arsonist will be caught, but the withdrawal of outer defenses from Fort Quiver troubles me more," Thaniel replied.

"We're returning to Cyanakin Hold?" Garrick asked, the sword at his waist forgotten for the moment.

"What happened to the determination, Thaniel? I thought you said he wouldn't get away," Hyde said pointedly.

"If my father knows something of our outer defenses that I don't, then that could mean that the entire west is in danger as we know it, which is a lot more concerning for us than some troublesome pyromaniac," Thaniel replied.

Garrick crossed his arms. "I disagree, I think we need to finish what we started here tonight."

"Considering that he is already gone and that we would have to track him in the dark, I would rather continue this pursuit another time." Thaniel's tone left little room for argument.

"Let me stay behind with Mavis and await his return then," said Garrick. "After the Arsonist is done doing whatever it is he is doing at the cemetery, he will return here to the cathedral space. When he does, I will be waiting for him."

"I'm not staying here, especially not with you," Mavis replied.

"I'm not staying here either. I'd rather sleep in my comfy bed than in this light-forsaken place," Hyde said.

"Some rangers you are," Garrick muttered.

"Very well Garrick," Thaniel said. "Feel free to stay here alone."

Thaniel, Hyde, and Mavis took off on horseback into the forest, leaving Garrick behind outside the destroyed cellar doors.

Garrick led his horse outside of the cathedral walls and tied it to a tree so that the Arsonist would not see it lingering near the cellar. He found a tree that he could climb that stood outside the broken front gates. As he climbed the tree, he heard a terrible sound coming from his horse in the nearby distance. He could hear voices of men coming from the same direction but could not make out any words.

He continued to climb the tree, thinking that it was just Hyde and Thaniel messing with his horse in an attempt to spook him. The terrible sound of the horse came to a halt as Garrick neared the top of the tree and found a branch big enough to sit on. He looked down below his feet that hung from the high branch to see a white-haired man walking past the tree and towards the cathedral gate.

Garrick quietly pulled his bow off from his back and took aim at the figure as he realized it was not one of his fellow rangers. As he prepared to let loose an arrow into his back, he began to wonder if this was the Arsonist. The descriptions of the Arsonist on the wanted posters of Prosperwood and Cyanakin Hold described him as wearing dark clothing and wearing a strange white mask.

Without further hesitation, Garrick let loose the arrow. It pierced into the white-haired man that crept beneath the tree. The man let out a shrieking scream and fell to the ground. Still alive, he attempted to crawl towards the gate. As Garrick regretfully let loose the arrow, he saw a man and a woman with similar white hair appear beside the one he had shot. The second arrow pierced the crawling white haired man, ending his life.

The man and woman with similar features looked up at the tree to see Garrick sitting atop it. Their red eyes faintly glowed in the dark as they charged towards the tree.

Garrick attempted to shoot the white-haired woman, but the arrow flew clear. Before he could draw another one from his side quiver, he felt something grab his left foot and pull him down.

Garrick's face smacked a tree branch on the way down and he landed badly on his right arm and leg. The arm let out an unpleasant cracking sound that echoed deep in the pit of his stomach. The bow lay in two pieces next to him.

The man and woman with white hair and red eyes stood above him. They each let out a shrieking sound as they opened their mouths to reveal fanged canine teeth. Garrick screamed in both fear and pain as he lay helplessly on the ground at their feet. From behind their frail and pale bodies, he could see several more walking through the trees towards them. They all looked very similar, a grotesque pale complexion, faintly glowing red eyes, fanged canine teeth, and stringy white hair that appeared to be falling out.

The stringy white-haired men and women charged down at Garrick and began to tear into him with their teeth. Garrick's screams of agony were quickly silenced as one of the white-haired men ripped out Garrick's throat with his teeth. The red eyed men and women dug into Garrick with such savagery that they were like a pack of wolves feasting on a fresh kill.

Thaniel, Mavis, and Hyde were too far gone to hear the painful screams of Garrick or the terrible cries of his grey horse. After they finished feasting upon Garrick, the stringy white-haired men and women began to stumble their way towards gates to the Forlorn Cathedral glade.

Chapter Ten

The druid recruits sat in a circle surrounding the Monolith that pierced through the earth like an arrow pointed toward the sky. The chirping sounds of crickets and other various bugs fell upon the ears of the recruits at a constant, thus breaking their meditative silence. Moths flew around the closed eyes of the men and women and tiny black beetles crawled off the tall pieces of grass and onto the crossed legs of the recruits. Nothing could disrupt their silence as they held each other's hands, making a ring around the sanctum while sitting on the grass with their legs crossed.

"Do not be distracted by the sounds and tickling sensations of the insects, they will not harm you here, they are as curious about you as you are about this Monolith," said Crane. He stood near them, slowly circling the Monolith on foot.

Lylah could feel a moth land on her nose and a beetle climbing in and out of the space between her toes. She refused to open her eyes or move a muscle because if she made any sudden moves then Crane would notice her movements. The recruits were being tested on their physical discipline to see how they would react to what Crane referred to as 'the forces of nature.' Although Crane circled the whole Monolith to get a good scope of all the recruits, he never once stopped looking at Lylah unless she slipped past his vision from behind the Monolith. He was determined to catch her making a mistake so that he could fail her trial and send her home.

"Two more hours to go," said Crane.

Atop one of the largest willow trees that drooped over the Monolith was a small series of branches that were big and wide enough for a human to stand on or sit on. Sitting down on the branches were Juspen and two other elders with whiskery bearded chins. Their frayed purple robes moved with the fall breeze that seeped through the drooping branches of the large Salix tree.

"Lots of promising trials this year," said one of the elders.

"Yes, however, I fear that they will not be enough, Folisco," Juspen replied.

"Isn't the council of nobles planning to reinforce us?" Folisco asked.

"No," Juspen replied.

"Then we are doomed," Folisco replied.

"It would seem that way, but we cannot abandon our sworn duties," Juspen replied.

"Have they all gone mad?" one of the elders asked.

"They claim to be fighting internal battles and that the Weeping Grove is no longer a crucial part of the realm," Juspen replied.

"We'll see how crucial it is when it has been razed to the ground by savages and they find their peasants dying of fevers and other ailments with nothing to treat them with," the elder man replied.

Juspen cast his eyes down upon Lylah and watched her curiously as he lightly pulled on the hairs of his chin beard. It was not that he sensed a special purpose about her, but rather that he saw a lot of his mother in her. The old women that controlled the Weeping Grove with a matriarchal atmosphere had diminished with time. Most of the women were incapable of bearing children for whatever reason, some claimed it was the price they paid for guarding the Monolith over the course of their entire lives. The few women that were able to bear children usually lost their lives in the birthing process. The offspring of the female druids that were able to give birth were made up mostly of boys and thus a change to the matriarchal state of the druid order was changed for survivability purposes. Juspen's mother was one of the last great female elders and he saw a lot of her strong-willed and rebellious characteristics within Lylah.

***

"You wretch, I saw you itch your back," Crane's voice cracked through the quiet. A lost looking recruit opened his eyes to see Crane towering over him. "Get out of my grove this instant," he said.

The recruit rose to his feet quickly and stood at attention before Crane with his arms at his waist side. "I said," Crane's voice grated, "get out of my grove."

"I'm s-o-sorry," the man replied.

"Yes, yes you are sorry." He grabbed the recruit by his arm and began to drag him away from the circle. The man got loose of Crane's grip and took off running south toward Earth Arch Pass to leave the grove. Crane scowled but let him go. "Sorry and pathetic," he muttered. The remaining recruits did not dare move a muscle.

"Does anyone else here not have the will to sit quietly on the grass for four hours?" Crane snarled. "A task so simple, a mere child could accomplish it?"

The recruits remained silent, allowing only the chirping of insects to be heard. They made no indication they had even heard Crane speak.

"I didn't think so," Crane said.

As Lylah breathed slowly in and out of her nose. She could feel the presence of Crane standing in front of her as his bald head blocked out the sun above like an eclipse. She knew how badly he wanted her to fail, and knowing this fueled her willpower to succeed, for she would not let him have the satisfaction of sending her home.

***

The three elders continued to converse with one another from atop the great Salix tree.

"How much time left do you think we have?" Folisco asked.

"Enough," Juspen replied.

"Enough?"

"I may have sent a few masters to the Northern Reach to seek out aid," Juspen replied.

"You did what?" Folisco asked. The two elder men shook their heads and sighed as Juspen remained silent with his eyes fixed on Lylah, who sat two hundred feet below him.

"You had no right to do that without holding a proper vote, Juspen," Folisco said.

"I did what had to be done, we cannot afford to lose the grove, or the sanctum for that matter," Juspen replied.

"We are but few in numbers, and now we are even less because you sent some of the youngest and most capable druids we had to their deaths in the harsh north. Even if they return with help, it will just be a bunch of rugged mercenaries, or worse," Folisco replied.

The two elder men could not be more disgusted with Juspen as they brushed past him to make their way down the ladder of the tree.

Juspen's eyes closed as the cool fall breeze whistled past his body and into the distant tree leaves. He knew that even if the masters somehow didn't manage to return, the grove would still have an important ace up its sleeve.

What the other elders did not yet fully realize was that one of their new recruits was not just some girl from the north. She was Lylah Proditore, the daughter of the most renowned man in all the Realms of Light, Nielas Proditore. Juspen knew that Nielas was not capable of letting his daughter be subjected to war-torn violence and he knew that Nielas would not risk her life by sending her to a place such as the Weeping Grove without keeping a watchful eye on her. If the danger that the elders knew and were afraid of was to invade their sanctum, then it would force Nielas to get involved.

Chapter Eleven

The Glade Belt was a strip of open grassy and rocky land that started at the Yokel Fields and carved its way east through the Western Glades. It was a curvy area around the central glade regions of the realm and had a small stone road that led from the Yokel Fields to the Brooding Bridge. The sky turned dark as the sun went down after a long day of the Arsonist riding from the Forlorn Cathedral to the point of the stone road that curved north toward the Brooding Bridge glade. The Arsonist avoided riding horseback on the road whenever he could since they were always occupied by travelers and protected by Cyanakin rangers. The Arsonist slowly made his way through the Glade Belt while Glacier followed behind at a similar pace. They stuck to the southern border of the belt as it was easier to be concealed by the trees, thus making them less noticeable to the wandering eyes of traveling traders and the vigilant eyes of the watchful rangers.

    The Arsonist stopped Xenos so that he could dismount him and stretch his legs. He pulled a leather flask out of his saddle pack and lifted his mask to take a quick sip of water. He cupped his left hand as he poured water into it. He quickly lowered his hand to the ground where Glacier sat as the water leaked through the cracks of his gloved fingers. Glacier licked the water from the Arsonist's cupped hand without missing a drop, leaving the leather glove damp with wolf saliva and flask water. The Arsonist pet him before reaching into his pack for an old carrot he had stolen a few days prior from the Yokel Fields. He held the carrot in front of Xenos' mouth, who quickly snatched it and chewed it until it was gone.

The voices of two incoming travelers in the distance alerted Glacier, who let out a bark to let his master know. The Arsonist grabbed the reins of his carrot-eating horse and began to pull it to the nearby edge of the forest so that they could hide behind a few of the Amberwood trees. He could not help but find how odd it was for two men to be walking along this road so late at night, especially without a lantern or any other light sources.

As the two voices got within viewing distance, the Arsonist was able to make out their appearances more clearly. There was an old man in ragged pauper clothes and a young man in decorative robes. As they proceeded to get closer, the Arsonist was able to hide behind a tree and listen to their conversation.

"I'm just saying that if we're going all the way to the Eastern Vale, it would have made more sense to steal, if not purchase a horse before we left," Rhys said.

"There was no time for that," Farbris replied.

"It would have saved time, and our feet also wouldn't be covered in blisters by the time we make it to the city gates," Rhys replied.

"Yes, but we don't have money for a horse, and stealing one would have been too risky," Farbris replied.

"Have you been to Yokelshire recently? Those farmers are as dumb as rocks," Rhys replied.

Farbris startled at the sound of a twig snapping in the forest. He quickly put his hand over Rhys' mouth and quietly motioned them to be silent. "Listen, whatever happens here, I need you to remain calm and stay quiet," Farbris said.

Rhys nodded his head in response to Farbris without attempting to utter a single word. Farbris removed his hand from Rhys' mouth and began to set down the old bag that once was used to carry tomatoes and potatoes across Yokelshire. He reached into the bag and pulled out sealed glass jars filled to the brim with a red liquid. Rhys looked around anxiously. He hoped that whatever was snapping on the branches was a ranger or a lost trader.

"Farbris, why are you here so early? It is not the first of the month yet. It is only the twenty-third," a raspy man's voice said.

Farbris finished setting all the glass jars of red liquid onto the stone road and stood up before backing away from them. He looked at the dark forest north of the glade belt to see several white-haired men and women standing in the shaded clearing of the forest's border. They all wore bright colorful clothes, making them easy for Rhys and Farbris to see. Their eclectic clothing resembled that of royal nobility and accumulated wealth. Their pale skin and faces were the only parts of their body that were not covered by some type of richly designed article of clothing.

"I am making next month's delivery early, for I have a personal matter to attend to in the east," said Farbris.

"You never notified Lord Argentwald of this matter," the raspy voice replied. A long and thin-faced man with dark-colored lips and glowing red eyes that sank into his skull stepped ahead of the other white-haired men and women. His raspy voice sent shivers down Rhys' spine. The Arsonist stood behind a tree to the south of them holding Glacier's mouth shut tightly with both his hands. He did not understand what was happening here on the stone road of the Glade Belt, but he recognized the pale skinned men and their colorfully royal-looking clothes.

"I didn't have time since this matter was sprung upon me yesterday afternoon," Farbris replied.

"I count nine jars here, but you were instructed to bring twelve for next month's delivery," the raspy-voiced man replied.

"Yes, due to my early delivery, the suppliers were not able to gather the other three jars in time, but do not worry, I will bring you fifteen when I return," Farbris replied.

"Worry? You are the one that is surrounded by those you made a deal with—a deal that you are attempting to weasel your way out of. If there is anyone who should be worried here, it's you," the raspy-voiced man replied.

"I assure you that I am not trying to do any weasel business here," Farbris pleaded. "I just have urgent matters to attend to in the east."

Rhys began to feel the cold sweat of fear dripping down the sides of his brow. He noticed the same thing happening to his uncle; a long strand of sweat had started to drip down Farbris' left cheek, giving Rhys no assurance that things were going well.

"What is this urgent matter that you must attend to?" an elegant voice asked.

Farbris' eyes turned from those that belonged to the man with the raspy voice to those that belonged to the elegant voice. It belonged to a woman standing near him to his left, her curly white hair bouncing on her shoulders as she circled him and Rhys. Her red eyes were almond-shaped, and her smirking lips were a light shade of red, as if lipstick had been applied to their previous pale appearance.

"My son has been sent to the Festering Cage, and I seek to liberate him from its domain.".

"The Festering Cage? Sounds like he must have done something pretty bad to have been sent there," she replied.

"Yes, something pretty bad, and pretty foolish," Farbris agreed.

Rhys' heartbeat began to pound as he felt the whitehaired woman standing behind him. She traced her pointed fingernails along the back of his neck. "What's the matter with this one, Farbris? Has he never seen a lady before?" she asked.

"No, at least not one as lovely looking as yourself," Farbris replied.

The white-haired woman removed her tracing fingers from Rhys' neck as she glared at Farbris who was smiling nervously at her.

"Why have you never brought him with you before? He looks quite tender," the raspy-voiced man asked.

"He is my scholarly nephew who has traveled from the east to tell me what has befallen my son," Farbris replied.

Rhys' eyes snapped wide open as he looked over at Farbris.

"You lie," the white-haired woman said.

"I would be a fool to lie to you in your presence my lady," Farbris replied.

The woman lifted a pristine eyebrow, "Indeed."

The Arsonist felt Glacier fighting to get loose from his grip as he let out a whimper. The white-haired man with the raspy voice looked at one of the other white-haired men and nodded at them as if motioning them to go check out the noise.

"Is it just you two here?" the white-haired woman asked.

"Yes," Farbris replied.

"Is that another lie?" she asked.

"I swear we are alone."

"How about you leave us your so-called nephew here to make

up for the three jars of blood you owe us, and we'll let you be on your way to the Festering Cage."

"I can't do that, he is very important to me," Farbris said. "And, uh, I will not be able to free my son without his scholarly knowledge."

"You of all people should know better than to travel along the Glade Belt Road after the sun goes down," the woman said.

"I knew you would all be here at this time of night and I didn't want to make you think I had forgotten our agreement," Farbris replied.

The white-haired man that was sent to check out the whimpering noise now stood in front of the tree that the Arsonist hid behind. The Arsonist held Glacier with both his hands muzzling the fidgeting wolf. Xenos wandered off deep into the woods just out of sight of the white-haired man whose red eyes peered into the darkness of the tree-covered landscape.

"Although this road has become our favorite hunting ground, the Festering Cage has become our main source of food ever since Lord Argentwald made a deal with you. So, if you are planning to go and cause any disruptions to our little livestock operation then you would be disturbing the fragile ecosystem that you have somehow managed to create here in the Western Glades," the white-haired woman said.

"I can assure you, that is not my intent," Farbris replied.

The Arsonist could wait no longer for the white-haired man to get any closer. He let Glacier go as he jumped out from the tree to reveal himself to the white-haired man. As the man turned and opened his mouth to shout toward the others, he was consumed by a torrent of fire. The Arsonist knew he had only one vial of flamethrower fuel in his pocket, and he needed to make it count. The torrent of fire that was released had set three of the nearby trees on fire, thus alerting the other white-haired men and women that had been circling Farbris and Rhys.

"You dare try to cross us?" the white-haired woman asked.

"Never, I don't know what's going on," Farbris replied.

The raspy-voiced man with white hair opened his mouth to reveal his long, sharp canines. His red pupils dilated as he charged toward Rhys. Before he could reach him, Glacier lunged from the grass behind him and dug his sharp wolf teeth into the soft pale skin of the man's left leg. The man let out a raspy scream for help as Glacier dug his teeth deeper into the man's ankle. Xenos fearfully

took off deeper into the forest to get away from the burning trees.
"Kill them both," the white-haired woman said.
Farbris quickly picked up one of the jars of blood. He turned around to strike the woman in the face. The jar of blood shattered. Glass cut open her pale face. Her neck and dress were drenched in blood. She screamed in pain and disgust as Farbris grabbed Rhys and took off running toward the burning trees.

The other pale-skinned men and women wanted to chase after Farbris and Rhys, but they could not take their eyes off the white-haired woman drenched in blood. Black bubbling blood oozed out of the wounds on her face as she pulled out broken shards of glass.

"What are you fools doing?" she cried. "Stop them!"

Their dimly lit red eyes dilated as they slowly approached her with revealed fangs.

"Don't even think about it," the white-haired woman said.

Before she could let out a scream, they tackled her. The white-haired men and women that had previously been circling Farbris and Rhys with her finally gave in to their uncontrollable hunger as they dug their fangs into her. As they all clustered around her body and feasted upon her flesh and blood, they were quickly set ablaze by the Arsonist, who released another torrent of fire from his gauntlets. As the jet of fire consumed them, they immediately exploded into ash. The ash set in and then blew away with the nightfall breeze that crept into the Glade Belt from the southern part of the forest.

Farbris and Rhys turned away from the smoking fire of the forest that had begun to spread south to see the Arsonist standing triumphantly over the now dead raspy-voiced man. The Arsonist's foot was pressing down on the raspy-voiced man's throat, which asphyxiated him to death.

"Who are you?" Farbris asked.

The Arsonist kneeled to pick up a jar of blood that Farbris had set down on the road previously. "Is this animal blood?" he asked.

"Yes, I am pretty sure it is cow or pig's blood," Farbris replied.

The Arsonist turned to look at Farbris and Rhys while holding the jar.

Farbris was immediately surprised by what he saw on the Arsonist's face. It was a mask that he had seen many years ago. "I know that mask," Farbris said.

"There are many wanted posters of me along the walls of Prosperwood," the Arsonist replied.

"I have never seen them," Farbris replied.

"I have," said Rhys.

Farbris and Rhys made their way back onto the road to thank the Arsonist for his rescue but were immediately separated from him by the growling wolf that lay before them. Glacier was not interested in letting them near his master, his teeth were showing, and his hair was standing straight up as he ferociously growled at Farbris and Rhys.

"Why are you delivering blood to these fiends?" the Arsonist asked.

Farbris looked down in shame as Rhys also looked at him questionably.

"Uncle?" Rhys asked.

The Arsonist walked over to Glacier and began to pet and calm him down so that he would stop growling at Farbris and Rhys. "It's okay boy," he said. Glacier whined and licked his teeth but obliged.

"I made a pact with these sick people three years ago," Farbris said.

"They are not people," the Arsonist replied.

"Wait, so is that why you always disappeared in the night? You told me you were going out for drinks and to look for a good time with a lady," Rhys said.

"Well, most of the time I was doing just that, there were other times however where I came out here and did something similar to this," Farbris replied.

"Did you ever think of the risk? What if they had killed you? What would I have done without you?" Rhys asked.

Farbris' eyes and lips trembled as his heart grew heavy in the face of his worried and teary-eyed nephew, "I did it to protect Prosperwood, to protect us, to protect you," he said.

"You weren't protecting anything. You were merely delaying the inevitable," The Arsonist interjected.

"I beg your pardon?" Farbris replied.

"Look, we're very grateful for your assistance but we—," Rhys stopped.

Xenos had swiftly begun to ride in toward Glacier and the three men. His dark hair nearly blended in with the dark forest behind him. Rhys' hands began to shake. The sight of Xenos reminded him of the nightmares that had recently haunted his sleep.

"Rhys, are you okay?" Farbris asked.

Rhys looked at the Arsonist who stood hooded and masked in the near distance. It all started to make sense to him now, the dark hooded rider on the dark horse. "I know you from my dreams," he said.

The Arsonist didn't quite understand what Rhys was saying, as if it couldn't even be possible, "Did you not hear me mention the wanted posters before?" he asked. Glacier, now bored with the interaction of the humans, had found his place at the Arsonist's feet where he decided to lay down and stare at the forests in hope that a rabbit or squirrel would appear. Xenos restlessly walked around the northern part of the forest that the stone road trailed off into.

"I have seen many wanted posters on my way through town, but that is not where I know you from," Rhys said.

Farbris also found the Arsonist to be quite familiar for he had seen that white porcelain mask with the intricate red winged eyelid design before. He vividly remembers his sister Marathair making one that looked similar when they were young, this was weeks before he left the Eastern Vale to journey south and become a scholar.

"I want to know why you are delivering blood and what the deal you made was," the Arsonist said.

"The deal was that if I had animal blood harvested from Yokelshire and delivered to Prosperwood then I could exchange it for safety. On the first evening of every month, I deliver ten to twelve jars of blood to the men and women that lived within Argentwald Manor and occupied the Brooding Bridge glade," Farbris replied.

"There you go again, calling them men and women," the Arsonist said.

Farbris raised both his fists in frustrated anger as Rhys stepped away from him to avoid the swinging of his uncle's arms. "What else would you have me call them?" he demanded.

"They are fiends," the Arsonist replied.

"Fiends?" Farbris asked.

Rhys was shocked by his uncle's words, but was more concerned by the Arsonist's appearance as it carefully resembled the appearance of the hooded and mounted figure from his dreams.

"Yes, that is what I would have you call them, and if you're ever unlucky enough to see a starving one that has gone completely ballistic, then you may call those ones ferals," the Arsonist said. He pulled out his last vial and began refueling his gauntlets.

Both Rhys and Farbris were curious about what type of technology it was for and neither of them had ever seen anything like it before. "What is that strapped around your forearms?" Rhys asked.

"This is the defender of two unarmed idjits that tried to deliver blood to a group of fiends in the middle of the night," the Arsonist replied.

Farbris rolled his eyes and sighed in frustration as Rhys squinted his eyes in confusion at the Arsonist. "Thank you for saving us oh mighty defender of the Glade Belt Road. I am afraid that we must be going now. I will let you know that by sabotaging our deal with the so-called fiends as you like to call them, you have endangered the lives of every man, woman, and child that lives in this realm," Farbris said.

"Oh, as if your little blood jar deal was going so well before I showed up," the Arsonist replied.

"We were just about to leave until your wolf companion here," Farbris said, gesturing wildly at Glacier, "which is probably going to turn into a fiend now, by the way., decided to let the so-called fiends or ferals or whatever it is you like to call them know that you were here, and therefore, that we were not alone."

Glacier did not appreciate Farbris pointing at him and began to growl at him once again.

"Animals can't turn into one of them, and I tried to restrain and muzzle him with my hands for as long as I could," the Arsonist replied.

Farbris furrowed his sweaty brow as he cocked his head to the side, "What?"

"You didn't know that?" the Arsonist asked. A quiet chuckle came from behind the Arsonist's mask as he grabbed the reins of Xenos to keep him from wandering away again. Rhys remained quiet and overwhelmed as he took a seat on the grassy stone road.

"How does that work?" Farbris asked.

"You're the expert that likes to feed them, you tell me," the Arsonist replied. He pulled himself up onto Xenos and readied himself to leave Rhys and Farbris so that he could get back to his task. "You should be safe to travel from here to the Southern Abyss now, but I have no idea of what awaits you there," he said.

"You're leaving us?" Rhys asked. Rhys and Farbris couldn't see it, but The Arsonist's face wore a look of disgust and confusion hidden behind his porcelain mask. Farbris' attention was focused on Glacier, whose yellow eyes were fixed on Farbris and followed him every time he moved around.

"I have personal business to the east of here that I must attend to, just like you," the Arsonist said.

"You mentioned wanted posters before. Why are you wanted in Prosperwood?" Farbris asked.

"I am wanted all over the Western Glades," the Arsonist replied. He smiled behind his porcelain mask as he motioned Xenos to start walking.

"Are you one of them?" Rhys asked.

The Arsonist came to a halt and turned around on his horse to look back at Rhys. "No."

"Why do you have red eyes, then?" Rhys asked.

Suddenly, Farbris' vision went blank as he disappeared into his memory. The mask and the red eyes were starting to build a picture within his mind. He remembered the two babies that had appeared before him. They were the result of the ritual he performed on his sister's newborn child. Nineteen years ago, in the Southern Foothills, he held them together on a rug like tapestry. He shook his head to clear his vision.

"How old are you?" Farbris asked.

"Nineteen, almost twenty," Rhys replied.

Farbris scowled. "Not you!"

The Arsonist turned back to face forward. He motioned Xenos to move. Xenos delayed the departure for a moment and then suddenly took off at a full gallop, and within moments, he was already well over a mile away.

Chapter Twelve

Rhys helped Farbris gather their cloth bags of supplies that had been dropped during the commotion. The sacks had food, water, and other various objects such as a writing quill and container of black ink that had been spilt everywhere.

"What an arsehole," Farbris said.

Rhys remained silent; he was too busy dwelling on the Arsonist and trying desperately to scour his memories for some sort of connection between him and his past dreams. Farbris sat on the ground and took a swig of water from his flask. Rhys was angry with his uncle for not telling him about the blood deliveries he was making all this time, but he didn't want to show it, for they both had a long journey to share ahead of them.

"Are you alright my boy?" Farbris asked.

"I'm fine," Rhys replied.

Farbris gave him a suspicious look. "That's what Faelina used to say to me when she was piss drunk mad at me."

"I just don't understand why you never told me about all of this," Rhys replied.

The smell of cow blood filled the air, the odor so potent that

Rhys could taste it on his tongue if he held his mouth open long enough. He desperately tried to delay the breaths he was taking with his mouth as a result.

"I don't know why I didn't tell you either. I think part of me felt that I was protecting you from the dangers that lay outside Prosperwood," Farbris said.

"I'm not a child. I am aware of the scary things that dwell within this world," Rhys replied.

"No, my boy, you really aren't." Farbris took another swig from his flask as if he was trying to empty it out with one gulp.

"Well, we best get a move on before any more of those fiends show up," Farbris continued.

"Oh, so now you're going to start calling them fiends now?" Rhys asked.

"It's starting to grow on me."

The two of them gathered their cloth sacks off the ground and then they were off. They went off the stone road path that led north towards the Brooding Bridge glade and instead headed east into the last forest they would see for days. As they entered the forest, the snapping of branches was the only sound that the two could consistently hear. The occasional bat would fly past them and make Rhys jump and Farbris laugh.

"I wonder if we will see him again," Rhys said.

Farbris ignored Rhys' comment. The idea of seeing the Arsonist again caused his mind to twist and whirl with possibilities. He started to wonder if the boy could actually be the child that his sister Marathair gave birth to. If the Arsonist was the other child from the day of Severance, then that would mean that Alarick failed to kill him as he had said he would. Was Alarick even alive? The two had not spoken or seen each other in seventeen years. Farbris made peace with the idea that his sister and her husband might both have died long ago. In his mind, they were both victims trapped in a cruel web of fate that had been spun by that bastard Zersten all those long years ago.

"Uncle?" Rhys asked.

Farbris shook his head as if he had just woken up from a dream or trance-like state. He had completely stopped walking in the forest and was staring at a moss covered rock on the ground for a few minutes while lost in deep thought.

"Yes?" Farbris asked.

"Are you alright? You stopped and have been looking at that

rock for a few minutes now, at first, I thought you were going to relieve yourself but…"

"Yes, sorry my boy I just have never seen a rock covered in so much moss before, it almost looks like a giant ball of grass, doesn't it?"

"Yeah, sort of, I guess," Rhys said.

Rhys had been drifting off into his thoughts too and so he could tell that his uncle was as well. He knew that something wasn't right with his uncle since their encounter with the Arsonist. It was almost as if his uncle was not telling him something, but after discovering his uncle's last secret, he almost didn't want to know what it possibly could be. The one question Rhys found peculiar that Farbris had asked the Arsonist was his age. He wanted to ask his uncle why he asked that question, but he knew his uncle would avoid it, or give him a fake answer.

"I know we have never been to the Southern Abyss before, and I know that everything you have probably heard about it is that it's this desolate wasteland of dead grass and dirt. I want you to know that everything you have heard is true," Farbris said.

"It was historically described as once being a lush and fertile land of golden rolling hills," Rhys replied.

"At one time it might have been that but now it is just a depressing bowl of dust that collects the bones of fallen men and women from past conflicts," Farbris replied.

"The Trinity Kingdom War?" Rhys asked.

"Aye, the Trinity Kingdom War," Farbris replied.

"You were alive during that time, weren't you?" Rhys asked.

Farbris laughed and nearly let it slip that he was the prince of one of the three kingdoms. He caught himself and tried to play it off as if he had forgotten what he was going to say. Farbris could tell by the look on Rhys' face that he was clearly not impressed. Farbris raised his brow as if surprised and excited that he had just remembered what he was going to say.

"I was alive yes, but I was down south learning to be a scholar. I was completely away from all the conflict," Farbris said.

"You once told me that my father was a great warrior that fought in the war," Rhys ventured. "Is that how he died?"

"Yes, and your mother brought you to me in Prosperwood when you were a baby," Farbris replied.

"What happened to her?" Rhys asked.

Farbris paused again but this time consciously. The image of his older sister being dragged away by Zersten's men and then carried off into the woods to never be seen again still choked him up.

"I'm sorry, uncle. I didn't mean to upset you," Rhys said.

"No, it's quite alright my boy," Farbris replied.

Farbris wiped the single tear from the corner of his right eye and continued to walk with Rhys. Suddenly, with a cheery tone in his voice, he continued. "She lived with us, but she was quite old and one day she just passed away in her sleep, she was living with us when you were only two years old," Farbris said.

Rhys didn't believe him. It just didn't make sense or add up in his mind. He clenched his fist in anger but then released it as soon as he noticed what he was doing. Deep down he knew his uncle was lying but he almost wanted to believe him anyway. It was as if he knew the truth was far more painful and dangerous than his uncle was leading him on to believe.

"Wow, she must have been quite old when she had me," Rhys said.

Farbris nodded at Rhys as if he were confirming his statement and then agreeing with it.

"My father must have really had a thing for older women then, seeing as how he had to have been young and in his prime to have been such a brave warrior during such a dark time," Rhys said.

Farbris could somewhat tell what Rhys was trying to do but rather than question why his nephew was attempting to poke holes in his false narrative he instead chose to use this moment for his own personal entertainment and comical relief.

"Oh, why yes, he did. Your father had quite a thing for women that were much more mature than him," Farbris said. Farbris noticed the cringing face of Rhys from the corner of his eye and smirked as he continued.

"It always confused me, because your father was a young stallion with muscles as big as my head. He could have had any girl from the Eastern Vale in his bed at an instant and yet he chose my old and feeble sister," Farbris said.

"I think I've heard enough about my parents and their tastes for one day," Rhys replied.

"Oh, speaking of tastes. I remember your father once told me that he saw women as bottles of wine and that the older they were the better they tasted," Farbris replied.

Rhys stuck his tongue out in disgust and began to make gagging sounds as if he was going to throw up. Farbris couldn't help but laugh, it was a long time since he had the pleasure of teasing and mocking his older sister. As they continued through the forest, Farbris began to get lost in the memories of his sister and the wonderful times they had together. He remembered the time that she used to chase him around the Moran Citadel when they were children, and it nearly brought him to tears.

"I wish I could remember them," Rhys said.

"I wish you could too," Farbris replied.

The two stopped and embraced one another with a hug.

"I'm sorry that you got stuck having to raise me," Rhys muttered.

Farbris pulled away from hugging Rhys so that he could look him in the eyes. Rhys' grey eyes were swollen so badly with tears that Farbris could not see the tiny flecks of blue within them.

"I wasn't stuck raising you, my boy. Never apologize to me for that again," Farbris said.

Rhys nodded as he dug his crying face into his uncle's shoulder. Farbris was never good at dealing with emotional people, especially emotional men. Something was different this time, it had something to do with the fond memories of his older sister and the bond he had with his nephew as a result of her disappearance.

"We're almost to the Whistling Prairie," Farbris said.

Rhys dried his face with the sleeves of his grey scholar robes as his uncle Farbris patted him on the back.

"Try not to get mucus on those robes, they're one of a kind," Farbris said.

Both Rhys and Farbris continued to walk through what felt like a never ending dark forest of amber colored tree leaves and broken twigs that snapped at the lightest footstep. The sun had not fully come out yet, so their vision within the forest was quite limited. Farbris could tell they were going the right way by the amount of wind that was blowing west from the Whistling Prairie and into the Amberwood forest. A gust of wind swept over Rhys and Farbris, blowing their hair back as dozens of amber colored leaves danced in the air around them.

The fallen leaves that danced within the cool nighttime breeze reminded both Rhys and Farbris that winter was approaching the Realms of Light. Winter was Bregan's favorite season due to the solstice festival that would take place within the streets of Prosperwood Village. Rhys remembered how excited his younger cousin would get every year when fall came to a sudden end. Fabris could never forget the joy that Bregan had in his eyes when he saw snow for the first time. Rhys and Farbris continued to walk through the dark forest while meditating silently on the memories of family members they both missed dearly.

Chapter Thirteen

Winter arrived early in the northeast of the Northern Reach. Icy waters now engulfed the rocky sand beaches of the Festering Cage. The salty and freezing cold ocean spray drenched Viti and Bregan as they dragged large wooden planks through wet sand. The guards laughed at Bregan as he struggled to lift the planks from the ground to carry them into the shipyard.

Alarick would often notice Bregan and help him. He occasionally got yelled at by a guard to get back to work and to stop helping the little rat. Bregan often saw Hobart lurking about within the corner of his eyes like some wild predator.

Viti's arrival at the prison had reignited hope within Bregan's mind, for he felt like he might actually have a chance to escape this terrible place.

The shores of the Eastern Vale and Windfall Harbor were out of sight. When Bregan first arrived, he could look out at the sea, and notice the outlines of the land masses, but now due to the winter weather that had come, he could no longer see them. Winter used to be his favorite season, but now that he was standing barefoot on the cold and wet sand, his feelings about it had changed. He no longer longed for the solstice festival anymore. The only thing he longed for now was a nice warm bed with a thick fur blanket. The chilling ocean winds that blew through his soaking-wet blue prison jumpsuit made him feel as if he was fully exposed. Whether he was wearing clothes or not made little difference, for he felt completely vulnerable to his surroundings more than he ever had in his entire life.

When Bregan returned to his cell with Viti and several other men, he often wondered if his father and mother even knew where he was or what had happened to him. Tears would run down his face onto the damp prison cage floor when he started to think about how the people of Windfall probably didn't even notice he was gone. It was as if his life never had any meaning before, nobody knew who Bregan Moran was, and nobody cared.

At night when he would finally ignore his growling stomach and give in to his exhaustion, he would dream of his mother answering the door at the crab shack. As she opened the door, a pale-skinned man would tell her that her son was dead. Bregan used to hate the crab shack. He shared the upstairs portion of it as a small living space with his mother. The people of Windfall Harbor called it a restaurant attic, but Bregan never understood why. To him, it was just the living space where his mother made wigs out of horse hair and nail polish out of ground-up plant petals that she had imported from the south.

Viti had noticed that this sleeping young teenage boy Bregan beside him was not just some degenerate from Windfall Harbor. He felt sorry for getting him mixed up in all this piracy business by showing up at his crab shack down by the docks. He sat down and leaned against the cage bars while trying to think of Captain Saesh and the crew and how much he missed being with them. He couldn't think of them, no matter how hard he tried to imagine being with them when he closed his eyes. All he could hear, see, and think about was the fragile and innocent child that was asleep by his side.

The cage that Viti and Bregan shared was damp, cold, and reeked of a fierce and foul body odor. Bregan would always fall asleep while lying on his left side while on the stone ground of the cage. In his sleep, he would have nightmares. He shook and mumbled things in his sleep. Viti tried to comfort the boy as he slept without showing too much attention. He didn't want to seem weak or feminine to the other cell mates that sat nearby in the corners of the cell.

Viti had noticed that Bregan's feet were pitch black and scraped up from the days he had spent walking around the prison's brutal environment. He suspected he would get in trouble with the guards for any acts of generosity, but he did not care, for it pained him to see a young boy like Bregan suffering in such a dark and horrid place. Viti ripped off the sleeves of his blue prison jumpsuit and wrapped them around Bregan's feet one night while he slept. The ripped off sleeves didn't conceal Bregan's toes. They kept the bottom portion of his feet wrapped and warm. It helped protect the previously exposed wounds that had developed within the arches of Bregan's feet.

When Bregan awoke to see the kind generosity that his cellmate Viti had done for him, he wanted so desperately to hug him, but he knew that Viti would reject the affectionate offer. Viti rubbed his rough dirty hand on Bregan's golden curly haired head, creating a messy mini knot nest. The guards marched the shackled prisoners outside in their chain gang fashion. They were all ready to meet the sun but were immediately disappointed by the cold and heavy rain downpour that stormed against the shipyard work site in the distance.

Viti and Bregan looked at one another with such disappointment as they stood shackled in their chain gang line. Lightning struck against the rising tides of the ocean as the waves crashed against the jagged rocks along the shore. A dark ominous sky loomed ahead of the prisoners as they nailed the planks of wood together at the base of an incomplete ship. Bregan could see the faint light of what appeared to be the Windfall Harbor lighthouse. Its beam of light rapidly paced back and forth through the foggy mists of the stormy northern coast.

Seeing this faint trace of light pierce back and forth through the terrible weather of the Seething Sea reminded Bregan of his home. The warm memories of his mother's embrace was all it took to remind Bregan that there was still hope for him to see her again someday.

Chapter Fourteen

With both Hyde and Mavis following closely behind him, Thaniel walked through the fortified gates of the Cyanakin Hold. As they neared the hall where dozens of rangers were shouting and laughing as they ate breakfast, both Hyde and Mavis trailed off from Thaniel's path and made their way for the chow line.

Thaniel continued up the stairs to the war room located on the third and highest floor of the stronghold. As he entered the war room he saw his father Renson and several other high ranking ranger officials gathering around a series of detailed Western Glades maps that were unfolded out onto a circular wooden table.

"Back from your task already?" Renson asked.

"I just got back at sunrise," Thaniel replied.

"Good, we are quite busy discussing some important matters right now so if you want to wait for me in my study I can—"

"Why are you withdrawing troops from Fort Quiver?" Thaniel interjected.

Renson moved his attention away from Thaniel and back down at the Western Glade maps. "Leave us," he said.

The other ranger officials began to empty out of the war room leaving Renson and Thaniel alone in the space.

"Who told you I was recalling forces from Fort Quiver?" he asked.

"Mavis mentioned it after I bumped into her at the Forlorn Cathedral," Thaniel replied.

"You trespassed on the cathedral grounds?" Renson asked.

"No, not really. We tracked the Arsonist's whereabouts to the cathedral glade," Thaniel replied.

"I see. Where are the others I sent with you now?" Renson asked.

"Garrick stayed behind to await the Arsonist's return and both Mavis and Hyde returned home with me. They are both currently in the chow hall eating breakfast," Thaniel replied.

"Garrick stayed behind alone? What about the Arsonist?" Renson asked.

"The Arsonist was gone. I felt that knowing the reason for emptying our outer defenses took more precedence over capturing a loose criminal," Thaniel replied.

"That is not your authority to know. It is also not your authority to abandon a task assigned to you so that you can run back home and question your superior officers" Renson replied.

"Father, I meant no disrespect. I am just concerned," Thaniel replied.

"I understand but I think you need to remember that just because I am your father does not mean you can bend the rules to a way that you see fit," Renson replied.

"Understood," Thaniel replied.

"Good. Now that we got that out of the way I will tell you that we are actually discussing the possible reinforcement of Fort Quiver," Renson replied.

"Reinforcement? Why did you empty it to begin with?" Thaniel asked.

Renson motioned Thaniel to come over and look down at the detailed maps as he pressed his finger down on one near the Waning Forest glade that bordered the west to the south. "We have had numerous scouting reports that described a roving threat of southern savages that were surrounding the forests of the Amberwood Village people. They are easy to track for they leave behind a trail of death in their wake. Dead animals and villager remains have been found in multiple regions and these savages continue to roam unchecked while killing everything at will. They have come to destroy our way of life and everything we hold dear," he said.

Thaniel couldn't believe what his father was saying. It was a lot for him to take in all at once. "It still doesn't make sense to me though. If you know that this enemy is at our border then why withdraw the border defense?" he asked.

"Because they weren't at our borders anymore. By the time we figured out what was happening, they had already infiltrated half the glades and were beyond Fort Quiver's sight," Renson replied.

"I see. So what do we do now?" Thaniel asked.

"As I said, I have decided to reinforce Fort Quiver with the forces that occupy Cyanakin Hold here. The forces I withdrew from Fort Quiver have already dispersed into groups throughout the glades and are attempting to hunt down and slay the roaming savages," Renson replied.

"Where is my place in all of this?" Thaniel asked.

"Where do you want to go?" Renson asked.

"I want to fight with my friends and my kin," Thaniel replied.

Renson hesitated to respond but he knew that his son was too stubborn, an apple that fell close to the fatherly tree. He swallowed his pride and the lump in his throat as he gave in to his son's wishes. "Very well, you shall be sent to reinforce the defenses of Fort Quiver and await further instructions," he said.

"Thank you, father. I won't let you down," Thaniel replied.

"I know you won't," Renson replied.

Thaniel left the war room to return to Mavis and Hyde in the chow hall to discover that they had already left. They were both given orders by a commanding officer to leave immediately for Amberwood Village. Thaniel made his way to the armory to gather more supplies and rations before his departure from Cyanakin Hold.

Outside the gates he mounted his grey horse for the day long ride ahead of him that would take him south to Fort Quiver.

Chapter Fifteen

Lylah awoke from a surreal dream that left her feeling shaken. A light breeze had swept in and had made the trees sway back and forth above her as she lay wide awake in her bedroll.

The remaining druid trials lay in similarly fashioned bedrolls all around her. After a long day of strenuous tasks, the trials had been given bedrolls by Crane so that they could retire underneath the Salix trees that surrounded the monolith.

She sat upward in her bed roll and looked at the monolith that seemed to call to her through the whispering wind that floated through the air and tree branches above her. In her dream, she stood before the Monolith in the Weeping Grove. As she approached the Monolith, she reached out to touch it, but before her fingertips could touch the Monolith, she awoke from her dream.

Now sitting up in her bedroll, wide awake and facing the Monolith, she felt the same temptation she had experienced in her dream. She slowly made her way toward the Monolith with stealth to carefully not awaken her fellow trials that were asleep nearby. As she approached the Monolith, she reached out to touch it with her fingertips, expecting something to startle her or deny her physical contact. She closed her eyes as her fingertips pressed into the cool metallic obelisk, and as she did this, she experienced the same pulsating experience from the first time she had touched it.

The overwhelming and soothing experience was short-lived. She suddenly heard a ghostly and unfamiliar voice inside her head. She could not make a sound nor let go of the Monolith that her hands were now fully pressed against. The voice whispered into her mind repeatedly as her shut eyes squinted in fear.

"Do not wake the dreamer," the voice repeated in her mind.

Suddenly Lylah was grabbed behind by a familiar pair of female hands and was ripped away from the Monolith. She fell to the ground and was finally able to open her eyes.

She sighed in relief as she saw Celosia standing over her with a big grin on her face. She reached down with her right hand to help Lylah stand up.

"You just couldn't resist touching the thing, could you?" Celosia asked.

"Something about this Monolith was drawing me in and I couldn't resist it," Lylah replied.

"I knew a girl in Harvestshire that had the same effect on me. It's alright girl don't be ashamed. I take it that you haven't had much luck with men in the past?" Celosia replied.

"No, wait what? No, I had a dream and the Monolith was in it and then I awoke and I heard a chilling voice calling to me through the wind," Lylah replied.

Celosia stood in front of Lylah smirking as if she was not convinced.

"I swear to you," Lylah said.

Celosia was unconvinced, and as she rolled her eyes at Lylah, she began walking back toward the lake where she previously was before finding Lylah pressed up against the Monolith.

"Wait, you weren't sleeping?" Lylah asked. As she followed Celosia toward the lake, she noticed an indent in the dirt that met the water as if someone had been sitting there for a few hours.

"I can't sleep," Celosia said.

"So you've just been sitting here staring out at the lake all night?" Lylah asked.

"Don't judge me, you're the one that woke up in the middle of the night to go and touch the massage rock over there," Celosia replied.

"I told you already that's not what I was trying to-"Lylah stopped. She could tell there was no use convincing Celosia of what truly happened. She sat down next to her in the dirt.

"Those lights over there across the lake have been multiplying all night long, they almost look like torches or something," Celosia said.

Lylah squinted her tired eyes as she looked across the lake to see multiple dim lights floating atop the fog of the cold lake, "They look like tiny candle flames dancing above a cloud."

"Yeah, I can see that," Celosia replied.

"I wonder what they are or where they're coming from," Lylah said.

"Well, I know that the island in the center of the lake over there is called Solus Isle and has pretty much been abandoned for decades, but the lights seem to be coming from the right of it, which makes me think that maybe it's just row boats departing from Footman's Refuge," Celosia replied.

"Footman's Refuge? I was always told by my father that the place was abandoned," Lylah replied.

"So many beautiful structures and settlements abandoned and lost to time," Celosia replied.

"I wonder why there's flickering lights over there if those places are abandoned," Lylah said.

"It could just be a bunch of fisherman from the north," Celosia replied.

"So, why can't you sleep?" Lylah asked.

"I'm homesick or something," Celosia replied.

"Where is your home?" Lylah asked.

"The Eastern Vale, in a small cottage atop a hill looking over Revelry Lake," Celosia replied.

"Sounds peaceful," Lylah replied.

"Yeah, but only when your drunk father doesn't come stumbling home in the middle of the night while tracking mud all over your damn bed as he tries to crawl into it to touch you," Celosia replied.

"I assume that's why you left?" Lylah asked.

"Pretty much, my mother always told me that her grandmother and thus our ancestors were tied to the Evenfall Tribe that inhabited the southeastern valley and cared for this place. So, one day when I was tired of guarding myself from my sick father I decided to abandon everything and everyone I knew and loved and made my way here on foot," Celosia replied.

"I think that's pretty brave of you. You sound like one hell of a strong woman," Lylah replied.

"I try to be," Celosia replied.

"Well, as for me, I got sent here from the north by my mother and father," Lylah said.

"Neither of them are abusive I hope," Celosia replied.

The two girls smiled at each other before giggling quietly. "No, thank goodness, and to answer your question from earlier, no, I have not had much luck with men, and I don't want to, anyways," Lylah said.

Both the girls grew quiet as they sat in the damp dirt, looking out at the flickering flames in the distance. They both were eager to ask each other many questions and share stories, but something kept them silent. It was as if they were afraid to seem vulnerable. The eagerness to open up to one another and befriend each other gave each of them a form of anxiety that they couldn't bring themselves to act on.

The calm wind, the waving of tree branches, and the scent of lake water surrounded them as the sun slowly crept up from behind the Dreary Mountains that towered over them from across the Fisherman's Channel that fed out of the lake and toward the sea.

Chapter Sixteen

The Arsonist arrived right outside the Krastoff Family Mill. A familiar feeling of frustration surged over him as he dismounted from Xenos, and sunk his cavalier boots deep into the mud. If there was one thing that the Arsonist hated more than his socks getting damp, it was his boots getting caked in mud.

As he trudged through the dirt sludge toward the mill, his wolf Glacier followed closely behind him. Before he could even knock on the door to let the residents of the mill know that he had arrived, the heavy wooden door swung open as two young men embraced him with excitement. It was the two Duitbror brothers. They had both moved from Amberwood Village to the mill after the Krastoff family that owned the mill had mysteriously disappeared shortly after the Severance event of the Foedus Bridge.

Both the brothers wore similar garments that were very plain and casual. Their brown shirts were not tucked into their pants, but they were covered by white butcher aprons that were stained, but not by the blood of any animal. Strapped to each of the brother's foreheads was a pair of goggles. If it weren't for their difference in hair color, they could easily be considered twins. They each had the same line of freckles that went over their cheeks and across the bridge of their nose. They both had a tiny gap between their front teeth and the same style of bowl cut. One had orange-like hair, and the other had light brown hair, but they both had light-brown eyes.

"Ah, Felix and Clive, the two brightest minds in all of the Realms of Light," the Arsonist said.

"It's about bloody time that you showed up, we were starting to worry about you," Felix said.

"Yeah, we started thinking that we may have to auction off that weapon you ordered," Clive added.

"I know, it has been quite a long time, and I am so sorry for the delay," the Arsonist replied.

"Come in, come in, we have lots to discuss," said Clive.

The two brothers welcomed the Arsonist and Glacier into the mill as Xenos wandered through the mud that surrounded the structure. Inside, the dim light revealed a cluttered assortment of cabinets, rough-hewn tables, and sagging bookshelves, their wood darkened by years of dust and damp. In one corner, against the cold stone floor, lay a narrow straw mattress—a crude, threadbare sack stuffed with chaff and draped with a patched woolen blanket, its edges frayed and stained with the grime of countless nights. The base beneath it was a low, warped plank of oak, splintered and gouged, as though salvaged from some forgotten ruin. It was barely wide enough for one, forcing the brothers to trade sleep for work-one laboring through the night while the other sank into the lumpy, mildewed embrace of their meager rest.

The brothers were bright students of the Amberwood Academy, and the scientific discoveries made by scholars in the south had piqued their interest.

"I assume you are out of juice?" Felix asked.

"Aye, I am currently running on the fumes of my last vial," the Arsonist replied.

"How much coin do you have on you?" Clive asked.

"After I pay you for the weapon I ordered, I won't have much left. Mercenary work has been hard to come by these days ever since the rangers decided to start doing their job of protecting the woods," the Arsonist replied.

"Well, I'm sure we can work something out," Clive replied.

"Did you see the giant balloon vessel tied down above the Goose Egg Pub in Prosperwood by chance?" Felix asked.

"No, I can't say I have been to Prosperwood in months," the Arsonist replied.

"Ah, well it's of our design, we constructed it for Mayor Winter, it's supposed to be a wedding gift to his daughter and her soon-to-be husband Dorian," Felix replied.

"Yeah, we got paid pretty handsomely for that one. The mayor said he wanted something that would allow his daughter and her lover to be able to fly over the glades. Said that it was always his daughter's dream to be able to fly," Clive said.

"Wait, this balloon thing of yours can actually fly?" the Arsonist asked.

"Aye, it can fly, it's slow but it works," Clive replied.

"That's bloody brilliant, I don't know how you guys come up with this stuff," the Arsonist Replied. He stood back as Clive and Felix tinkered with a few heated vials and some type of mechanic tool that the Arsonist couldn't quite understand the purpose of. While Clive poured a strange transparent and odorless liquid into a vial that matched the same ones that the Arsonist used to fuel his flamethrower gauntlets, Felix made his way up a short ladder to a small platform.

"That's new," said the Arsonist.

"Yeah, we installed this platform last month. It is pretty sturdy," Felix replied.

Felix began jumping up and down on the wooden platform to give a physical example of how sturdy it really was.

"So, when do we get to see you without your mask?" Clive asked.

"Never, you couldn't handle my beauty. You both would fall madly in love with me," the Arsonist replied.

The two brothers laughed so hard that Clive nearly spilled the fuel onto the table, and Felix nearly fell off the platform above. As Felix made his way down the short ladder, he carried a cloth-wrapped object under his left arm.

"Is that it?" the Arsonist asked.

"Yes, this is the weapon you ordered," Felix replied.

The Arsonist's red eyes gleamed from behind his mask as Felix unwrapped the weapon in front of him.

"We call it the Daybreak Hand Canon," Felix said.

"We? You mean you call it that," Clive interjected.

"Whatever," Felix said.

"How does it work?" the Arsonist asked.

Felix picked up the weapon by its handle and aimed it toward Clive.

"Don't point that damn thing at me. Have you lost your mind?" Clive said.

"Oh, sorry," Felix replied. He aimed the weapon at the ceiling of the mill before pressing his right index finger down on the trigger with a slight amount of pressure. The barrel of the weapon fired off and left a hole in the ceiling of the mill as a piece of debris came falling behind Felix.

"Impressive," the Arsonist said.

"If it can put a hole that big in the ceiling, I can't imagine what it will do to those damn ferals that you're always complaining about," Felix replied.

"Perhaps, may I see it?" the Arsonist asked.

Felix handed the pistol over to the Arsonist. He couldn't believe what he was looking at. From behind his mask, his mouth lay wide open in admiration at the beautiful craft of the weapon. It had a long dark wooden grip that was smooth to the touch. The metal barrel was dark and matched the same metallic appearance of the trigger that hung below.

"It's a flintlock mechanism, which means that a piece of flint is struck against the steel plate there in the back, it creates a spark which ignites the explosive powder that you load it with. It can only fire one shot at a time," Clive said.

The Arsonist listened carefully to Clive's words, but his eyes were fixed on the beautiful design of the dark-looking flintlock pistol. He reached deep into his inner coat pocket and pulled out a sack of coins, the same sack of coins that were given to him by the farmer in the straw hat.

"I'll start counting if you want to show him how to load and fire it," said Clive.

Felix began to head toward the door to lead the Arsonist outside for some shooting practice until he was startled by a sudden heavy knock on the door. Clive, Felix, and the Arsonist all looked at the door curiously in silence as another heavy knock fell upon the door.

"Well? Answer it you fool," Clive said.

"I'm going, I'm going," Felix replied.

The Arsonist gripped the flintlock pistol tightly as Glacier began to snarl and slowly creep toward the door.

Chapter Seventeen

Felix opened the door to find Rhys and Farbris standing on the front porch step to the mill.

"Good evening sir, we were just passing through and we were wondering if you had room for two travelers to stay the night," Rhys said.

Farbris' eyes widened in disbelief as he noticed the snarling wolf Glacier nearing him. Rhys looked past the brown-haired head of Felix to see Clive and the Arsonist standing behind Felix.

"You have got to be kidding me," said the Arsonist.

"Well, isn't this a surprise," Farbris replied.

Glacier began to bark and howl as if ready to strike out at Farbris and bite his ankle. The Arsonist handed the pistol to Clive as he walked toward the doorway and nudged Felix to move aside.

"Are you two following me?" the Arsonist asked.

Rhys and Farbris stood nervously in the doorway as the whistling prairie wind swept through their bones leaving them chilled and shivering under the moonlit sky.

"I told you that the dark horse wandering near the edge of the forest looked familiar," Rhys said.

Farbris sighed and rolled his eyes as he turned away from the windmill and began to make his way back through the mud from whence he came.

"Where are you going?" the Arsonist asked.

"Away from you, it's obvious that we're not welcome here and that we are going to freeze to death in this bog from a lack of hospitality," Farbris replied.

Felix looked back at Clive who shrugged in confusion.

"We didn't mean to cause you anymore trouble," Rhys said.

"You have not caused me any, it was merely a question," the Arsonist replied. He turned to Felix and Clive who both nodded as if they understood what he was going to say before he could even say it.

"I have to go track down my wandering horse but I will return, please count and collect all the coin, and I will return for the vials and the..." the Arsonist trailed off, realizing he had no idea what the weapon was called.

"The pistol," Clive replied.

"Ah, yes the pistol," the Arsonist replied.

Rhys turned away from the doorway and began to follow after his uncle through the mud as the Arsonist followed closely behind him. Glacier stayed behind with Clive and Felix as they shut the door to the mill behind the Arsonist.

"So, what's the story with those two? Are they your family?" Rhys asked.

"No, they are friends that I have made during my travels. They are quite brilliant, and I visit them from time to time to purchase supplies from them. They are both brothers that have studied the industrial sciences that have been flooding north from the south as of late," the Arsonist replied.

"I see, so I assume that is where you got that device which allows you to spew fire from your hands?" Rhys asked.

"Aye, it is a flamethrower gauntlet according to them," the Arsonist replied.

Farbris stopped so that the two following him could catch up after having overheard the conversation between Rhys and the Arsonist.

"So where did you see my idjit of a horse wandering off to again?" the Arsonist asked.

"When we exited the edge of the forest north of the mill we saw it wandering toward the woods," Rhys replied.

"Aye, it looked familiar to us but we didn't connect it to you. I assumed it was just a wild horse that had gotten lost or was looking for food," Farbris replied.

"Well, he usually does this quite often but never gets far. I was planning to return to the Western Glades after I gathered some supplies, so I guess I'll have to look for him then if he has not returned to this area by sunrise," the Arsonist replied.

"You mean you aren't staying in that mill?" Rhys asked.

"Oh, no. There is no room, the two brothers that inhabit the mill can barely exist in it together as is. I'm afraid there is no place of hospitality between here and the east as far as I know," the Arsonist replied.

"We'll be sleeping in the mud as the winter wind slowly takes us then," Farbris replied.

"Don't be so dramatic, uncle," Rhys replied.

"My bones are too old for this shit, Rhys," Farbris replied.

"There is a place not that far west of here that could provide you with a room and potentially some food and drink," the Arsonist replied.

"That would require us to go backwards and our time is already short. The longer we take to get to the Eastern Vale, the less time my son has to live," Farbris replied.

"Right, I recall overhearing you say something about your son being imprisoned when you were making a deal with the ferals," the Arsonist replied.

"Wait, why are you even helping us all of the sudden? You were a complete arse to us earlier and you abandoned us on a trail surrounded by the ashes of bloodthirsty savages that tried to kill all three of us," Farbris replied.

"We weren't the most approachable or polite people either, uncle," Rhys interjected.

"I'm just saying, why should we suddenly trust anything this asshole says?" Farbris asked.

The Arsonist adjusted the coat sleeves that covered his gauntlets and looked up at the sky to see a full moon. His red eyes trembled behind his porcelain mask as the cold wind nearly blew his thick cloak hood off. His long black hair flopped out from behind his mask and rested on his shoulders as he entered a deep thought. There was something about the silver-haired young man that stood before him. As he looked at Rhys, who was busy trying to calm his furious uncle down, he noticed something strange about him. It was as if the Arsonist was peering into a crystal clear mirror that revealed a cleaner image of himself. With the moonlight shining down upon the face of Rhys, it allowed the Arsonist to analyze his facial structure more clearly. The way his cheekbones raised and his lips pressed together reminded him of himself, but he couldn't believe it to be possible.

"I am nineteen years old and almost twenty," the Arsonist said.

Rhys and Farbris both stopped arguing as they turned to the masked and hooded figure. It was as if the calm collected voice of the Arsonist had revealed an entirely different person to them. The whistling cold winds could suddenly be ignored as both the men focused on what the Arsonist had to say.

"I am wanted all over the Western Glades for a crime I did not commit," the Arsonist said. His red eyes closed tightly as he pulled his gauntlets up toward his face to remove the white porcelain mask that covered it. As he removed his mask from his face, he opened his eyes. His burning red irises glinted in the moonlight. "I have red eyes because I was born cursed with them," he continued. "I am not a feral or any type of blood thirsty savage that you may have encountered or heard stories about."

Farbris and Rhys could not believe what was happening, the fierce figure from the glade belt road that saved their lives was now revealing his true identity to them. Rhys looked upon the pale-skinned face of the Arsonist and began to experience the same strange familiarities that the Arsonist had about Rhys' complexity and facial structure.

"How is this even possible?" Rhys asked.

"It can't be," Farbris said.

The Arsonist stood before them in silence as the prairie winds blew off his hood revealing a long mane of unkempt black hair that danced within the breeze that surrounded his head.

"What is your name?" Rhys asked.

"I was given a name by my father, Alarick Kalon." the Arsonist replied.

"Alarick?" Farbris asked.

The Arsonist nodded in confirmation at Farbris who was now panicking to search for his pipe in his sack of supplies that he had been carrying on his back up to this moment.

"Where the blazes did I put that damn thing?" Farbris asked.

The Arsonist squinted his eyes in confusion at Farbris who was now dumping his entire bag of supplies into a dry patch of weeds that grew out of the muddy terrain. Rhys suddenly approached the Arsonist slowly while looking at his face as if it were an ancient painting or text that he was studying.

"Are we..." Rhys stopped.

"You noticed it too?" the Arsonist asked.

Farbris finally found his pipe and began to quickly pack it with the loose tobacco that he had left. It was just enough to get a small bowl burning. The wind continued to blow the matches out that Farbris attempted to light his pipe with. After stressfully going through six matches to light the pipe, the smell of Yokelshire grown tobacco filled the air around him. He covered the bowl of the pipe with his right hand as he puffed on it a bit before interrupting Rhys and the Arsonist's facial study.

"Don't be alarmed," Farbris said.

Both Rhys and the Arsonist looked at Farbris who was now taking a heavy drag of his pipe to calm his nerves.

"You know something about this, don't you?" the Arsonist asked. He looked back at Rhys' face and as his grey eyes turned to meet the Arsonist's red eyes it suddenly became clear to him.

"Your face is lighter than mine," Rhys said.

"You both are related," Farbris interjected.

Rhys' eyes became as big as the full moon that hung above them. The Arsonist's brow furled in disapproval of what Farbris' interruption had revealed.

"Explain," the Arsonist said.

"Can we at least return to the mill first? This damn chill will be the end of me if this pipe goes out" Farbris replied.

"Fine," the Arsonist replied.

"Why didn't you tell me I had a brother?" Rhys asked

"You don't have one," Farbris replied.

The three men trudged through the mud and back to the mill where the Arsonist knocked on the door to let Felix and Clive know that they had returned.

"Any luck with the horse?" Felix asked.

"No," the Arsonist replied.

"Alright, well we've got six vials of fuel for you and the flintlock pistol with eighteen rounds that you ordered," Clive said.

The Arsonist grabbed the six vials and carefully placed them into individual holsters that were attached to his belt loops that were located below his lower back. The flintlock pistol was placed into a special leather holster and handed to the Arsonist by Clive. The Arsonist then attached the holster to the left side of his belt therefore giving his right hand an easy access to unsheathing it in the face of danger.

"Let's go outside and show you how to use it," Clive said.

"I think I get the idea," the Arsonist replied.

"Alright, suit yourself," Clive replied.

"Is that a southern firearm mechanism?" Farbris asked.

"No uncle, his gauntlets are firearms," Rhys said.

Farbris nearly choked on his pipe smoke as he shook his head in disappointment at what Rhys had just suggested.

"So where are you off to next? Still on the revenge quest?" Felix asked.

"No, I think I might be traveling to the Eastern Vale next after I find my wandering idjit of a horse," the Arsonist replied. Farbris and Rhys looked at each other with surprise.

"You're coming with us then?" Rhys asked.

"Yes, I have a lot of questions that I am sure your uncle here will be glad to answer if I were to accompany you on your jailbreak journey," the Arsonist replied.

"We would love to have you with us. I too would like some answers," Rhys replied. He glared at Farbris as he approached him. Farbris sat quietly and looked down at his pipe that was slowly dying out from being smoked too quickly. Rhys nudged him with his elbow to get him to say something.

"Ah, yes, it would be a delight to have you come with us," Farbris said.

"Good, then leave anything that isn't essential here. We will find Xenos and head out," the Arsonist replied.

As Rhys, Farbris, and the Arsonist departed the windmill they were given thankful praise from Felix and Clive. The two genius brothers wished them all three good luck and that they hoped to see them again soon. The Arsonist took the lead of the three and began to make his way toward the Western Glades while Farbris and Rhys followed slowly behind.

"Where are we going? The east is the other way," Rhys said.

"Yes, but we need to rest and gather our strength for the long road ahead," the Arsonist replied.

"So where are you taking us then?" Farbris asked.

"To the Glades Maids Bordello, I have a friend who works there and she will gladly tend to our restless needs," the Arsonist replied.

"A whore house. You're taking us to a whore house," Rhys said.

"I prefer to call it a brothel," the Arsonist replied.

"More like a flesh peddlers den," Farbris said.

"Set aside whatever predisposed feelings of it that you may have for it is the only place nearby that will take us in for a night and give us a bed to sleep in. That is, unless you would suddenly prefer to lay out in the damp mud with the freezing cold winds blowing over you," the Arsonist replied.

"No, we will go with you to this bordello you speak of," Farbris replied.

"We have to find my horse first anyways," the Arsonist replied. He stopped as they neared the forest's border so that he could carefully place his mask back on. The three men pressed onward into the Western Glades border. Rhys gulped as he anxiously followed the Arsonist into the dark Amberwood forest. Farbris sadly dumped the ashes of his pipe bowl out onto the mud as he entered the forest behind them.

Chapter Eighteen

The collapsing of stone walls and sounds of cannon fire awoke the starving and physically fatigued Bregan from his cell floor slumber. The gate to the cell was open. All of the cellmates except for Viti had flooded out of the space. Bregan attempted to stand but failed to gather the strength required to lift his bruised body up.

Viti noticed that his friend was struggling and decided to pick him up and toss his light young body over his shoulder. Bal could be heard shouting at the guards from outside as the Festering Cage prison took its battle stations. Viti peered through a large hole in the stone wall to see a magnificent and enormous ship outside. Its black and red sails could be seen from miles away as they floated above the dark wooden vessel. Every few moments a torrent of cannonballs would be released from the ship, annihilating the prison guards that attempted to shoot it with crossbows and mortars from the shore. The prison was being bombarded, and Viti needed to find a way to escape with his nearly unconscious friend.

"Get back in your damn cell, you wretch," a familiar female voice said.

"Ah, are you trying to get some alone time with me now?" Viti asked.

"Don't make me put a hole in your throat," she replied.

Viti held tight to Bregan as he jumped through the hole in the wall, falling into the sand. The female guard quickly ran toward the hole to take aim on Viti with her crossbow. She pulled the trigger to let loose a bolt but missed as Viti took off running toward the ocean.

"Stop those two prisoners! They're getting away," she said.

Viti could see a rowboat departing from the ship and heading toward the beach. He set Bregan down on the sandy shore and began waving his arms around to get their attention.

"Over here, over here, it's me Viti, I'm over here," Viti said.

A shadow was cast on Viti from behind by the large figure of Hobart that stood behind him. As Viti slowly turned around to see Hobart he was quickly struck down in the face with a piece of wood leaving him unconscious on the beach. Bregan who was now somewhat awake due to all the commotion taking place on the beach could see Hobart standing over his friend Viti.

"Get away from him you bastard," Bregan said.

Hobart looked over to see Bregan shouting at him from the floor. As he neared Bregan he began to grin as he pulled out his wooden shank from their last encounter. Bregan knew that it was over and that Hobart would have his way with him if not kill him. Before Hobart could reach down to Bregan to grab him, a cannonball suddenly flew from the ship and decapitated Hobart, thus knocking his fat head clean off. Bregan tried to scream in fear at the gruesome sight but lacked the air and energy to do so.

Viti remained unconscious as a rowboat of dark-skinned men with unkempt braided hair and rugged clothing came stomping onto the sandy shores.

"Yup, that's Viti alright," one of the men said.

Viti's eyes slightly opened as he tried to mutter something to one of the men that had picked him up.

"What's he trying to say?" one of the men asked.

As the man carrying Viti to the rowboat leaned his ear toward Viti's mouth his eyes squinted in confusion.

"He wants us to grab that boy over there and bring him with us," he said.

"Alright, you're coming with us then lad," the other dark-skinned man said.

Bregan's eyes grew heavy as he lay on the beach in shock at what had just occurred. He felt his body become lighter as the strong dark-skinned man lifted him up and began to carry him toward the rowboat. He set Bregan down next to Viti's limp body and began to row the boat back toward the ship that continued to release a torrent of cannon fire at the prison walls. As the rowboats arrived alongside the dark wooden hull of the ship ropes were tossed overboard to tie to the rowboats. The strength of many men onboard the ship would be used to pull the rowboats up the side of the ship allowing Viti, Bregan, and the sailors who saved them, to be pulled onto the deck. Bregan could barely stay awake, and as the familiar face of Alarick blocked out the blinding sun like an eclipse, he couldn't help but suddenly feel safe. Bregan tried to keep his weary eyes open but failed as he quickly gave into exhaustion and faded away into dreams.

Chapter Nineteen

The moon was full of grey in the sky. Thaniel's horse stopped outside the stone brick walls of the fortress. As he dismounted, several rangers greeted him. Fort Quiver was the southern bastion of defense that the West had left intact. It was responsible for defending the bottom hemisphere of the Western Glades, which included places like Amberwood Village.

Fort Quiver was occupied and fortified by several dozen rangers that lined its outer and inner defenses, including the four watchtowers, which secured the walls of the fort. Foxholes and trenches had both been dug out in the front and back dirt regions of the glade where the Fort Quiver resided. Thaniel had never seen anything like this before. It was as if the men and women surrounding him were preparing for an all-out war. He remembered his father telling him about the southern savages. He remembered how important Fort Quiver was for the West's strategic defense. Yet it never occurred to him that they were at war with the South or anyone, for that matter.

As he made his way up the winding wooden stairway inside the fort's inner keep, he couldn't help but wonder what had led to all of this. Why was it that these savages were invading the Western Glades?

The Arsonist

"Ah, the general has sent his son to aid us," an orotund voice said.

Thaniel entered the war room at the top of the stairs to see several veteran rangers sitting around a large round and empty table, "good evening gentleman," he said.

"What word does your father send with you to us?" the orotund-voiced man said.

A hooded man with a scar above his left eye stood before Thaniel at the doorway entrance. A thick but short black beard covered most of his lower face.

"He has sent me to help win this fight," Thaniel said.

"Fight? This is not a fight. This is our last stand," the bearded man with the orotund voice replied.

"Last stand?" Thaniel replied.

"Aye," a brown-haired female ranger in the background said.

Thaniel looked around to see the grim looks on all the veteran rangers' faces. He drew out his bow and carefully unwrapped it with one hand while holding it with the other.

A few of the rangers furled their brows while others that recognized the bow were shocked in amazement as their eyes became as wide as the moon that hung outside the nearby window.

"This will not be our final stand. This will be the final blow that we deal to our enemies. Behold, Arrowguard, the Ward of the Wilds," Thaniel said.

"Your father's legendary longbow," The female ranger said.

"I heard the stories, but never saw him use it with my own eyes," The bearded man said.

"It's magical arrows will illuminate the darkness that has loomed over Fort Quiver for far too long," Thaniel replied.

"Sounds like we need to roll out the perimeter maps one last time and show Lord Cadere here what we're dealing with" the bearded man said.

"That would be lovely, and I don't believe I got your name," Thaniel replied.

"The name's Nosodul, and these are the last remnants of my ranger company that was charged with scouting and protecting the Waning Forest which is now lost and overrun with bloodthirsty cannibalizing savages," Nosodul replied.

"My name is Gwenith," the older female ranger said.

"Nice to meet you, Gwenith," Thaniel replied.

As Thaniel finished shaking Gwenith and Nosodul's hand he,

made his way to the round wooden table as another nearby ranger rolled out a few maps of the Fort Quiver glade. It was a large piece of parchment paper with a series of detailed drawings that showed the trenches and the keep among other little hidden traps and defenses that the rangers had in place along the forest borders.

"We have three dozen men and women scouting during the night and we have just as many if not more scouting on high alert throughout the day. Our enemy has remained silent although they have not retreated. We know they are not gone, for our scouts have reported sightings of them lurking about in the bordering woods between the fort and the Waning glade," Nosodul said.

Thaniel studied the words of Nosodul carefully as he listened. He examined the map with squinting eyes as he watched Gwenith drag her left index finger across the map pointing to positions of importance within the glade, "How many times have they failed to assault this fort? Do the scouts know how many of them are left out there? We need to know what we're up against and if meeting them in open combat whether we use guerilla tactics from the trees or not is an option," Thaniel replied.

"This fort has survived one full assault from them that took place a week ago. There were over two hundred of their corpses plus the sixty or so of our own men and women. We piled the corpses and burnt them near Lake Eerie a few nights ago. The black bubbling blood that left their pale-skinned bodies has tainted the soil. Unless we get help from the Weeping Grove druids, I don't believe that the Yokel people will be able to expand their crops this far south," Nosodul replied.

"Interesting," Thaniel replied.

"The last report we got was from four days ago. The scout was soft spoken and frightened when they told us that they saw at least two hundred more red-eyed fiends with pale skin skulking within the Southern Foothills. They feast off of the unsuspecting travelers that have come from the east, as well as the wildlife, whose population now dwindles as a result of their presence," Gwenith said.

"Dwindles? What has become of the wildlife of our lands?" Thaniel asked.

"These savages have a hunger that knows no bounds, they are bottomless pits of bile and they know only how to kill and feast upon the lifeblood of their victims. They have been here for at least two months and their numbers are growing as the one common and noticeable wildlife has nearly disappeared entirely. It is their hunger that draws them here to the fort and toward Amberwood Village. As the wildlife suffers, so do we, for when all the deer and other animals are gone they must seek out an alternative food source which is where we come in," Gwenith replied.

"I had no idea, my father mentioned savages as if they were vicious foreigners crossing our borders and invading our lands with brute force as a means of gathering resources that they lacked," Thaniel replied.

"I'm afraid not Lord Cadere, your father has been made aware of the threat that comes from the south for quite some time. We have asked him for reinforcements but he has informed us that he has given us all he can spare for the northern part of the west is still in danger as well. We have no idea how many of these bastards have slipped through our defenses and have made their way toward Yokelshire or Prosperwood," Nosodul said.

"Very well, I guess we have a lot of work cut out for us then. We best make haste and prepare all our defenses, if these creatures are skulking around us in the dark woods then we need torches and every able body to take twelve-hour watch shifts. If you're not standing watch at night then you are in your rack quarters sleeping," Thaniel replied.

"Already on it, we have torch posts lit everywhere outside, I am sure you saw some of the men lighting them as you entered the glade. These things aren't afraid of the light but they're not fond of it and will only come near it if they're desperate," Nosodul replied.

"Excellent," Thaniel replied.

"I will post the new watch bill at sunrise and get everyone onboard so they can adjust their sleep schedules as necessary," Gwenith said.

"Feel free to put me somewhere on the front lines like in one of those foxholes," Thaniel replied.

"As you wish," Gwenith replied.

Thaniel made his way down the stairs to the veteran living quarters to rest. He found the general's rack that was reserved for his father and placed his bow on the ground underneath it before falling onto its silk sheets. As he quickly fell into a deep sleep his body tensed up with stress and remained restless as he began grinding his teeth.

Chapter Twenty

"Lylah, wake up," Celosia said.

Standing above the waking Lylah was the terrified-looking Celosia.

"What's going on?" Lylah asked.

"We're being attacked," Celosia replied.

Lylah stopped rubbing her eyes as they opened wide in disbelief. "By who?" she asked.

"I don't know yet, but we need to move," Celosia replied.

She helped Lylah stand up and then the two were off as they made haste toward the Monolith Sanctum. Lylah could see smoke stirring in the distance when she looked behind her. The sound of a horn being blown from above could be heard over the sounds of charging battle cries and terrified screams. When they both looked to their left toward the Lake Moran beach they could see over a dozen row boats lined up in the sand. As they both entered the Monolith Sanctum space they could see a handful of the trials standing behind Master Crane as he held a spear with both hands.

"Hurry you two. We don't have much time," Crane said.

Both Lylah and Celosia followed the handful of trials up the ladder to the largest of the Salix trees that towered over the Monolith. The sound of Crane screaming in agony could be heard and as Celosia turned her head to look down she saw and felt an

The Arsonist

arrow fly past her face as it pierced the tree bark in front of her.

Lylah didn't look back; she just kept climbing with determination to reach the top before it was too late.

Celosia looked down to see two pale-skinned men piercing Crane with their swords as he fell to the ground in a pool of his own blood.

"Celosia, keep climbing," Lylah said.

An arrow struck a trial in the back as they approached the top of the ladder. The other trials tried to hug the ladder and push inward to avoid the falling corpse that was descending from above them. Juspen and two other elders could be seen at the top motioning the trials to hurry and climb faster. The other trials made it up the ladder and were quickly lifted up and embraced by the elders.

Taunting voices could be heard from beneath Lylah and Celosia as they finished their climb. Arrows were now firing toward the top of the Salix tree as one of the pale-skinned invaders took a torch to the rope ladder setting it ablaze.

The fire began to climb up the ladder as Celosia made it to the top wooden platform of the tree. Lylah followed closely behind Celosia as she placed her right hand up on the ledge of the platform to help lift herself up. An arrow struck Lylah in her right hand as it pierced into the wooden platform. Laughter could be heard from the pale-skinned invaders bellow as Lylah let out a scream of agony. She couldn't climb up as the arrow had her hand stuck to the platform and the fire below her was quickly approaching her bare feet.

Without any hesitation Juspen kneeled and pulled the arrow out of Lylah's hand, freeing it from the platform. Juspen dropped the arrow off the ledge as he grabbed the bloody right hand of Lylah and helped pull her up onto the platform safely with the others. As Lylah lay on the platform screaming in pain, one of the elders pulled out a knife and cut the rope ladder loose before the fire could reach the platform.

"Bring me the Salix salve, quickly," Juspen said.

The trials cowered in fear as they huddled in a corner of the platform together with horror-struck faces.

"We never got that far in our training elder one," Celosia said.

Juspen let out a sigh of frustration as he arose to his feet and made his way into a nearby cloth tent. Although Lylah was in pain gripping her blood-soaked hand, she felt a sudden despair in her mind, she couldn't help but wonder where her father's protection was. Her father Nielas Proditore was responsible for the Footman's

Refuge settlement that lay across Lake Moran opposite of the Weeping Grove. When she sat on the beach with Celosia and saw the rowboats in the fog with their torches she thought nothing of it. Could an enemy of the south have invaded the settlement the night before? Where was her father's forces if he were not only responsible for the settlement but also for the protection of his daughter who now resided in the Weeping Grove itself?

Juspen returned with a transparent vial that was filled to the brim with a dark amber liquid in hand and with a fine thin piece of wood.

"Bite down on this and do not pull away from me," Juspen said.

Lylah inserted the small piece of wood into her mouth as Juspen took her bloody hand. He pulled the vial cork out with his teeth and held it upside down over the hold in her hand. He lightly shook the vial up and down a bit as a thick sludge of amber colored liquid oozed out from the vial. Gravity took its course and the thick liquid fell onto the hole of her wounded hand.

Lylah's failed attempt to scream could be heard from her mouth that was clenching the wood tightly. The fine thin piece of wood looked like it was about to snap like a twig under foot.

"What is that stuff?" Celosia asked.

"Salix Salve," Juspen replied.

"A healing ointment?" she asked.

"Yes, the sap of these trees can act as a remedy for almost any wound, it can treat fevers and stop the spread of infections," he replied.

"Wow, that is amazing," she replied.

"Indeed, why do you think we guard this place and tend to the trees as druids my dear?"

"I guess I just never knew the full truth of this place."

"There are few who do."

Lylah quieted down as the salve worked its way through the wound. Juspen ripped off a piece of cloth from his frayed purple robes and began to wrap it around her hand like a bandage.

"She should be fine now," Juspen said.

Celosia kneeled beside Lylah and attempted to give her some water from her pouch flask, "you need to drink some water," she said.

Lylah spat out the piece of wood that she dented with bite marks. "I'm fine," she said.

A fiery arrow struck the platform and another one hit one of the

The Arsonist

elders in the left side of his hip. He let out a painful cry as he lost his balance and fell off the platform to his death. Juspen grabbed a nearby frayed robe that was not being used near the tent entrance and used it to put out the fiery arrow that was stuck in the platform's ledge.

"They're trying to burn us out of the tree now," Juspen said. He peeked below to see several pale-skinned men and women placing torches at the base of the great Salix tree. As he turned to Celosia, Lylah, and the rest of the trials he continued, "Our time is short."

"What are we going to do?" Celosia asked.

"Not stand in visible sight near the ledge that's for sure. Come on, let's gather near the tent," he replied.

"Yes, let's just gather for our demise," she replied.

"What would you have me do, girl? Summon a flock of birds to carry us away to safety? They have taken the grove and none of the help I asked for has come. We are alone in this tragic demise that we now face" he replied.

"You knew this was coming? And you didn't tell us?" Lylah asked.

"I didn't want to alarm you. You are fragile trials after all," he replied.

"Don't talk to us like we're children. You're not Crane," she replied.

"Both of you stop. Look, out there in the lake," Celosia said.

The two elders and the trials could not believe what they were seeing. It was a dark wooden vessel with dark red and black sails floating above it.

"It cannot be," Juspen said.

"Is that the help you requested?" Celosia asked.

"We're about to find out," he replied.

Two rowboats could be seen dropping from each side of the large ship as several different humanoid silhouettes repelled down a rope onto each boat. The pale-skinned invaders turned their attention from the burning of the trees to the lake where their scouts cried for help. They noticed the large ship and its incoming rowboats and made their way toward the beach to defend their hold on the grove.

As the pale-skinned men neared the beach, a sudden torrent of cannon fire was released from the dark wooden vessel. The pale-skinned men and women took cover behind their beached rowboats as they aimed their crossbows at the incoming rowboats and opened fire. The incoming torrent of cannon fire obliterated their beach defenses as the incoming rowboats from the lake made their way to shallow waters.

The silhouettes became clearer from the top of the Salix tree and Juspen and the others were able to make out the appearances of some of the incoming sailors. They were all of different statures and skin colors, some of them wore tricorn and bicorn hats that were small and brimmed. Some of them wore thick coats with too much extra clothing and some of them wore very little clothing making them appear more savage in appearance. They drew their swords as they neared the beach and met the pale-skinned invaders where the Salix trees met the sand as they engaged in combat.

A battle was now taking place beneath Juspen and his druid trials, but they had no way out of the tree that was now slowly burning at the base. Crossbow bolts were flying, and swords were parrying as blood sprayed onto the sand and the nearby tree bark. Screams and roars of battle filled the air along with the smoke from the Salix trees carried away by the afternoon breeze.

"There has to be some extra rope up here or some way down," Lylah said.

"It is a long way down," Celosia said.

"I am afraid we do not have enough rope to reach the bottom," Juspen replied.

"So we're just going to wait up here for those flames to cook us?" one of the trials asked.

"No, those new invaders look somewhat friendly. I am sure they have to come to our aid," Juspen replied.

"And if they aren't here to help us?" Celosia asked.

"Why else would they be here?' Juspen replied.

"They could be opportunists," she replied.

"Perhaps," he replied.

Lylah babied her wounded right hand as she picked up a pile of the rope she found near the tent entrance, "someone help me unravel this and find a place to tie it so we can try to get out of this tree," she said.

"There's no use, my dear, the rope isn't long enough," Juspen replied.

Why do you have an extra pile of rope up here then if it isn't long enough? What is the point?" she asked.

"It was extra that we had from when we made the ladder and I had them store it up here so it wouldn't get moldy or chewed up by field mice," he replied.

"Great, that's fantastic. So, we'll just sit here and burn alive or take a leap of faith and hope the flames don't catch us before we kiss the ground," she replied.

The pale-skinned invaders could be seen retreating south out of the Monolith Sanctum space and through the Salix forest that led to the Earth Arch Pass. Instead of chasing after them into the forest, the men and women that fought them off stayed behind in the Monolith Sanctum space. They grabbed the bodies of their wounded and dead and tossed them carefully into the beached rowboats and prepared to push them back into the war toward the massive dark sailed ship. A handful of the men grabbed buckets from the rowboats and filled them up with water from the lake and ran to the Salix trees to toss the water on the fire in hopes of slowing the burn or dousing the flames. Back and forth, they ran from the rowboats to the Salix trees with big tin buckets of water in their hands.

Juspen and Celosia watched them from the tree with amusement as if the men and women below were ant size people scurrying at their feet. Lylah seemed to be the only one that had not forgotten that they were trapped atop a very tall willow tree with no way down.

"How did you manage to build the rope ladder up here before?" Lylah asked.

"I didn't, the first elders established these platforms. The elders before me reinforced them and when I took their place, I switched out the rope for something new and firm," Juspen replied.

"I see, well how close to the ground would this spare rope of yours get us?" she asked.

"I would be surprised if it gets you any closer than twenty-four feet away from the ground," he replied.

"Well, it doesn't seem like we have much of a choice other than to roll this thing down and try," she replied.

"Those sailors from that ship out on the lake seem to be friendly, they are actually putting out the fires," he replied.

"Well, when I get down there, I'll let you know if they decided to cut my head off or not," she replied.

"Maybe these ones won't shoot you in the hand," Celosia interjected.

"Too soon," Lylah replied.

"Sorry," Celosia replied.

As Lylah hung the spare rope off the ledge of the platform, she tied her end of it to a secure column that had been erected for the original rope ladder. A loud shout could be heard coming from down below and when she looked down from the platform she could see two men, one was holding a long roll of rope, and the other a bow and arrow. The one with the rope held it in the air and waved it around like a white flag for surrender. She watched from the high platform as they set it on the ground and unraveled it. One of the men tied an end of the long rope to an arrow and used a bow to shoot it to the platform. The arrow stuck to the bottom of the platform as the man pulled the rope down making it tightly secured on his end as Lylah carefully untied the rope from the arrow and began to wrap it around the secure column with the original rope.

Celosia handed Lylah a leather cloth that she had found in the tent, it appeared to have once belonged to a piece of Juspen's clothing. Lylah used the leather to keep her hands safe as she held onto the rope for dear life and began to slide down. She screamed in terror as she neared the two sailor men at the bottom. They were both prepared to catch her as she came crashing into them. As she did, they all three fell to the ground and released a series of sighs and grunts that were quickly interrupted by the screaming coming from Celosia as she held onto the rope and went sliding down to them as well.

"Well, that could have gone a lot worse," Lylah said.

The two sailors helped Celosia to her feet as she was greeted by the already-standing Lylah.

"Indeed, but we must hurry, my lady," one of the sailor men said.

"Where must we go?" she asked.

"Captain Saesh awaits," he answered.

Juspen could be heard yelling incoherent words to them from above.

"Is he going to come down here and join us?" Celosia asked.

"I think he's too afraid," Lylah replied.

The two women's joking and laughter were interrupted by their disbelief as Juspen came soaring down from the treetops while hanging onto the rope. The two sailor men learned from their prior mistakes and jumped out of the way before Juspen's feet could land on their respective faces. Celosia fell to the ground as she caught the old man in her arms.

"Well, that could have—" Juspen began.

"Don't say it," said Celosia.

"I didn't think you had it in you, old man," Lylah said.

"I didn't think I had it in me either," he replied.

"Please, we cannot tarry here any longer. Those things are still out there," the sailor said.

"Alright, take us to Captain Saesh then," Lylah replied.

The two sailor men hurried their way to the banks of Lake Moran where a wooden rowboat awaited them. Lylah, Juspen, and Celosia followed right behind them. The rowboat was only big enough to fit four adult-sized bodies and so one of the sailor men was motioned by the other to stay behind on the shore.

The sailor grabbed the oars and began to paddle them toward the dark wooden vessel. A ship of this stature had never entered Lake Moran before, and although the lake was deep enough to host such a ship in its waters it was still unbelievable to the eyes of Juspen who had lived near the Lake his entire life. Lylah began to feel sick as the rowboat bounced up and down in response to the amount of wake that the large vessel had unleashed into the lake.

The stress of all the cannon fire and rowboats made the short voyage from shore to ship quite miserable. By the time they reached the ship, they were all sick to their stomachs and drenched with salty lake water. Two large and fierce-looking sailors pulled the rowboat up by a rope that had tethered it to the ship. Celosia, Lylah, Juspen, and the paddling sailor all rushed to get out of the rowboat and one by one they flopped out of it onto the dark wooden ship deck like a bunch of fish falling out of a fisherman's net.

"Get them some blankets. They're probably freezing," a man said.

The sailor who had paddled them to shore denied the offered blanket and made his way down below to change his clothes. Celosia and Lylah bundled their blankets up together and huddled around the small and shivering Juspen to keep each other warm.

A man with warm dark skin and a smooth shaved head approached them with a wide smile barely tucked behind his big black bushy beard. "Welcome to the Southern Whimsy, the fastest ship in all the Realms of Light. I am your very handsome and very gracious host, Captain Saesh."

"I don't think I've ever heard of the Southern Whimsy before," Celosia replied.

"Well, we're in the process of renovating the ship as both it and its crew's reputation needed a bit of a makeover," Captain Saesh replied.

"What for?" she asked.

"Well, this particular ship used to be known as the Ebony Reaver," he replied.

Celosia's face went pale as she struggled to gulp in disbelief with eyes wide open like cottage windows on a hot summer day.

"Oh, so you have heard of us before, then? Well, we're not pirates anymore, really. Does that comfort you?"

"Tell me, Captain, what business does a pirate have saving keepers of the Weeping Grove?" Lylah asked.

"Why don't you ask your headmaster here, he's the one who asked for my services," Captain Saesh replied.

"Well, not directly of course," Juspen said.

"Not directly?" Lylah asked.

"No," a booming voice said.

Captain Saesh and a few of his men moved out of the way to reveal the source of the booming voice behind them. Alarick Kalon stood towering over the pirates-turned-sailors like a glimmering steeple bestowed upon a peasant village.

"Alarick!" Juspen exclaimed. "It is good to see you old friend, I only wish it were on better terms like old times."

"Indeed, these are grim days for us all, it pains me to see even the fathers of the forest struggling to ward off such evil," Alarick replied.

"My men will have the grove secured by nightfall and hopefully we can get out of here right after that with any of the survivors that are willing," Captain Saesh said.

"Aye, we best load up the rowboats with anyone we can find hiding out in the trees," Alarick replied.

"There was only a handful of us but they were too scared to propel down the rope with us," Juspen said.

"We will find a way to get them down," Saesh replied.

"Alarick, I have heard this name before," Lylah said.

"Lylah, look how much you've grown. I remember when you were as small as a Swollen River Vineyard grape and I could fit you in the palm of my hand," Alarick replied.

"You know who I am?" Lylah asked.

"Yes, I am a forgotten friend of your father's," Alarick replied.

"You know my father? How come we have never been properly introduced?" Lylah asked.

"I assume your father has mentioned very little of me, probably only mumbling my name behind closed doors as he buries his face in a book. We never had the chance to meet because he and I had a falling out when you were too little to remember, I'm afraid," Alarick said.

"Well, this conversation is getting quite cheery, would anyone like a bottle of wine?" Captain Saesh asked.

"A whole bottle?" Celosia asked.

"Oh, sorry I must have been thinking about myself. I meant a glass for any of you who would partake in my cellar and a bottle for me," Captain Saesh replied.

"I'll take water if you have any," Juspen said.

The surrounding crew members exploded and roared with belly-aching laughter as Captain Saesh shook his head and made his way down to the cellar of the ship.

"Pirates don't drink water," Alarick said

"Sailors," Captain Saesh said from below deck.

"He has ears like a fox," Alarick said.

"So, what do we do now?" Juspen asked

"Well, I think it would be in our best interest if I not only provided you the assistance you asked for, which I think I have, but if you came with me down the Seething Sea" Alarick replied.

"The Southern Wastes?" Juspen asked.

"Aye, the Southern Wastes," Alarick replied.

"Why would I go there?" Juspen asked.

"I need someone with your particular talents and knowledge to come with me in search of something that could help turn the tide in this age of terror," Alarick replied.

"I have never abandoned my post at the Monolith Sanctum," Juspen replied.

"I know you haven't but I'm afraid that if you stay here you will die, by tomorrow night this grove will be crawling with bloodsucking fiends that will rip apart your flesh like a pack of wolves feasting on a stray horse," Alarick replied.

"And what of my pupils?" Juspen replied.

"They will be going west with my nephew or we can drop them off in the Bay of Calamity with a rowboat and some supplies. It's their choice," Alarick replied.

"You know Lylah's father, why not take her to him?" Juspen asked.

"That would not be wise," Alarick replied.

"You three haven't been the same for many years, what happened?" Juspen replied.

"We best save that story for the journey ahead," Alarick replied.

Captain Saesh and a few of his men returned from the cellars with crates filled with wine bottles. Among the crate carriers was Bregan Moran who squinted his eyes together as he looked upon Celosia and Lylah.

"Can we help you, little man?" Celosia asked.

"Be nice," Lylah said.

"So, who will be having wine?" Captain Saesh asked.

Alarick, Juspen, Lylah, and Celosia looked at Saesh with blank expressions and silence.

"More for me, then," he said.

"Bregan, can I have a word with you?" Alarick asked.

"Of course, uncle, what is it?"

"The time for us to part ways has come, now, don't forget what we talked about when I woke you up from your dehydrated state like the beaten jailbird you were," Alarick said.\

"The sword in the cathedral, yes, I will not forget, but are you sure my father will understand and help me?" Bregan replied.

"Yes, I'm sure your father will be delighted to hear that you were taken care of by me, and let us not forget your new best friend, Viti," Alarick replied.

Viti stood nearby behind Bregan while also holding a crate of wine.

"Are you sure you want to go with him?" Alarick asked.

"I would be honored, besides I owe him for getting him into so much trouble," Viti replied.

"Nonsense, I got myself into the trouble, don't be so hard on yourself Viti, you owe me nothing, and even if you did I would consider us even by now," Bregan replied.

Alarick, Bregan, and Viti made their way to a nearby rowboat to begin the preparations for their departure. Juspen had finally decided to take part in the wine that Captain Saesh was going on about and within two glasses he fell asleep on the deck leaning against a potato barrel like the lightweight he was.

Celosia and Lylah as curious as they were had decided to approach Alarick and Bregan to see what they were up to.

"Alarick, is it?" Lylah asked.

"Yes, what can I do for you Lylah?" he replied.

"Are you going back to the shore with these two?" she asked.

"No, I am afraid not. I will be staying here onboard the Southern Whimsy with Juspen, and that reminds me of something I have been meaning to talk to you girls about," he replied.

"What's that?" she asked.

"Would you both like to accompany Bregan and Viti here to the Western Glades to find something of great importance to me?" he asked.

"Depends on what it is we are searching for I suppose, and also what the other options are," she replied.

"My son," he replied.

"You have a son?" she asked.

"Yes, and he is with my brother right now, there is also an old possession of mine that my son must find and claim, an heirloom if you will," he replied.

"What other choices do we have?" Celosia asked.

"You can go with these two boys or we will drop you off in the Bay of Calamity with a rowboat and supplies, and from there you can paddle your way to Voyage's End and find a carriage to wherever it is you'd like to go in the Eastern Vale," Alarick replied.

"Sounds like we're going with Bregan and Viti then," Celosia replied.

"The Western Glades would bring me closer to my father, and I do wish to ask him why he did not come to our aid," Lylah said.

"I'm sure he was preoccupied with urgent matters, don't hold it against him," Alarick replied.

"He is the most insightful man I know, and I will be damned if I let him get away with this, he already gets away with too much as it is," she replied.

"He is just lost right now Lylah, I would find comfort in your mother and wait for him to find his way again," he replied.

"My mother is almost worse," she replied.

"I see, well, I can't stop you from seeking confrontation, do what you must, but first I ask that you help locate my son, he is in great danger whether he is aware of it yet or not," he replied.

"I suppose it's the least we could do since you rescued us," she replied.

"Great, that makes me happy to know that my nephew won't be alone in his travels," he replied.

"Nephew?" she asked.

"Aye, Bregan here is my nephew. His father is currently with my son. I guess we sort of swapped children by accident," Alarick replied.

Bregan, Alarick, and Lylah laughed as Viti and Celosia got

acquainted with one another. Captain Saesh began to work on his second bottle of wine as he approached them drunk and awkwardly as if he had two left feet.

"I must say, I am so glad to have seen you after so long, Alarick," Captain Saesh said.

"I know, this is all so surreal, it's like a long-awaited reunion that I only wish I could have assembled under better worldly conditions," Alarick replied.

"There I was, my face buried between a nice pair of tan breasts whilst soaking in the southern sun with all its tropical fruits and passionate denizens. Then you come up and tap me on the shoulder and ask me for help," Captain Saesh replied.

"Funny how things like that happen," Alarick replied.

"Yes, funny indeed, I still can't believe you purposely got yourself thrown into that light-forsaken place, I wince at just the thought of the place alone, what a nightmare it would be to get locked up inside there," Captain Replied,

"And now we're back together just like old times," Alarick replied.

"Just like old times, but you're lucky I didn't forget what you said about showing up to break you out in two months after your sentencing," Captain Saesh replied.

"I should have said one month, I figured out what I needed to know within two weeks of arriving in that shit hole," Alarick replied. "Though it's lucky, really. I had time to wait for my nephew to get himself into a heap of trouble."

The two men laughed as Captain Saesh took a long sip from his bottle. He wiped the red wine off his lips and chin before continuing the conversation. "Never did I expect to have to assault the Festering Cage of all places though. I don't think our ships' sails will be able to safely fly high in these parts ever again. We're going to be hunted for the rest of our lives because of you, say, why did you want to go there anyways?" Captain Saesh replied.

"My informant that knew of the last location of Zersten's whereabouts had been thrown in there and I knew he was as good as dead, but I needed to see for myself," Alarick replied.

"And? Was he dead?" Captain Saesh replied.

"Yes, unfortunately, I was too late, they had drained him dry for bottling just days before I arrived," Alarick replied.

"Those sick bastards, I'm glad we gave their little distillery a black eye before we pulled you, Viti, and Bregan out of there,"

Captain Saesh replied.

"Yes, luckily for me however, the Warden Bal has loose lips, and I was able to pinpoint where Zersten is most likely headed," Alarick replied.

"The Southern Wastes," Captain Saesh replied.

"Aye, the Southern Wastes," Alarick replied.

"Well, the light-forsaken wasteland awaits us, and hey, listen, I want to send a second rowboat with your nephew and his new friends. I have two men that are dying to see trees again, the damn land lovers that they are, we've got fake sailors here in our midst Alarick," Captain Saesh replied.

"Who might those two be?" Alarick replied.

Two fair-skinned men stood a few feet away, chatting with one another and drinking wine.

"Vred and Fargo, come here," Captain Saesh said.

The two men sat their cups down atop a nearby barrel and brushed their hands off on their pants before making their way to Alarick, "nice to meet you, Alarick, we have heard many great things about you," Fargo said.

He had blue eyes and was of medium height, his face was big but his body was thin, and he wore clothes that stood out from the rest of the crew members onboard the ship. They were fine-tailored clothes, dark blue with fine silver thread weaved throughout the tunic. His boots looked as if they had never touched the earth and his face looked as if he had never shaved but never needed to for his facial hair was dark, fine, and patchy. His hair was short as if it were shaven bald months ago. He had a polished-looking bow strapped to his back in a finely woven quiver.

"Aye, the legends of both the Northern Reach and the Western Glades have made their way far beyond the Seething Sea and Southern Abyss," Vred replied. He was also of medium height, but much stouter looking than Fargo. His long brown hair was pulled back in a ponytail creation that resembled that of a fox's tail. His lips and neck were concealed behind a very large beard that reached down beyond the collar of his leather cuirass. His brown eyes peered into Alarick's with sincerity and respect, and as they shook hands, each of them knew they were touching palms with a man of honor.

"It is an honor to meet both of you, but why do you wish to go west?" Alarick asked.

"I grow tired of humidity and stumbling drunk over other drunks every night," Vred replied.

"I never wanted a sailor's life. I was always just seeking adventure wherever I could find it," Fargo replied.

"I see, well if Captain Saesh has no qualms about it then I don't see how more bodies could hurt, there is no harm in wanting a change of pace in life, I of all people understand and respect the desire to change what you are doing with your everyday life," Alarick replied.

"Aye, I will gather my things and load up a second-row boat with supplies then," Fargo replied.

"Before I take my leave, I have one question for you," Vred said.

"What might that be?" Alarick asked.

"Is it cold in the west?" Vred asked.

"Yes, although it is nothing in comparison to the great northern reach," Alarick replied.

"Finally, a place I can praise for its weather and not its fine drinks and easy women," Vred replied.

They both smiled as Vred followed Fargo down below deck to gather his supplies.

"I'm starving," Celosia said.

"I am packing extra food for you, don't worry," Bregan said.

"Oh? What a charmer," Celosia replied.

"I told you to be nice," Lylah said.

"I am being nice, thank you Bregan," Celosia replied.

"It's no problem," Bregan said.

"Are you all just about ready to go?" Alarick asked.

"Yes uncle," Bregan replied.

"Alright then, you know which way you're going?" Alarick asked.

"Yes, we will paddle our way to the banks of the Whistling Prairie and then head northwest past the Krastoff Family Grain Mill as you instructed," Bregan replied.

"Perfect, and don't forget to say hello to the brothers in the mill if you come across them, they're timid and strange but they won't harm you," Alarick replied.

"How far into the glades are we going?" Lylah asked.

"You shouldn't have to go beyond the old Forlorn Cathedral that borders the glade belt, but you may have to venture into Prosperwood Village," Alarick replied.

"Should we seek aid from the rangers in the glades?" Lylah asked.

"No, absolutely not. Do not seek their aid under any circumstances," Alarick replied.

"Why not?" Lylah asked.

"It is for the best that we do not get them involved," Alarick replied.

"Weren't you one of them?" Bregan asked.

"Yes, but that was a long time ago, I'm afraid time has not been kind to that order and their leader has fallen ill under a dark curse that I see there being no end to," Alarick replied.

Fargo and Vred made their way back with a sack of supplies for the journey. They began to load up into a second rowboat that would be lowered into the sea alongside the other one that held Celosia, Lylah, Bregan, and Viti. Vred grabbed the oars and began to paddle the rowboat as Viti grabbed the oars in his respective boat and began to do the same.

"Bregan, when you see your father and Rhys, tell them that I love them," Alarick said.

Bregan nodded in compliance as he waved farewell to the crew of the Southern Maiden.

"And Bregan, if you come across a dark hooded and broody-looking fellow with red eyes, tell him I said to stay sharp," Alarick said.

Chapter Twenty-One

The Glades Maids Bordello was located in the wide open, triangular-shaped glade that occupied the space to the northeast of Amberwood Village which was the chief village of The Western Glades due to their central heartland location.

"The Amberwood Glades" as the area would be known as, was a small and quaint inhabited region that was much like an island surrounded by an ocean of empty forests. The Arsonist, Rhys, and Farbris trod lightly as they approached the knolls that surrounded the front exterior of the bordello.

"Still no sign of the horse?" Rhys asked.

"His name is Xenos," the Arsonist replied.

"If my stomach rumbles one more time I think I may have to eat your dog," Farbris said.

"My dog is a wolf and his name is Glacier," the Arsonist replied.

"Do you have any more animal companions or just these two?" Rhys asked.

"No, but why do you ask, have you dreamed of me with more than these two?" the Arsonist asked.

"There's no need to get snarky, and my dreams are more like nightmares, and they're apparently more like visions than dream states" Rhys replied.

"You're right, I'm sorry. I'm just dangerously hungry, I've been on edge since I arrived at the grain mill with the twins and all this walking on foot has me bent out of shape," the Arsonist replied.

"For once, I think you and I are on the same page or at least are thinking alike," Farbris said.

"Listen, when we get inside please do not do anything that would bring any unwanted attention to us," the Arsonist said.

"Understood," Rhys replied.

"I'm sure everyone's gaze will be fixed on the flesh peddlers anyway," Farbris replied.

"Would you please stop calling them that?" Rhys asked.

"Fine," Farbris replied.

The Arsonist knocked upon the iron door lightly and waited for the door guard to open the sliding slit that was a little higher than the Arsonist's eye level. The tall man behind the door looked down upon the Arsonist, Rhys, and Farbris with keen dark brown eyes.

"Just you three?" the man asked.

"Aye, just three of us," Farbris replied.

"What brings you to the bordello during this midday hour?" the man asked.

"We're travelers from the east seeking warm foods and beds, and potentially the western glade's comfort and hospitality that we've heard so much about during our travels" the Arsonist replied.

"I recognize your mask, stranger," the man said.

"It's a hard one to forget," the Arsonist replied.

"Indeed, you have a lot of business here in the west, it seems strange that you would travel to this place all the way from the east so frequently as you do, although I do not recognize your companions from any previous visits," the man replied.

"My business is none of your concern. Will you let us in or will you be refusing us service?"

"I will let you in, but you best not cause any trouble, some of Lord Argentwald's court members are still here from the night before, but they won't notice you if you don't notice them" the man replied.

"Yes, yes, I already know how desperate the Bordello's owners are to stay in business and not get drained of both their money and blood," the Arsonist replied.

"One last thing, you have to remove your mask if you are to enter. We don't allow any patrons to wear masks, hoods, and any other face-obscuring objects that you might fancy" the man replied.

"Very well," the Arsonist replied.

"Oh, and the dog has to stay outside," the man said.

"Fine, just let us in already," the Arsonist replied.

"It's a wolf," Farbris said.

With the removal of the Arsonist's porcelain mask, the iron doors to the Glades Maids Bordello opened like a tomb being unsealed from the world. The three men stepped into the dark building and left their virtues behind them.

The man at the door greeted them and tipped his top hat to them as he sealed the iron door behind them. Clouds of pipe smoke filled the air and a couple of dozen booths filled the walls as one single giant bar with many stools towering over the booths in the middle. There were four columns inside, one per respective corner, and in front of each column were several flat platforms with steps that led up to them, and on these platforms, beautiful women danced with very little clothing on to cover themselves.

The strong scent of Brightwater perfume lingered in the air and killed any other smell that would oppose it. Behind the bar was a kitchen and Rhys, Farbris, and the Arsonist couldn't even tell that some fresh bread was being let out of the brick oven due to the overpowering scents of perfume and pipe smoke.

The sound of a nearby drum and fiddle band that occupied a space in front of the bar had laid siege to everyone's ears as the sight of revealed female flesh blinded their sight in desire. The three men were lost in the lustful haze as all their senses were assaulted by pleasures newly discovered.

"Hey there Arsy," a soft-spoken woman said. She stood atop one of the flat platforms near the front left column of the bordello, near the entrance.

"A friend of yours?" Farbris asked.

"An acquaintance," the Arsonist replied.

The three men were immediately approached by a woman wearing very little clothing while carrying a silver platter of drinks in small lidless glass jars, "can I get you anything, hun?" she asked.

"No, I'm good, thanks," Rhys replied.

"What's the matter with you? Where are your manners? I raised you better than that," Farbris said.

"I'm not thirsty, I'm starving," Rhys replied.

"I bet you could sink your teeth into her if you were hungry enough. Deliverance knows that I surely could," Farbris replied. He winked and waved at one of the nearby female patrons that were dancing on a nearby platform.

"Afraid not, I only hunger for Lady Winter," Rhys said.

"Oh, for pity's sake," Farbris muttered.

"Lady Winter? She's a noble's brat, too vain and prude for the likes of you. Only the self-absorbed crown themselves with titles to foist upon the rest of us," the Arsonist said.

"Says the man who calls himself the Arsonist," Farbris shot back.

"Don't talk of her like that—you don't even know her, and you're no different from me. Who's to say her beauty wouldn't catch your eye too?" Rhys replied.

"Look around you, wretch. I'm the one with taste here. If it's company you want tonight, they've got plenty of men and women to spare," the Arsonist said.

"There isn't a wine or mead strong enough to convince me to touch any of these people," Rhys replied.

"Suit yourself," the Arsonist replied.

"Aye, come find me after you locate your balls," Farbris said.

Rhys stood there alone at the entrance to the bordello letting all of its debaucheries soak into his mind. Farbris packed a bowl in his pipe and made his way to one of the dancing patrons that had been trying to get his attention. She held a lit match in front of her glimmering blue eyes as Farbris approached her with the pipe hanging out of his mouth. As she lit the pipe bowl for him, they both grabbed a drink from a nearby waitress and got lost whispering in one another's ears.

The Arsonist made his way up the steps to the bar platform and took a seat on one of the stools. The bartender began to wipe down a small wooden drinking glass with a towel while smiling at him.

"I knew you'd miss me," she said.

"Miss you? You're like a disease I can't get rid of," the Arsonist replied.

"How rude," she replied.

"Oh, come on Seranda, you know I'm just kidding," the Arsonist replied.

"How could I forget the classic humor of Alarick Kalon?" she asked.

"That's not my name, so it's obvious that you've forgotten me," the Arsonist replied.

"I'm not going to refer to you by your silly little nickname,"

Seranda replied.

"It's not a nickname, it's a real name, and a title if anything," he replied.

"Why do you let those wanted posters get to you? Just go by your real name and let that incident go," she replied.

"People will never forget the Arsonist, so why should I? I keep the name close to my heart with all my other promises that I've kept," he replied.

"That name must be pretty lonely then because I don't know many promises that you've kept," she replied.

"I see you still haven't lost the talent for making everything about you," he replied.

"What can I say? I learned from the best," she replied.

"I'm the most selfless person I know," he replied.

"Whatever you say Alarick," she replied.

"What time are you departing from this place?" he asked.

"Forgotten my bartending schedule already?" she asked.

"It's always fluctuating, so how am I supposed to know?" he asked.

"I never knew working all day and being off all night counted as fluctuating," she replied.

"So, you'll be free this evening?" he asked.

"If you want a bed warmer, just ask any other woman that works here. I'm sure at least one of them will know exactly how you like to be taken care of. Deliverance knows that I certainly don't know," she replied.

"That's not fair," he replied.

"You, of all people, shouldn't be complaining about fairness," she replied.

"Do you have anything to drink that's as cold as you are?" he asked.

"We're fresh out of sympathy and ale I'm afraid," she replied.

"Wonderful," he said.

The Arsonist pulled out a sack of coins and tucked his dark bangs behind his pale-skinned ears. He looked up from the sticky wooden tabletop at Seranda, whose red eyes had met his own. The dark circles under the Arsonist's eyes bespoke exhaustion, unlike Seranda's, whose eyes were alert, intense, and alluring. He peered into them and remembered how her pallor flesh was devoid of warmth. It looked as though she hadn't seen the sunlight in years. Her now snow-white colored hair was once a dark crimson color that matched the blood she now consumed. When she became infected with the black blood, she became pale to the point of opalescence. She now had a face of eternal beauty that was preserved by immortal blood. She set a glass jar of room-temperature water on the sticky bar table and slid it toward the Arsonist.

"Only because I pity you," Seranda said.

"Thank you, you're too kind," the Arsonist replied.

"I know," she replied.

"I always loved playing the game where I would have to guess what color your eyes were before they became red," he said.

"I always loved telling you that they were green, and then you'd get too drunk to remember the next day," she replied.

The Arsonist was not amused, and as he grabbed his glass jar of water, he turned to see Rhys standing behind him.

"Now it all makes sense," Rhys said.

"We have a complicated history," the Arsonist replied.

"Complicated? Don't be such a cliché, Arsy. Hey, can I call you Arsy?" Rhys asked.

"I would prefer it if you didn't," the Arsonist replied.

"What happened to these pale-skinned people being fiends?" Rhys asked.

"These ones are different," the Arsonist replied.

"I can't help but think that all these poor women that work here have been victims to your self-destructive personality for Deliverance knows how long," Rhys replied.

"You know nothing of which you speak," the Arsonist replied.

"Oh, but I think I do. In fact, I think I have read enough literature and poetry about the womanizing man to know your complicated history here," Rhys replied.

"Watch yourself, Rhys," the Arsonist replied.

"What? Are you going to throw a punch at me? Wouldn't that be hitting yourself?"

"Don't tempt me."

"Why don't you boys shake them off or take this pissing contest outside," Seranda said.

"Actually, I've been carrying this runt all day, and my back is pretty sore. I probably shouldn't be doing any heavy lifting right now. Do you think you could shake mine for me?" the Arsonist asked.

"I've seen it plenty of times already to know that it isn't as heavy as you think," she replied.

"Ouch," Rhys said.

"Alright, well, here you go, take this coin and order me and my companions here a couple of hot meals, won't you?" the Arsonist said as he handed Seranda a small cloth bag.

"I like her. Hey Arsy, do you have any Salix tree salves to treat that? She got you pretty good," Rhys said.

The Arsonist pretended to strike Rhys with his fist making Rhys flinch and cower in fear as a result, "yeah, that's what I thought," he said. As the Arsonist stepped away from the bar stool platform with his glass of water he noticed a group of red-eyed men looking at him in one of the nearby booths. Their skin was pale like Seranda's but much more foul looking.

"What's it cost to get a private room in this joint?" Farbris asked.

"Too much for you to afford, old man," the Arsonist replied. He kept his gaze fixed on the pale-skinned men with red eyes that sat in their booth with grimacing looks on their faces.

"Remember what the doorman said, pay no attention to them and they won't pay attention to us, now let's not ask or look for any trouble, yeah?" Rhys said.

"Trouble is all that I know how to attract, I'm afraid," the Arsonist replied.

"You're going to get us kicked out and we'll be sleeping in the mud with the cold winter winds blowing over our faces as we freeze to death," Rhys replied.

"Nonsense, I'm just going to wander over to that booth over there and make some friends," the Arsonist replied.

They're the same kind as the one you love. Don't do anything foolish. Remember, you're the one that told Farbris and I not to do anything that would invite unwanted attention," Rhys said.

"I don't know what you're talking about," the Arsonist replied.

Rhys was nervous but he noticed that all the patrons with red eyes also had white hair just like he did, although he didn't have red eyes, the Arsonist did. He wondered if they were somehow related to these fiends as the Arsonist referred to them.

Suddenly, the smell of anger choked the air of the bordello premises, and the Arsonist remembered why he recognized the hooligans sitting at the booth. They were part of the same group of fiends that attacked Amberwood Village a few years ago and had set fire to the schoolhouse while the children were still inside. The Arsonist was lost in the memory and the smell of perfume and pipe smoke was now replaced with that of burning flesh and wood, the music in his ears was replaced with the screaming of children, and his vision became as red as his fiery eyes themselves.

A hand gripped his right shoulder from behind as if it were that of a sailor pulling a man overboard back onto the ship. The Arsonist was drenched with shame and anger as he turned to see the shoulder-touching hand connected to a concerned-looking Farbris who was standing alongside an equally as concerned Rhys.

"They're not worth it lad," Farbris said.

"I'm getting tired, we should get a room and catch some sleep before heading out, maybe if we're lucky we can just hire a nearby carriage to take us east," Rhys said.

"Alright," the Arsonist replied. He complied and surrendered his anger as he began to walk back to the bar to order a room for himself and his companions.

"I knew that wasn't him," a voice said.

The Arsonist recognizing the voice turned back to the booth of foul looking pale-skinned men to see where the voice was coming from. A man with long dirty white hair draped around his red almond-shaped eyes sat leaning back at the booth smirking with his legs crossed and his feet kicked up on the table. His arms folded back behind his head with a small pipe hanging from his mouth. His face was pale like the rest of his kind, but his complexion was grave-looking much like the feeling he contributed to the bordello's sudden new atmosphere.

"The real Arsonist is a bloodthirsty killer and would have set this whole tavern ablaze," the man said.

Seranda was pouring a drink for another customer when she heard the pale-skinned man's voice and looked over to see the space between his booth and the Arsonist, which had begun to shrink.

"The real Arsonist should have defanged you and left you for dead inside a rotting hole, just like the one that you crawled out from," the Arsonist replied.

"Damnit, don't be a fool boy," Farbris said.

"Strong words for a weak boy. Listen to your old man here. He's wise and has lived a long life because he probably doesn't pick fights with those who outnumber him," the man replied.

"I only count six of you here. Maybe you should go outside and slay a defenseless villager to rally two or three more of your friends to the cause. Then it might be an even fight," the Arsonist replied.

"Your arrogance has left you blind to your surroundings. Take another look around you, boy, this time of day is when the bordello belongs to us, and just as the sun has set outside, it has also set on you. Your courage has failed you," the man replied.

Seranda whistled to get Farbris and Rhys' attention. As they turned around to see her motioning them, they were approached by a handful of pale-skinned patrons.

"I really don't want any trouble," Rhys said.

One of the pale-skinned men lunged toward Rhys and Farbris with fang and claw but was intercepted by a bullet blowing a clean hole through his face. The limp body of the deranged fiend went flying back into a pale-skinned woman who caught the lifeless remains of his body. The music stopped the patrons screaming and swarmed the iron door to the bordello to escape and flood outside into the dark forest that awaited them.

The Arsonist stood with his red eyes intensely gleaming from behind the smoking barrel of his pistol. He grinned wickedly as he turned his attention back to the booth to set his aim upon the men who occupied it. The pale-skinned men sat nervously while clenching their fanged canines together like two swords parried in combat.

The screams grew louder outside but this time they were accompanied by a very loud wolf-like howl.

"What in Deliverance's name was that?" Farbris asked.

"I've heard that howl before but not from here," the Arsonist said.

"That didn't sound like your average wolf," Rhys said.

"Sounds like your friends are here to save you again," the Arsonist said.

"That howl came from no friend of mine," the pale-skinned man replied.

"Seeing a blood-drinking fiend that could fight its own battles alone. Now wouldn't that be a sight to see," the Arsonist replied.

"Damn you, I told you that it came from no friend of mine. How about you lower your weapon, and we see how you hold up alone against me," the pale-skinned man replied.

"I like where it is right now, actually. It looks good when it's aimed toward a couple of thugs, and besides, fear is a good color on you," the Arsonist replied.

"You must be looking in a mirror, boy. I'm not scared of you. I know how your fickle devices work. I remember those fiery gauntlets of yours, and I know that just like them, you have to reload at some point, and there's enough of us here to swarm you before that can happen. You can't kill all of us," the pale-skinned man replied.

"You're right, but the only one I care about killing is you. I could care less what happens to me afterward," the Arsonist replied.

"Have you gone mad?" Farbris asked.

"Well, do it then, boy. What are you waiting for? Take your shot and prepare for many fangs to pierce your frail body," the pale-skinned man replied.

The guard door closed the sliding slit on the iron door to the bordello and ran to the inner room of the bordello where the bar was kept, "we need to get out of here now! There is a giant beast outside ripping people apart," the door guard said.

"What?" Seranda asked.

"We should leave now while we still can," Rhys said.

"You go on ahead, I have unfinished business here," the Arsonist replied.

"A giant beast you say?" Farbris asked.

"Aye, a giant beast covered in blood and fur," the door guard replied.

"Oh, Deliverance, save us all," Farbris replied.

"Arsonist, we need to leave, let these fiends go, they're not worth it," Rhys said.

The Arsonist's red eyes twitched as he clenched his jaw. The fantasy allure of killing these fiends had taken hold of his mind. "Damnit," he said.

"Come on, we can slip out the back door," Seranda said. She put on her long black cloak and flipped the hood up over her white-haired head. The door guard sealed the iron door to the bordello shut and made his way toward Seranda awaiting him at the back of the Bordello behind the kitchen. Farbris and Rhys quickly followed behind the guard, seeing no end to the standoff between the Arsonist and his pale-skinned rivals.

"Just going to abandon your friends like that?" the pale-skinned man asked.

"They're not my friends," the Arsonist replied.

"Right, a bloodthirsty criminal such as yourself doesn't have any friends," the pale-skinned man replied.

"You're one to talk Victoyos, you probably kill and betray all of your so-called friends," the Arsonist replied.

"Oh, but I have plenty of friends. Here, meet them for yourself,"

Victoyos said. He quickly pushed the two pale-skinned men that sat respectively on each side of him toward the Arsonist, who fired a gunshot in response.

Victoyos swiftly stood up and leaped through the glass window behind him. The Arsonist's gunshot blew through one of the pale-skinned fiends, and before the rest of them could reach him, he unleashed a torrent of fire from his left-hand gauntlet, turning them to ash and setting the bordello space between the Arsonist and the broken window ablaze.

The Arsonist cursed Victoyos as he saw him leap through the burning shattered window glass. As the Arsonist finished reloading his pistol, he pointed it up at the broken window to set his aim on Victoyos, but he was gone.

The Arsonist ran to the back of the bordello, where the others had already taken off out the back door. They had not gotten far into the woods as he could still see the white pulled-back hair of Rhys in the distance. He started to run in their direction to catch up to them. As he left the screams of people behind him, the smoke of the burning bordello began to climb upward toward the full moon that lit up the night sky.

Glacier, who had not only heard but witnessed the troubles of the beast outside the bordello, had already darted away from the bordello to the woods out back. He saw his master fleeing the burning building, into the woods, and toward familiar faces. He charged forth after him with haste.

"What was that thing back there?" Rhys asked.

"In all my long-lived years I have never heard of a hairy howling beast," Farbris replied.

Seranda, the door guard, Rhys, and Farbris came to a swift halt as they noticed the Arsonist approach them panting and sweating while attempting to catch his breath. Seranda's red eyes lit up like glowing cherries at the sight of Glacier.

"Well, except that one of course," Farbris said.

Rhys and the door guard laughed for a bit as Seranda kneeled to pet Glacier.

"How are you, boy? I sure did miss you," Seranda said.

"If we're all done crowding my wolf now I'd like to get a move on before that thing comes after us," the Arsonist said.

"Oh, are you done having a death wish now?" Farbris asked.

"What was that all about anyway?" Rhys asked.

"Nothing, we need to move, now," the Arsonist replied.

"Where are we heading?" the door guard asked.
"East," the Arsonist replied.
"They're coming with us now?" Rhys asked.
"It would seem so," Farbris replied.

The Arsonist stepped in front of Seranda with Glacier by his side. The two led the companions from the front while Rhys and the door guard followed in the back with Farbris and Seranda paired up in the middle of the group. They trudged through the cold frozen ground as they made their way east of the bordello and back toward the grain mill.

"We never got that food or drink," Farbris said.
"Or bed," Rhys said.
"Quit your bellyaching, we had no choice but to leave," the Arsonist replied.
"It would be nice if we could stop and rest, I feel as if I am going to faint at any moment," Rhys replied.
"I think there's some bread and a few drops of water in my supply bag," Farbris said.
"We can't afford to stop with that thing still out there," Seranda replied.
"Aren't you afraid of being out here when the sun comes out? I can't imagine that it will be very good for your skin, I've heard it makes your kind slow and tired," Farbris said.
"The consequence of sun exposure to my kind is nothing more than a bad sunburn and a terrible headache. So how about I worry about me, and you worry about yourself," Seranda replied.

The door guard laughed as he took off his top hat and wiped his brow.

"Are we headed back to the grain mill then?" Rhys asked.
"Yes, and unfortunately we will most likely stay there, although I have no coin to give them in exchange, so it's going to be awkward," the Arsonist replied.
"I've been in far worse cramped places in my lifetime," Farbris replied.

As the group wandered for hours toward the edge of the woods, they continued to bicker. When they got near the bordering edge of the Amberwood forest, their side conversations were interrupted by a fierce howl in the distance. It was much like the one previously heard at the bordello.

The sound was let loose from the beast again. Except this time, it was followed by a familiar man's voice screaming in agony as the sound of a gunshot went off in the far distance "Was that what I think it was?" Rhys asked.

"Felix," the Arsonist said.

Glacier and the Arsonist darted swiftly ahead of the group toward the edge of the forest where the whistling prairie clearing could be seen beneath the wide-open southern plains sky. The others picked up their feet, hoping to match the haste and keep up with them.

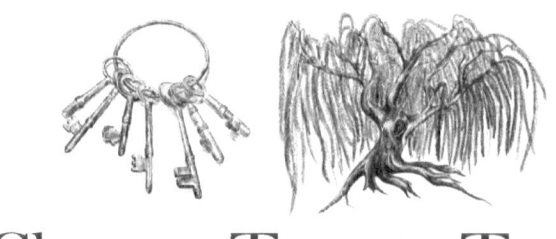

Chapter Twenty-Two

Celosia, Lylah, Bregan, Viti, Vred, and Fargo crowded into a rickety paddle boat, its oars slicing through Lake Moran's murky waters as they headed toward the Western Glade. Across the lake, the Weeping Grove flickered with chaos—flashes of steel and bursts of shouting cut through the distant tree line, the clamor of battle echoing over the water. The unsettling din lingered as they reached the muddy shores of Lake Moran, just south of the Footman's Refuge, and emptied out of their rowboats. They trudged through miles of high grass and dead weeds that littered the Whistling Prairies' golden fields. No wildlife could be seen or heard. There was nothing but flying insects to be found as blades of spiky grass were trampled underfoot.

The company made their way over a couple of rolling hills covered in weeds, and as the sun went down behind them, they could barely see a large grain mill in the distance. As they grew closer to it, they heard a loud and fierce howl followed by a gunshot going off.

As they hurried their way through a field of grass, they saw a man on the ground crying his eyes out while holding a limp and ravaged body of a man. As he approached the crying man, Fargo pulled out an arrow and prepared to draw his bowstring. Vred followed a few footsteps behind as he unsheathed his sword from the scabbard on his back. Celosia, Lylah, and Bregan huddled behind Viti, who tightly held a knife in each of his hands.

"Get away. It's still out there," Clive said.

"What is?" Fargo asked.

Before Clive could say another word Glacier leaped from the darkness of the forest and into the dirt space between Clive and Fargo. Fargo aimed his bow at Glacier, ready to pull back an arrow into the wolf's skull.

"If you let go of that arrow it will be the last thing you ever do," the Arsonist said. He was now standing behind the crying Clive with his pistol aimed at Fargo.

"His eyes, he's one of them," Vred said.

Vred gripped his sword with both his hands as he charged toward the Arsonist, but his heels dug into the dirt as he came to a swift halt as Bregan shouted.

"Stop, this is a friend of Alarick's. His appearance matches the description that I was given," Bregan said.

The Arsonist tilted his head to the side in confusion as he squinted his eyes at Bregan. Rhys, Farbris, Seranda, and the door guard finally caught up to the Arsonist and stood behind him as they leaned forward with both hands on their knees as they attempted to catch their breath.

"You know my father?" the Arsonist asked.

"Aye, I know him, he said to keep my eyes out for a dark hooded broody-looking fella with red eyes, and you look like just the figure he described," Bregan replied.

"Broody?" the Arsonist asked.

"Sounds about right," Seranda said.

Fargo lowered his bow and placed the arrow back in his quiver. Vred lowered his sword and sheathed it back into the scabbard on his back.

"My apologies, friend, you can't be too careful these days," Vred said.

"Indeed, I thought it was a wild wolf that had attacked these two," Fargo said.

"It was. Just not Glacier, the damn thing is still out there. I don't even think my hand cannon hit it. I think it just scared it off, but it got my brother. It got Felix," Clive said.

"The damn thing already got here from the bordello?" the Arsonist asked.

"Bordello? They have those here?" Vred asked.

"Which way?" Fargo asked.

"I don't know, somewhere over there in the woods," Clive replied.

"No, not the wolf, the bordello," Fargo replied.

"Would you idjits take this seriously? This man just lost his brother for Deliverance's sake," Lylah said.

"Aye, sorry we're just making light of the situation," Vred replied.

Viti and Celosia shook their heads at Fargo and Vred as they approached the Arsonist. Bregan noticed his father and cousin Rhys standing behind the Arsonist and as they noticed Bregan they could see a crazy calm in his face.

"Bregan?" Farbris asked

"Father," Bregan said.

Farbris pushed the Arsonist out of the way and rushed toward Bregan. The two met each other with open arms and hugged one another tightly as Rhys slowly approached them with open arms as well. The three of them hugged one another and laughed with tears running down the sides of their cheeks.

"It's so good to see you both again," Bregan said.

"I'm so glad we don't have to break you out of prison now," Rhys replied.

"I beat you to that one I'm afraid," Viti said.

"Actually, we beat them to it," Fargo said.

"Well, this is all very nice and all but what is going on and what are we going to do about the disaster that sits here before us?" Celosia asked.

"I was wondering about the same thing," Lylah said.

"This beast is unstoppable," the bordello door guard said.

"I have never seen anything like it before," Clive said.

"I'm going to put a hole in its head and then we'll be on our way," the Arsonist said.

"On our way where? My cousin stands here before us now, so there is no need to go east. You can return to picking fights with pale skins and brooding alone in the forest with your animal companions. It's clear you're not concerned about anyone else," Rhys replied.

"You're right. Perhaps I will head back into the woods and leave you here to reason with the monster. I am sure it will respond well to history lessons and witty words," the Arsonist replied.

"Do you two ever stop fighting?" Seranda asked.

"No, the bitching never ceases, I'm afraid," Farbris replied.

"Would all of you shut up and help me get my brother's body inside? The damn thing wrecked my arm as I shot my pistol. I think it broke the damn thing," Clive said.

"Your arm is broken?" Celosia asked.

"No, the pistol you fool," Clive replied.

"I don't understand, why are you here? How did these people break you out?" Farbris asked.

"Come Father let us go sit inside the mill and I can tell you everything," Bregan replied.

"No, I don't think so, none of you are welcome here, you can stay out here and deal with that damned beast for all I care," Clive said. He began to drag his dead brother Felix's body in the windmill only to slam the door behind him. A series of many locks being activated could be heard from outside.

"Great, now we can freeze to death out here in the fields," Rhys said.

"Not if that thing over there kills us first," Viti replied. He pointed toward the forest with his knife, and as all the others turned to look, they all saw a large dark figure standing at the edge of the forest.

"It's almost like the damn thing is daring us to come after it," the Arsonist said.

"What is it?" Seranda asked.

"It looks like some kind of wolf," Fargo said.

"That is no mere wolf, it is too muscular-looking, and it's also standing upright," Farbris replied.

The beast was tall. It was at least six foot five and completely covered from top to bottom with thick black hair that was saturated with blood. It stood on two hind legs that were attached to large claws that dug into the frozen mud.

Its hands stretched out, revealing large claws that looked like daggers for fingers. The head of the beast looked wolf by design with no humanoid features. The mouth was wide and filled with many sharp teeth that were stained red with the blood of a fresh kill. The eyes were red and motionless as they locked their sight upon the men and women that stood before them outside the windmill.

"We're in for one hell of a fight if it attacks us," Viti said.

"It is nothing more than a feral fiend that will die by my hand just like the rest," the Arsonist replied.

The beast lowered itself to the ground on all fours and began to circle them smooth and almost catlike.

"I think Clive was right. The thing doesn't even look injured. He must not have hit it with the hand cannon," Rhys said.

The companions readied themselves again for combat as Fargo

The Arsonist

readied his bow and Vred readied his sword. The Arsonist aimed his pistol at the beast but was ready to unleash fire from his left flame gauntlet again if necessary. Viti gripped his two knives, and Rhys grabbed a quill from his satchel. Farbris started to pack his pipe as Lylah and Celosia each grabbed a large nearby rock that they could throw. Bregan stood with Seranda and the door guard near the windmill entrance.

"I can't believe this is my last pipe bowl. If we survive this, the first thing I'm doing when I get back out of here is making a special trip to Yokelshire," Farbris said.

"Is this really the time for that?" Rhys asked.

"You really think we're getting out of this alive?" Celosia asked.

"I have faith in you all," Farbris replied.

The beast lunged its way high into the air and then disappeared before their eyes.

"Where did it go?" Lylah asked.

The group slowly started to huddle back toward the door to the windmill. The screams of the door guard startled them as they turned to see large claws dug into the sides of his face as he was pulled up above and away from them.

"No," Seranda said.

"Run," Viti said.

The group took off heading toward the forest as the beast crouched atop the doorway to the windmill and feasted upon the bordello door guard. As they all used the swiftness of adrenaline to dash through the forests on foot, they could hear the howls of the beast coming from behind them.

"It's following us," Lylah said.

"No, it's hunting us," Vred replied.

"What is this damn thing?" Fargo asked.

"We'll find out when it's dead," the Arsonist replied.

The beast could be heard like a stampede of horses coming from behind. It leaped through the forest from branch to branch pursuing them as they ran. The Arsonist turned to see it and aimed at it with his pistol before squeezing the trigger and letting loose a gunshot. The beast feinted before disappearing into the darkness of the treetops.

"Did you do it? Did you kill it?" Farbris asked.

"I think I hit it," the Arsonist replied.

The beast lunged from behind a nearby tree and attacked the

Arsonist. Before the beast could dig its claws and teeth into his flesh, it was attacked from behind. Glacier dug his fangs deep into the back of the beast. The beast let out a wail of pain as it reached back to grab Glacier. Glacier let out a whimper as he was flung across the forest and into a nearby tree.

"No," the Arsonist said.

The Arsonist went to ignite the flesh of the beast with his flamethrower gauntlet, and as he pressed on the lever in his palm, he heard an empty fuel line dripping as a flame as small as a match was emitted from the gauntlet's vent. Fear washed over his face as his red eyes faded into the dark rings around his eyes. The beast's wolf-like face neared the Arsonist as it prepared to feast upon its prey. The Arsonist closed his eyes, ready to accept his fate. They snapped open from the sound of bones cracking as a rock struck the beast across the face. An arrow soared past the beast's canine-like ear, barely missing it as it let out a whimpering howl, this one was different than the others, and it expressed pain and discomfort, not the thrill of the hunt like the others before it. Vred charged in behind the beast, with his sword moving quickly in front of him. He was preparing to stab it into the beast, but before the steel could meet the black fur, the beast leaped into the tree branches above them.

"Are you alright?" Vred asked.

Lylah who had thrown the rock at the beast quickly ran over to the Arsonist to help him get up on his feet, "come on we've got to get moving," she said.

Vred noticed that the Arsonist was struggling to pick up Glacier, so he picked the wolf up himself and tossed it over his shoulder as he and the Arsonist ran deeper into the woods with everyone else. The beast continued to pursue them, but it was more cautious and hesitant to strike at them than before.

"I can't keep going," Rhys said. "My feet are giving out, and I'm exhausted."

"I can feel myself fading," Bregan said.

"We have to keep moving, the damn thing is still hunting us, and it will kill us in our sleep," Farbris said.

"These forests are ripe with monsters seeking to spill our blood," the Arsonist said.

"Then we cannot linger here for too long," Vred replied.

"How long until the sun comes up? Will that have any effect on it?" Farbris asked.

"Long enough for it to pick us off one by one," Seranda replied.

"How far are we from the cathedral?" Bregan asked.

"An hour by horseback," the Arsonist replied.

"And on foot?" Bregan asked.

"No idea, but why does it matter? Why do you ask about the cathedral? What has my father put you up to?" the Arsonist asked.

"He told me to find my father and cousin and then located something within the cathedral," Bregan replied.

"No, we're not going there," the Arsonist replied.

"I don't think we have a choice, it's the only nearby place that can provide us with shelter," Farbris said.

"That doesn't change the fact that we have a bloodthirsty beast chasing us right now," Lylah replied.

"It's not chasing us anymore. It's just up there somewhere watching us," Rhys said.

"What's the plan then?" Fargo asked.

"There is another place, one that is nearby, closer in fact," Seranda said.

"No, we're definitely not going there either," the Arsonist replied.

"I think I know of which you speak, and if my suspicion is correct, then I would have to agree with the Arsonist on this one," Farbris said.

"Don't be foolish. I wasn't suggesting that we all go there. I was talking about me," Seranda replied.

"How does you going there help us?" the Arsonist asked.

"What is it that you are talking about?" Bregan asked.

"Argentwald Manor, it is home to many loathsome fiends," the Arsonist replied.

"Ah, so my suspicions were correct," Farbris said.

"If I go, it will draw the beast off of you and give you enough time to make it to the cathedral," Seranda replied.

"Who will take this suicidal journey with you?" the Arsonist asked.

"No one. I will go alone. As I said, it will draw the beast off you as it will see me alone. It should give you the couple of hours you need to get away. If anything, it will at least give you a lengthy head start," she replied.

"It will kill you," the Arsonist replied.

"Nonsense, you can't get rid of me that easily. I'm a disease, remember?" Seranda replied.

The Arsonist smirked but was still unamused by her proposal.

"There seems to be no other better way," Rhys said.

"Shut it. You have no say in this matter, just close your eyes and take a nap while thinking of Lady Cold or whatever her name is," the Arsonist replied.

"Stick it up your arse, Arsonist, I know you're afraid now, just like the rest of us, and I know that you know that there is no other option right now. This damn beast has left us with no other alternative," Rhys replied.

"We could tie you to a tree and leave you here," the Arsonist replied.

"Both of you, stop it. There is no more debate on this matter. I will take my leave now. Catch your breath, tighten your boots. When I say go, you will take off toward the cathedral. Do you understand me?" Seranda replied.

"Let me go with you," Lylah said.

"No, I am to do this alone," Seranda replied.

The Arsonist approached Seranda and reached out to the loose hair strands that floated beside her pale cheeks. He tucked them behind her ears so he could see the oval shape of her face.

"I have very few reasons left to want to live in this world anymore, don't do anything stupid that would take away one of the last reasons I have left," he said.

"I can't even tell if I'm dead or alive anymore, but if my heart is still truly beating, then you're the reason it still is," she replied. The Arsonist leaned his head in to kiss her, and as he neared her lips with his own, she pulled away from him.

"Go," she said. As she took off running away from the group into the forest, the Arsonist stood in the dark forest clearing, looking extremely troubled and confused. A couple of branches could be heard breaking, and they could be seen falling from above as the beast let out a howl and headed toward the direction of Seranda.

Lylah, Rhys, and the others began running in the opposite direction as Bregan tugged on the Arsonist's trench coat, motioning him to come with them. The Arsonist put on his porcelain mask and flipped the hood over his dark mane of hair as he took off running after Bregan and the others.

Chapter Twenty-Three

A young man lightly tapped Thaniel on his chest to awake him.

"Lord Cadere Sir, first wake up," the young man said. Thaniel knew that there would be two more taps and wake-up warnings left to come before he was forcefully removed from his rack by a superior.

This was the way of the Rangers and their watch rotation. An apprentice-like figure, that was usually the youngest in the regiment, would be sent throughout the forts to issue wake-up warnings to those whose time it was to stand watch. So, instead of rolling back into a dreamless sleep and delaying the inevitable second wake-up Warning, Thaniel decided to sit up and drag himself out of bed.

After he put his leather boots on, he could hear the the young man from earlier returning down the hall to issue the second wake-up warning. As the young man opened the door to Thaniel's quarters, he saw him standing beside his bed with his bow strapped to his back.

As Thaniel finished strapping his bracers to his wrists and adjusting his cloak, he turned to see the young man peeking in from the cracked open door that emitted the only light source within the room.

"Thank you for waking me," Thaniel said.

"It is an honor sir," the young man replied.

Thaniel made his way out to the front of Fort Quiver to relieve one of the two rangers in the farthest back to the front gate foxhole, "I am here to relieve you of your post," he said.

"Thank Deliverance, I don't think I could keep my eyes open much longer," the ranger said, climbing out of the foxhole.

"Get some rest," Thaniel replied.

Thaniel slid down the dirt walls and into the foxhole to take his seat next to a grizzled-looking ranger who was smoking a pipe with his eyes fixed on the dark forest that lay in front of the fort, "you know smoking will give away your position if they have sharpshooter archers," Thaniel said.

"You must be new if you think that these things can fire arrows," the grizzled-looking ranger replied. His face looked grim. His complexion was weather-beaten from too many woodland skirmishes that took place before the uniting of the realms.

"These things are really that savage, huh?" Thaniel asked.

"Savage? That would be a compliment," the man replied.

Thaniel was surprised by the words of the grizzled-looking ranger, but he was not shocked. He let the silence in the foxhole grow until he could no longer stand it, "so, when is your relief?" Thaniel asked.

"I am the relief."

"You must have arrived here moments before me, and I thought I was early," Thaniel said.

"No, you were just on time." the grizzled-looking ranger replied.

"My father always says that if you are on time, you are late," Thaniel replied.

"You must be Renson Cadere's boy," he replied.

"Yes, I guess he must have said that to a lot of people in his long line of duty," Thaniel replied.

"Aye, I knew the bastard. He was a sharp one," he replied. He dumped out his pipe bowl and began packing it again to light another one. As the pipe bowl began to smolder, he reached his left hand out to greet Thaniel officially, "the name's Carlyle, by the way," he said.

"Nice to meet you, Carlyle. I don't think my father has ever mentioned you before. You look like a Cyanakin veteran to me. Say, how many skirmishes have you had with these things out there?" Thaniel replied.

"Skirmishes? Ha! That's what we used to call the petty squabbles and trading of blows back before the uniting of the realms.

That was a name given to the small feuds and battles that took place here in the West before you were even born," Carlyle replied.

"Alright then, if not skirmishes, what would you call your encounters with these things instead?" Thaniel asked.

"Carnage," Carlyle replied.

The wind began to rise in the glade, and the flames emitted by the torches started to sway back and forth, dancing with the southern breeze that crept out from the trees.

"It will be morning soon, and then we'll be able to see the bastards better if they're out there anyway," Thaniel said.

"Oh, they're out there, and they're probably frothing at the mouths as they watch us right now, the bastards," Carlyle replied.

"Deliverance will protect us," Thaniel said.

"Deliverance? Ha! You best stop believing in fairy tales, boy. That bow in your hands is the only thing capable of protecting you," Carlyle replied.

"There's no non-believers in a foxhole, is what my father always said," Thaniel replied.

"I knew your father. He was never in a foxhole," Carlyle replied.

As the hours grew longer, Thaniel's alertness started to dwindle. He kept thinking of his mother and what she would think about all of this. He wondered how she would feel about his father letting him defend the frontlines in a foxhole at Fort Quiver.

These thoughts carried his mind away until he was no longer there, his body leaned forward in a foxhole while gripping the cold grass surrounding its front perimeter, but he was no longer there. Pipe smoke and bread rations were all Thaniel could smell and taste in the foxhole as he drifted off into memories of his mother and how he discovered her body the night she was murdered.

"The bastard will pay," Thaniel said.

"What's that?" Carlyle asked.

"Nothing," Thaniel replied.

Both Gwenith and Nosodul could be heard shouting from the fort walls down to the rangers in trenches. Gwenith stood upon the rear fortress walls while Nosodul stood on the front walls.

"Look alive out there, two more hours to go until the sun rises," Gwenith said.

"Those hydration flasks better be empty, if I send an officer down there and they see that you haven't been drinking any water you will be reprimanded by me personally," Nosodul said.

Thaniel suddenly felt a burst of energy and reached down into his satchel to find his hydration flask.

"Move over, I've got to take a piss," Carlyle said.

"You must be joking, you can't seriously think to relieve yourself in here," Thaniel replied.

"Oh, yes, I can, and yes, I will. Unlike you, I drank my hydration flask roughly an hour ago," Carlyle replied.

"I don't think I'm going to be able to drink my water to the sound of you doing that right next to me," Thaniel replied.

"You're going to have to try or figure something out then," he replied.

As Thaniel opened his flask to take a chug, he was interrupted by the sound of Carlyle's urine stream hitting the ground a few feet away from him. Thaniel put the lid back on his hydration flask and tucked it back in his satchel while maintaining an annoyed and disgusted look on his face.

"Much better," Carlyle said.

"You have no dignity or self respect, do you?" Thaniel asked.

"This world doesn't respect us, so why should we?" Carlyle replied. He sat down into a dry portion of the foxhole and pulled out a small knife to clean his fingernails out with. Thaniel looked away in further disgust as he tried to find his way back to the memory trance that he was previously in.

"Something's drawing closer to the trench," a ranger said.

"Nonsense, I see nothing from here," Nosodul replied.

"Sir, there's definitely something heading this way," he replied.

Nosodul pulled out his telescope to look at the forest in the distance, "I can't see anything," he said. Thaniel's senses once again became suddenly alert, and he readied his bow.

"Here we go again," Carlyle said.

"They're actually coming?" Thaniel asked.

"Nosodul's eyes have failed him with age, or he's accidentally covering the end of his telescope with his hand," Carlyle replied.

"What do you mean? I don't see anything out there either," Thaniel replied.

"They're coming," Carlyle replied.

The rangers in the forward trench began to panic like a stomped-out ant hill as they unsheathed their swords. The archers on the walls started to dip the tips of their drawn arrows into a burning cauldron.

"They've never attacked us this close to daylight," Nosodul

said.

"If this is a false alarm you can cut my eyes out sir," the ranger replied. Silence rolled through the fortress walls, trenches, and foxholes like a fog setting in on an eerie road.

"Time to go to work," Carlyle said.

Thaniel watched as Carlyle threw his pipe on the ground and unsheathed his sword. Carlyle then reached into his back pouch to pull out a vial of transparent liquid.

"What is that?" Thaniel asked.

"The blokes from the windmill sold a couple vials of this stuff to me a few months back, it's like liquid fire," Carlyle replied.

"What's it called?" Thaniel asked.

Carlyle pulled the cork out of the vial and poured the liquid onto the steel of his blade, "they called it Daybreak fluid, but I hated the name, so I call it Western Glade hospitality, or comfort rather," Carlyle replied.

Thaniel watched in astonishment as Carlyle pulled out a small limestone to strike the blade. As Carlyle struck the blade with the small flint like rock, the entire soaked portion of the steel blade went up in flames like a city guard's torch.

"That has to be the most impressive thing I've ever seen," Thaniel said.

"Really? You have a weapon that generates arrows at the draw of its bowstring, and you think me setting a steel sword on fire is more impressive?" Carlyle replied.

The two rangers laughed for the first time together in the foxhole, but the joy was short-lived as the cracking voice of a nearby trench ranger called out to open fire. Carlyle and Thaniel couldn't turn their attention back to the forest fast enough before the whole sky lit up with a volley of flaming arrows. As the arrows hit the forest perimeter and set fire to the trees, an endless wall of silhouettes appeared within the forest. As the volley made contact with the forest, the dark silhouette figures became that of pale-skinned fiends with red eyes.

The trees quickly caught fire from the arrows, but the flames did not affect what looked like a rapid white tide of red-eyed invaders crashing into the trench full of rangers. They extended their arms with claws dangling in front of their frothing-fanged mouths as they charged out from the forests. Their bodies squirmed like a swarm of eels through the trenches as the screams of dying rangers were drowned out by the screeching of the pale-skinned fiends.

Thaniel did not hesitate to let arrows fly as he stood within the foxhole and aimed at the incoming invaders.

"Don't let them bite you," Carlyle said.

The front gate to the fort opened as a dozen rangers came charging forth to reinforce the failing outer defenses.

"There's so many of them," Thaniel said.

"This is smaller than the group I saw heading toward the prairie when I was scouting down south a month ago," Carlyle replied.

Within minutes the front trench was overrun, and the foxholes began to disappear within the endless crowd of stringy white-haired savages. Their red eyes and pale skin were all that could be seen as Thaniel continued to let arrows fly into their skulls.

"Gwenith, we need more men up here," Nosodul said.

"We're a little preoccupied back here," she replied.

"They're flanking us?" Thaniel asked.

"Looks like the bastards are learning," Carlyle replied.

Thaniel and Carlyle started to retreat with a handful of other surviving rangers as the foxholes became overrun.

"The front line is lost. Retreat to the fort and close the gates. We must hold," Nosodul said.

"I sent word to Amberwood's forces two days ago requesting immediate aid," Gwenith said. Thaniel and Carlyle stood behind the now sealed gate, awaiting orders for what to do next.

"Good. I hope to Deliverance that your messenger did not get intercepted," Nosodul replied.

The gate to the fort was now under siege as the fiends crashed their scrawny bodies into it, killing themselves in the process. As the bodies quickly piled up on the gate, they began to tower toward the wall. The integrity of the iron-reinforced wooden gate began to fail as the surviving fiends would use the corpses of their fallen kin to climb up the front gate and toward the wall itself.

"I have never seen anything like this," Nosodul said.

The gate suddenly burst open as the fiends nearly reached the wall. As it did, the large number of deceased bodies came crashing through into the fort's entryway. The few rangers that attempted to reinforce the gate with their body weight were now crushed under the piles of dead pale-skinned fiends.

Thaniel began to fire arrows into the destroyed gate opening as more and more pale-skinned invaders rushed through its crowded entrance. Carlyle charged into them with his burning sword as handfuls of other rangers joined him.

The Arsonist

"Gwenith, status report," Nosodul said.

"They've taken out our rear defenses. The fort is getting surrounded. It looks like a white ocean out there," Gwenith replied.

Nosodul unsheathed his sword and motioned a few of the archers on the front wall to follow him, "to hell with this, let's get down there and hold the gate or we're as good as dead," he said.

Thaniel couldn't believe what was happening. It was like nothing he could have ever imagined. He knew there was only one way he was getting out of this alive. There was not any amount of skilled rangers that could handle a threat this terrible. There was not any amount of Cyanakin training that could have prepared them for this type of force.

As his arm grew tired from firing arrows into the endless wave of red eyes before him, he knew that only help from his friends Hyde and Mavis could save them. He started to quietly mutter a prayer to Deliverance, "please, god of liberation, declare your light and deliver us from this menace," he said.

The rangers defending the gated entryway began to falter as the pressure surrounding the fort's walls began to bottleneck at the front gate.

"There is no end to them," Carlyle said. Before he could lose hope and fall to the pale fiends surrounding him, his second wind arrived at the sight of Nosodul joining the fight at his side.

Dozens of archers now stood alongside Thaniel with longbows in hand. As they aimed at the gate, they shouted for Carlyle, Nosodul, and the others to duck for cover. They responded to this command by dropping to the ocean of pale bodies before their feet. As they fell to the ground, the archers let loose a torrent of arrows that shot through the red-eyed horde. A worthy effort, but it did not halt the ever-growing advancement that the fiends continued to make as they crowded the entrance to the fort.

"Gwenith, get down here and help us or get up to the front and shoot them down as they try to enter," Nosodul said.

The fire of Carlyle's sword began to die out as the resolve of the rangers started to dwindle. And as the sun rose above the treetops, a small sense of relief washed over Thaniel,

"Deliverance hasn't forsaken us yet," he said.

The remaining southern wall archers had now moved their positions to the northern wall above the gateway itself. Gwenith and a handful of rangers from the southern wall unsheathed their swords as they joined the entryway defense with Nosodul and the others.

"We will not lose Fort Quiver today," she said.

"I'm more concerned about losing the will to fight," Carlyle said.

"Keep your head held high, brother. We rangers are all that stands between these monsters and the people of the Western Glades," she replied.

"How can we hope to stop such a foe?" he asked.

"We are the children of Deliverance himself. If there is a light out there, then it will find us, there are people out there depending on us to protect them, and we will not fail them," she replied.

"It's almost as if the entire southern wastes have emptied across our lands. It feels as if the ground is shaking as they assault our fort. It's like a stampede of wild horses charging toward us," he replied.

Before Gwenith could reply to Carlyle, they were startled by the bodies falling from above. As they both looked up to the sky, the light in their eyes turned dim as the hope in their heavy hearts shrank.

"Look out," Thaniel said. The pale-skinned fiends had finally made it up the front wall by climbing up the bodies of their fallen kin. They had killed the archers that guarded the wall itself and started to rain down upon the defenders of the entryway.

"They've breached the wall," Nosodul said. Before he could utter another word, a pale-skinned body came up from behind him and sank its large fangs into his neck, ripping out a chunk of flesh in the process. His body fell to the ground, but Thaniel and the others lost sight of it immediately as a swarm of pale-skinned bodies piled up on top of it.

"Retreat," Gwenith said.

Without a second to waste, Thaniel and the other rangers followed Gwenith and Carlyle up the stairs and toward the rear half of the fort. As they sprinted away to make their escape, Thaniel turned to let loose a few arrows into the pale horde as he ran away from them.

"There is no escape. This fort has become our tomb," Carlyle said.

"If my messenger made it to Amberwood, then help should be nearby," Gwenith replied.

The dozens of rangers left made their way up the rear watchtower stairs and to the rear wall. They huddled together to make their final stand against the horde that surrounded them. Carlyle stood on the left side facing the watch tower in front of the archers with his sword no longer burning, while Gwenith stood on the right side with her sword drawn, ready for the pale skin fiends that had begun to rush up the watch tower stairs after them.

Thaniel looked out from the rear fort walls to see that the pale-skinned forces had thinned out as they had all made their way to the front gate. He knew there was no way he would survive the jump down, the walls of the fort were too high, and the grass below was too thin to break his fall. The impact with the ground did sound like a more peaceful way to go than the cruel fate that awaited him to his right and left. He was ready to make peace with dying by falling to his death instead of being ripped to shreds by fanged monsters.

"Look, the reinforcements are here," a ranger said.

Thaniel looked up from the walls toward the forest to see an army of rangers on horseback standing by. Gwenith, Carlyle, and the others began to cheer with joy as they waved their arms back and forth from the stone walls motioning to the rangers for help. Hyde was among them but more forward, as if he were in charge of this group of horseback rangers.

"Hyde, you must hurry, they're overwhelming us up here," Thaniel said.

"Please, hurry and flank them at the front," Gwenith said.

Hyde sat on his horse, looking up at the walls with a motionless face covered by a hood and mask. As the other horseback rangers behind began to creep forward out of the forest with swords in hand, he raised his right hand and made a fist, signaling them to stop.

"What are you waiting for?" Thaniel asked.

Hyde turned his horse away from the fort and made a knife hand with the previous fist that he held, signaling the rangers to move out.

"Where are they going? I don't understand," Gwenith said.

"They're leaving us," Thaniel replied.

The pale-skinned fiends had now made their way through the watchtower doors and were pushing into Gwenith and Carlyle. Thaniel watched in disbelief as Hyde, and the other rangers disappeared into the brush of the forest.

"You bastard, we're all going to die up here," Thaniel said.

Carlyle fell to the ground as several fiends overwhelmed him. Gwenith sensing the inevitability of her demise, decided to embrace it by dropping her sword and climbing onto the stone walls, only to take a step off it and into the earth below. Her collapsed body lay still in a pool of blood after making an impact on the grass beneath her. As the bodies of fallen rangers spilled over the wall and piled up around Thaniel, he closed his eyes, ready to join them.

Chapter Twenty-Four

"We finally made it," Farbris said.

After a long night of trudging through the dark Amberwood forest, they finally arrived at the iron fence surrounding the Forlorn Cathedral. As they approached the gate, the Arsonist noticed it was slightly open. "Someone else is here," he said.

"Let us move into the Cathedral with caution then," Rhys said.

"No, we will go around back to the cellar door," the Arsonist replied.

"Fine," Rhys replied.

The group huddled together in exhaustion as they followed the Arsonist. It was as if they were his very shadow.

"The cellar has been left open, too," the Arsonist said.

"Are you sure you didn't just forget to close it?" Rhys replied.

"Yes, I'm sure," the Arsonist replied.

"Okay, fine, I believe you," Rhys replied.

As they made their way down the steps into the cellar, a foul smell greeted their noses.

"Look out," Fargo cried. From the dark corners of the cellar, a pair of glowing red eyes came charging toward the group.

"Get out of the way," Vred said. As the group quickly moved away from the entrance to let Vred through, he tossed the limp body of Glacier to Viti before unsheathing his sword and beheading the pale menace that lay before him, "I hate those damn things," he said.

The Arsonist began to feel around in the familiar dark for a box of matches that he could use to light a nearby candle.

"Do we have lanterns or anything?" Lylah asked.

"The better question is, do we have anything to eat?" Celosia asked.

"Speaking of eating, this fellow doesn't look too good," Viti said.

"That's because he hasn't been eating. He's a feral now," the Arsonist replied.

"I was talking about your wolf," Viti replied.

"Ah, sorry, my mind is a bit troubled at the moment," the Arsonist replied. He finally found a familiar box of matches and was able to use them to light a candle near the entryway to the cellar. With the candle in his hand, he made his way through the cellar to light the other candles he knew of. Vred and Fargo carried the remains of the pale menace outside before coming back down into the cellar and closing the doors behind them.

"I wonder who broke into this place," Bregan said.

"Who cares, where is that bag of supplies at?" Celosia said.

"Right here my lady," he replied.

"Such a nice boy." Celosia grabbed the bag from Bregan and began rummaging through it for any food scraps that might be left.

"So what are we having?" Lylah asked.

"We've got an apple that someone took a bite out of," Celosia replied.

"That was me, sorry. I don't care for the green ones as much as I thought I did," Fargo said.

"We've got a quarter loaf of bread with a bit of mold developing on the crust, but we can just rip that piece off," Celosia said.

"Any meat?" Farbris asked.

"And that would appear to be all," Celosia said.

"No meat?" he asked.

"No meat," she replied.

"We're going to starve," Bregan said.

"Don't be so dramatic, boy," Farbris replied. He sat down beside Bregan, Lylah, and Celosia as they emptied their bags of supplies in hopes of finding some food crumbs.

"So, you said that thing was a feral?" Viti asked.

"Aye, they were humans once, and then they contracted the Sanguinism or Black Fire as some call it," the Arsonist replied.

"So why don't they all look this way? That woman who led the beast away didn't look like that," Viti replied.

"They don't turn into ferals unless they're starving," the Arsonist replied.

"We're all going to be ferals soon if we don't get some damn food in us," Vred said.

"I had some fruits and vegetables in here, but they're foul now, I'm afraid," the Arsonist replied.

"So what are we going to do?" Viti asked.

"Well, we could go into the woods again in hopes of finding a deer, and then maybe Fargo here can take it out, and we can bring it back," the Arsonist replied.

"The amount of time and work that will take is not worth it. I'd rather starve," Fargo replied.

"Suit yourself, the only other option we have is to head into a nearby town, but that's at least another six hours on foot," the Arsonist said.

"Six hours? Fargo, give me the damn bow. I will do it myself," Vred replied.

"I will go with you. I know these parts better than anyone here," the Arsonist replied.

"Aye, let's go then," Vred replied.

"Don't break my bow, or I'll break your neck," Fargo said.

As the Arsonist and Vred made their way toward the entry point to the cellar, they were stopped by Celosia standing up in front of them, "you know, we could always just eat that wolf of yours instead," she said.

"What?" the Arsonist asked. He looked over at Rhys sitting on the nearby bed with Glacier's limp body on his lap.

"Come on, he hasn't even moved since he was flung into that tree, and I'm pretty sure he's not breathing right now," she said.

"How could you even consider that?" Vred asked.

Farbris stood up from the cellar floor and approached Celosia with a sharp look in his eye, "there is a special place in the quaking darkness for people who eat canines, especially ones as loyal, faithful, and brave as that one there, and if you even lay a finger on this man's companion, I will not hesitate to throw that pretty face of yours outside there with the feral," he said.

"Okay, relax. I was just trying to be realistic here. We're all tired, hungry, and on edge. Maybe we just need to rest," Celosia replied.

Farbris patted the Arsonist on the shoulder, and the Arsonist looked into Farbris' eyes as if he were thanking him without saying it.

"Alright, let us not delay any longer. If I don't shoot a deer soon, we may have to eat Fargo," Vred said.

"You wouldn't dare," Fargo replied.

Laughter filled the cellar as the chuckling Vred and Arsonist made their way up the steps that led outside.

"Quaking darkness?" Bregan asked.

"Aye, a plane of fate that I would not wish upon my worst enemy," Farbris replied.

Celosia sat back down beside Lylah as Bregan and Farbris made their way to the bed where Rhys sat. As she sat down her cold hand was met by the warmth of Lylah's.

"It wasn't that bad of an idea. You were just looking out for everyone and trying to help," Lylah said.

"No, it was an awful idea. I don't know what has gotten into me recently," Celosia replied.

"Well, where can we start? Hunger, exhaustion, adrenaline-induced fear, and dehydration," Lylah replied.

"Speaking of awful ideas, why did you want to go with that woman? Seranda, I think her name was," Celosia said, laying her head on Lylah's shoulder.

"Because she was heading toward the Brooding Bridge, and that's the fastest way I could get to my father," Lylah replied.

"Why would you want to seek him out? I thought you were mad at him," Celosia replied.

"Oh, I am mad, but I am more curious as to why he did not swiftly come to my aid at the Weeping Grove as he always said he would," Lylah replied.

"I see. Well, these new friends of ours came to your aid, and I think they would be pretty upset if you abandoned them," Celosia replied.

"They wouldn't even notice if I was gone, I contribute nothing to this group," Lylah replied.

"That's not true. I would notice," Celosia replied, her hand was warm as it grabbed Lylah's.

"I don't remember the world ever seeming this dangerous before," Lylah said.

"That's because you were young and sheltered. This world of ours is ripe with monsters looking to drink our blood," Celosia replied.

The Arsonist

"I suppose that these new friends of ours need us as much as we need them. Perhaps it is best that I stick around," Lylah replied.

"I agree. I think you don't give yourself enough credit. That observantly conscious mind of yours is more valued here than anyone is willing to admit," Celosia replied.

"I do wonder what happened to Seranda, though. I hope that she made it to the bridge," Lylah replied.

"We can only hope," Celosia replied. The two snuggled up closer to one another as their eyes grew heavy. The comforting warmth of each other's bodies distracted them from the conversation that was taking place at the nearby bed.

"At first, I hated this dog, but now I see him like this, and I can't help but weep," Farbris said.

"That was a good thing that you said back there, uncle. I am sure the Arsonist greatly appreciates it," Rhys replied.

"Well, if you appreciate it, then I know he does too," Farbris replied. He gripped the fur of Glacier as if hoping it would help him fail less at holding back his tears.

"Cousin, I know this might be a bad time, but I met your father," Bregan said.

"What?" Rhys asked.

"He saved me from the Festering Cage prison. He told me to tell you he loves you," Bregan replied.

"That's impossible. I've never met the man before in my life," Rhys replied.

"Sure you have. You were just too young to remember," Farbris said.

"To be honest, I had no idea who he was until he explained everything to me as I rested in Captain Saesh's quarters. That boat ride to Lake Moran was a long one," Bregan said.

"Lake Moran?" Farbris asked.

"Aye, Lake Moran," Bregan replied.

"Interesting," Farbris said.

"Well, I would say tell him I love him too, but it wouldn't be sincere, and I doubt we will see him again," Rhys said.

"He went with Captain Saesh, and they were headed down south. They mentioned something about some ruins and a port town," Bregan replied.

"That is very interesting," Farbris said.

"Do you know something about this matter?" Bregan asked.

"What? No, oh, Deliverance's sake, no," Farbris replied.

"Liar," Rhys said.

Farbris stepped away from the bed to look around for a flask of water to drink.

"He knows something," Bregan said.

"Of course he does," Rhys replied.

Bregan sat down next to the sobbing Rhys and put his arm around him in an attempt to comfort him, "there was another thing, your father mentioned an artifact of great importance, and he said it was here inside this Cathedral," he said.

"This Cathedral? Like, above us?" Rhys asked.

"Aye, when we left the ship, he told me to find you and my father and bring you here to this Cathedral. It's kind of funny how everything worked out," Bregan replied.

Farbris, who had been eavesdropping on the conversation, had finally found some water and had begun to make his way back to the bed where Rhys and Bregan sat, "Deliverance must have been watching over all of us," he said.

"Well, I suppose we should go get that artifact then, hey?" Rhys replied.

"Don't you think we should wait until they get back with the deer? It's still really dark out, and I'm really hungry," Bregan replied.

"I mean, I can go alone if you want to sit here with Glacier," Rhys replied.

Bregan looked around to see Celosia and Lylah sitting asleep against the nearby wall with their heads leaning into one another. Fargo was asleep on the other side of the room, sitting against the opposing wall. Viti, who appeared to be plagued with exhaustion, was dozing off while sitting on the cellar entryway steps as his head dipped between his knees.

"Viti, do you want to lay here with Glacier for a bit?" Bregan asked.

"I would love that, my back is killing me," Viti replied.

Rhys removed the limp body of Glacier from his lap and left him softly on the foot of the bed where he lay still. Bregan, Rhys, and Farbris made their way out of the cellar as Viti flopped into the bed next to Glacier.

"I wonder if we can find a shovel around here somewhere to give the wolf a proper burial," Farbris said.

"We can always ask the Arsonist when he gets back," Rhys replied.

"Would you stop calling him that? Just call him Alarick. That's his real name, not this wanted poster nickname that he parades around town referring to himself as," Farbris replied.

"I'd rather not," Rhys replied.

Farbris shook his head in frustration as he rolled his eyes like a couple of marbles and stepped out of the cellar, "it's a bit chilly out here, maybe we should just get some rest and then come out here in the morning," he said.

"I was crippled with sleep depravity, but now after hearing what Bregan said, I have caught my second wind and am eager to see what is inside this Cathedral," Rhys replied.

"Cousin, you can barely even make it up the stairs. Why don't you just go lay down, and I'll go inside and check it out for you," Bregan said.

"The bed is a bit occupied right now, I'm afraid, and I wouldn't miss seeing what I think this artifact is for the world," Rhys replied.

"What do you think it is?" Bregan asked.

"A living weapon," Rhys replied. He proceeded to follow Farbris and Bregan into the cathedral.

Chapter Twenty-Five

Thaniel's blue eyes shot open, only to wince in pain as the fangs of a pale-skinned fiend dug into his right shoulder. The pain in his shoulder ramped up from stiffness all the way to a searing, blinding agony that pulsated faster than he could blink.

Just when the pain was at its worst, it dissipated like fog on a lake. With clenched teeth he gripped his bow as he felt his body falling over the edge of the stone wall. The bodies of pale-skinned fiends and fallen rangers came tumbling down over the wall like an avalanche of snow crashing down a mountain side. Thaniel felt weightless amongst them as the fiends' fangs pulled out of his shoulder.

As he began to fall, he saw the mutilated bodies of his brethren piled up on the pale-skinned bodies waiting for him to join them. As he braced for impact, he felt the bow in his hands begin to move and transform before his motionless eyes. The bow had transformed into a bulwark of vibrating light that was bright and metallic looking.

Thaniel held onto the inner handle of the shield in front of him as he met the pile of bodies that awaited him below. A tingling vibrating sensation went through his forearms as he felt the shield broke his fall, and as he slid through the pile of bodies, he trailed behind the shield while still hanging onto its handle. He was in shock and could feel the vibrating sensations transfer from his forearms to his skull and down his spine.

The bite wound on his shoulder burned. His whole body began to feel feverish. Pale-skinned bodies rained down all around him and collapsed into pools of blood as they hit the grassy earth beside him. Thousands of red eyes could see him from the tall stone walls. They knew that he was still alive, and they hungered for his life.

Using the shield as a crutch that he could dig into the ground, he put his aching body weight into it in order to stand up. He knew he had no time to waste. He began to limp toward the trees hoping to escape into the forest and leave behind the fiends as they leaped to their deaths from the wall behind him.

With shield in hand, he made it into the forest, only to turn back and see the fiends arriving to feast on the pile of his fallen comrades. Thaniel couldn't ignore the throbbing pain in his shoulder. Not even the strange sensation that pulsated through his entire body was enough to distract him from the pain.

As he limped through the amber colored forest, he sweated profusely. His mouth had become so dry that it felt like his tongue was stuck to the floor of it, incapable of moving. The sounds of birds chirping had once brought him comfort, but now it only brought him sharp pain in his ears as his vision began to spin.

No matter how hard he focused on a distant object that in his right mind he knew was immovable and inanimate, he couldn't help but notice it, moving side to side as if it were swaying with the wind. Rocks, hills, and trees were moving in and out of his vision as they stood still within the true reality that had abandoned him.

He came to a sudden halt at the sound of gnawing screeches coming from fiends up ahead. The sound grew louder as if it were getting closer, and then it was suddenly joined by the frightened neigh of a horse. The dizzy and fading vision of Thaniel, could make out a dark horse coming toward him from up ahead. Its dark tail swished as it unleashed the force of a back leg kick knocking a lunging pale-skinned fiend away into a nearby tree.

Thaniel stood within the shadows of the trees as the overhanging moonlight shined upon his wet face. As he watched the horse defend itself against the handful of red eyes fiends, he wished he could do something to help it. Being a protector was in his blood, the same blood that boiled at the thought of being helpless to save an innocent creature.

The shield in his hands reacted to this thought process by

transforming back into a bow. The bright metallic finish of the bow glimmered in the moonlight and caught the red eye attention of the nearby fiends. Once they noticed Thaniel in the distance, their senses became fixated on him. They could smell the blood from his shoulder wound, and their fanged drooping mouths began to salivate at the sight of him.

With their clawed hands extended out in front of them, they began to rake at the air around them as they charged toward him. Thaniel lacked the strength and energy required to aim the bow at them and pull the string back, but he watched in fearful curiosity as his arms arose before him and took aim upon the fiends.

He could feel his arm pulling back on the bow string, and even as he consciously told his arm to lower itself, it would not obey. He was aware of his body's actions, but he was no longer in control. He could feel his right hand's fingertips touching the bowstring, but he could not command them. The bow was no longer an extension of his body. It had become an actual part of him.

Within seconds, the fiends were ashes on the leaf littered ground before him. Thaniel was rooted in place with the shock of what had just happened. He was surprised to see that the horse was still alive. It had slowly made its way toward him and reached its head toward his own. The horse softly dug its muzzle into his neck as if trying to communicate with him. Thaniel noticed the saddle on the horse and realized it was not wild after all.

As he gently touched the horse, he saw the gleam of a canteen on the back right side of the saddle. He grabbed it as his sweat dripping face teemed with excitement. He quickly pulled the lid off and tilted his head back as he poured the cold water from the canteen into his mouth. He could feel a chill run down his esophagus as his head began to shake involuntarily.

The water ran down Thaniel's chin, almost freezing in the winter wind as it went down his tunic. He emptied the canteen and then inserted it back into the saddle. He could feel a small amount of his original strength returning as he wiped off his chin and pulled his weak body up onto the horse. With the bow in his right hand and the horse reins in his left, he began to motion the horse to go forward.

Thaniel's mind was too numb to contemplate his surroundings, to track where Hyde and the other rangers had gone. He had a general idea of which Western Glades region he was in despite not being able to use his ranger instincts to survey the land around him properly. He knew that he had to be heading northeast of Fort Quiver toward Amberwood Village, but he wasn't certain.

He was fighting sleep with a growling stomach and the sound of the horse's shoes hitting the earth below. He wanted to believe that he could close his eyes and let everything go dark. He trusted this horse to lead him to safety. He knew that horses were smart and careful creatures.

The fear he had was not due to a lack of trust in the horse but rather a lack of trust within his own body. The seeping wound on his shoulder burned. It was getting worse, and he feared that he would soon become that which he had recently tried to destroy.

Thaniel knew that he would eventually have to give into the temptation of sleep's allure as the trotting horse rocked his exhausted frail body like a matron rocking a baby to sleep. He decided to make peace with it. If this would be the last time he closed his eyes, then he was ready to take that chance. He knew the journey home to Cyanakin Hold was at least a day and a half out, and there was no way he could keep his eyes open much longer.

Thaniel prayed to Deliverance to watch over him and grant him the strength to beat this ailment that had befallen him. He stowed away the bow, and with both his hands loosely holding onto the reins, he leaned forward and sank into unconsciousness.

Chapter Twenty-Six

The Arsonist and Vred had made their way a couple of miles from the cathedral to a small open glade area. It was known for its active family of deer that would dwell within its tall grassy field.

"I don't think I quite caught your name. What was it again?" the Arsonist asked.

"Vred."

"Ah, well, it's nice to meet you, Vred."

Before Vred could exchange a greeting with the Arsonist, his attention was stolen by a heavy-horned buck making its way across the tall grass a couple yards away. The Arsonist noticed it too, and he lowered his hooded head down as Vred readied the bow's arrow for release. The elk lowered its head behind the grass and disappeared from their sight. "Damnit," Vred said.

"Have you ever done this before?" the Arsonist asked.

"No, I was always more of the gardening type."

"Really?"

"Aye, I grew up on a pumpkin farm down south in the Eastern Vale,"

"I would have never guessed."

"Most people usually don't." Vred lowered his bow and leaned back up against the tree near the Arsonist.

"Most men I come across that possess a similar stature to yours tend to be obsessed with death and killing," the Arsonist said.

"Not me, no way. I may have grown up on a pumpkin farm, but I was raised by the sword. I know how to kill a man as a result. That doesn't mean I enjoy violence or seek it out. It's not what I would consider a pleasure that I'd often fancy," Vred replied.

"I know how you feel, most people take one good look at me, and they assume I'm one of those blood-sucking fiends," the Arsonist replied.

"I'm sure the mask you wear doesn't help you much,"

"It's because of them that I wear the damn thing,"

"Sounds like you and I are both just misunderstood,"

The Arsonist removed his mask, allowing the long dark hair that it held back to fall loosely in front of his red eyes, "you could say that."

Vred was now greatly intrigued by the Arsonist and although his heart felt heavy in the presence of such dimly lit red eyes he couldn't help but feel somewhat sorry for the Arsonist. "What happened to you? Why do you look the way you do?" he asked.

"I was born this way," the Arsonist replied.

Vred's brows curled up in confusion as the Arsonist slouched down against the tree in a brooding fashion, his head hanging between his arms as they rested on each respective kneecap.

"So, you're not one of those things?" Vred asked.

"If I was, do you really think I'd be sitting here with you and not back there killing our defenseless friends?" The Arsonist replied.

"Damn, you're right. I just realized we have the only weapons with us," Vred replied.

"My eyes are similar to theirs, and although my skin possesses similar traits of opalescence, I am not dead like them, even if I feel like it sometimes."

"I have never heard of anyone being born this way."

"Neither have I, but yet here I am."

Vred turned his attention back to the tall grass that danced with the winter wind hoping to see another elk expose itself, "I really hope one of these damn things walks into my arrow soon so we can get back to the others. I feel uneasy knowing that we accidentally left them alone without anything to defend themselves with," he said.

"You've got a good heart, Vred, but just be patient. They'll show up soon. I have frequented this glade many times."

"Many times, huh?" he looked down at the Arsonist, who continued to brood with dark circles under his red eyes that bespoke exhaustion.

"Aye, it was easier back then, though, I would come out here with Glacier, and he would—," The Arsonist's throat began to tighten as he took in a short intake of breath. A great sob escaped him as he covered his pale face with his shaking hands. Vred lowered his bow once more and kneeled beside the Arsonist to hug and pat him on the back.

"It's going to be alright, friend, this too shall pass," Vred said.

"He was my only friend," the Arsonist replied, burying his tear-drenched face into the tough leather of Vred's tunic, "it's all my fault, I forgot to refuel the gauntlets, and I couldn't protect myself. Glacier wouldn't have even been involved if I could have just killed that damn beast myself," he said.

"It's not your fault," Vred replied.

"Seranda is out there alone and she's probably dead too now because of me, all because I forgot to refuel the gauntlet and scorch the beast," the Arsonist replied.

From the corner of his eye, Vred could spot the elk exposing itself once more. He patted the Arsonist again and stood up once more before aiming for the elk. "Got him," he breathed, letting loose an arrow that flew right into the ribs of the elk, knocking it down into the grass and injuring it but not killing it. The deer began to let out a loud distressful groan as Vred dropped the bow to the ground and charged forward.

He unsheathed his sword as he neared the deer and plunged it into the neck of the beast, thus ending its life. As he pulled out the arrow and flung the bleeding corpse of the elk over his shoulders, he turned to see the somber-looking Arsonist standing before him. He was no longer crying. The tears had gone cold and dry against his white cheeks. He held his porcelain mask in his left hand as a breeze blew his hood back, revealing a mane of messy black hair.

"I'm not the Arsonist. I'm just a fool behind a mask who can't protect the ones he loves, let alone himself. I deserve to be put down just like that elk," he said.

"Aye, you're not the Arsonist, but you're not some stupid elk, either. You're the crazy bastard that has some of the strangest weaponry I've ever seen. That had a pet wolf that loved him dearly and wouldn't have wanted his master, his friend, to carry on like this," Vred replied.

The Arsonist wiped his cheeks off with his sleeves and pulled himself together as he placed the mask back on his face and raised his hood over his head.

"I don't know if the love you have for that woman out there is unrequited, but she saved us all, she gave her life so that ours could continue, and I don't think she would have done that for you if she knew you were just going to roll over and die here in the grass," Vred said.

"You're right. We should get back to the cathedral so we can all eat, rest, and figure out what we're going to do about that beast that's still out there somewhere," the Arsonist replied.

"Aye, let's get going then," Vred replied.

The Arsonist picked up the bow and followed Vred through the forest and toward the cathedral.

"Hey, so what is your real name anyway?" Vred asked.

The Arsonist briefly froze up as his lips trembled behind his mask. "My real name is Alarick."

Chapter Twenty-Seven

Within the Forlorn Cathedral lay many empty benches caked in dust. As the sun rose outside, thin beams of light pierced through all the surrounding stained-glass windows. Tall candle stands that once held illuminating flames were now empty like scabbards without swords. Rhys, Bregan, and Farbris were barely able to open the creaking front doors to the cathedral before stepping inside.

"This place has seen better days. It is old. Very old," Farbris said.

"I don't see what makes this place so special, but then again, I've never been much of the religious type," Bregan said.

"This place isn't special just because it's religious," Rhys said.

"Oh, so because it has a few spires and buttresses, it's suddenly a religious space?" Farbris asked.

"Well, yes, of course. Why wouldn't it be?" Rhys replied.

"Father, you can tell that this place is some kind of church or temple by looking at its architectural design," Bregan said.

"This place hasn't been a religious sight in decades. They call it the Forlorn Cathedral due to its mysterious and sorrowful presence here in the Western Glades. The abandoned history of this place still intrigues me to this day," Farbris replied.

"Well, it smells awful in here, and places like this always made me feel uncomfortable," Bregan replied.

As all three of them made their way down the decorated aisle between all the pews, they could see a large stone coffin lying vertically toward the wall behind the podium.

"Whose grave is that?" Rhys asked

"Nobody important that I would know of. I don't recall anyone being laid to rest here," Farbris replied. As his brow furled, he squinted at the coffin. He was trying to make sense of what could be within it. Rhys and Bregan began to make their way toward it. They had the intent of unsealing it.

"I don't think that's such a good idea," Farbris said.

Rhys and Bregan stood tired before the stone coffin with wired eyes, "this has to be where my father kept it," Rhys said.

"I wish I knew for sure. I mean, your father said he had something for you in this place, but he never specified where or what exactly," Bregan replied.

"This has to be it. I'm sure of it," Rhys replied.

Farbris was worried now that the coffin might hold the remains of Rhys' mother, Marathair and that Alarick had requested Rhys to visit this cathedral to see his mother after all this time. "I really don't think you should open it," he said.

"Why?" Rhys asked.

"What's wrong father?" Bregan asked.

"What if it's someone's final resting place?" Farbris replied.

Rhys and Bregan hesitated only for a moment before giving into curious temptation. Farbris then approached them with nervousness in both his eyes and voice. "Maybe we should get out of here. It does smell pretty bad, actually. You weren't kidding. There's some kind of foul scent in the air."

"Just think of that woman from the bordello," Rhys replied.

"Bordello?" Bregan asked.

Farbris' nervousness suddenly subsided as he succumbed to his memory of the bordello and the humor that he found in it, "ha, that young girl just wanted my money. After I turned her down to go see what trouble the Arsonist was causing, I could hear her telling her friend that my breath reeked of pipe smoke so bad that she almost confused it for an ashtray," he said.

Rhys was pushing all his body weight into the coffin, but it wouldn't budge.

"Cousin, do you need some help?" Bregan asked.

"Yea, here, help me push this thing over. It's quite heavy," Rhys replied.

Farbris laughed as he saw the two young boys struggling to remove the lid. After letting out a few struggles, he came to realize that they were sweating and straining to remove the stone lid. As they both pushed with all their strength, they finally heard the lid begin to move, but their weight wasn't quite enough.

Farbris accepted that there was no stopping them from opening this coffin, and so he joined in to help them with their struggle, "one more big push lads. I will help you this time," he said.

As he pushed in with all his weight, so did Rhys and Bregan, and with the combined efforts of all three body weights, they managed to push the heavy stone lid off of the coffin. As the lid fell over to the decorated floor, it let out a loud thud that echoed throughout the entire cathedral.

"Finally," Bregan said.

Laying within the coffin was a sword that was all too familiar to the excited eyes of Rhys, "a living weapon," he said.

"What do you mean by a living weapon? There are only three of them. I would expect the one who was teaching their existence to young children to remember that," Farbris said.

"You're right. Which is why I can't believe that one is lying before me," Rhys replied. He stood above the coffin in awe as Bregan trailed off to look at the stained-glass windows.

"So now what?" Bregan asked.

Farbris began to scratch his beard as he pondered the situation, "I wonder why Alarick left his sword here, and I wonder why he wanted us to find it for him," he said.

Rhys reached into the coffin to pick up the sword. It was surprisingly lightweight, "Lightfang, the Wrath of Eldritch, is found once again," he said, admiring the sword he now held in his grasp. He was suddenly startled by the echoing yells of Bregan, who was now cowering behind the coffin near Farbris. His eyes were worried, and his body was trembling in fear as he gripped the cold stone coffin.

"What is it?" Farbris asked.

"Look, over there," Bregan said.

Rhys and Farbris both turned their attention to the hall of pews to see a handful of red-eyed creatures closing in on them.

"The pale-skinned bastards must have been lurking in the shadows. I bet the loud sound of that stone lid sliding onto the floor got their attention," Farbris said.

Rhys looked down at Lightfang as he gripped its dark hilt, which molded to match the size of both of his hands. He felt a strange vibration pulsating through his forearms, and up toward his neck, and down his spine as he watched the red eyes grow closer.

"It's eerie how the hilt molds to fit your hand," Rhys said.

"Yes, I am sure it is quite interesting. Now, how about you start swinging the damn thing before we all die," Farbris replied.

"I don't know how to fight with a sword," Rhys replied.

"You better learn quickly then, or we're as good as dead," Bregan replied.

Rhys suddenly felt the loss of control in his legs and arms as his body hurled forward toward the fiends that neared him. His movement was swift and elegant. He slashed through each one of the fiends with ease.

"Where did you learn to fight like that?" Farbris asked.

"I don't know. I have no idea what's happening," Rhys replied.

The sword had taken control of his actions, and with an artful technique, he was able to slash his way through every pair of red eyes in the cathedral before shutting them all for good as their pale bodies hit the floor around Rhys.

"Cousin, that was incredible," Bregan said.

"You're telling me," Rhys said.

Hand clapping started coming from the entrance to the cathedral. It was coming from the Arsonist's shadowy silhouette standing in the lit doorway, "Well, well. Look at you, killing pale fiends, now, are we?" he said.

"You're back already? Did you get any food?" Bregan asked.

"Yes, I got plenty of food. Vred is preparing it now with the others down in the cellar," the Arsonist replied.

Rhys felt the control of his body return to him as he looked over at the Arsonist whose curiosity couldn't be seen from behind his porcelain mask.

"Where did you find my father's sword?" the Arsonist asked.

"In the coffin over there," Farbris replied.

"I'm starving, and this place reeks," Bregan said. He hurried out of the cathedral toward the cellar to see how the food was coming along.

Farbris nodded at the Arsonist as he patted Rhys on the shoulder and started to make his way out of the cathedral to follow Bregan.

"Not so fast, old man, I have some questions for you, and you're finally going to answer them," the Arsonist said.

Farbris stopped and took a seat on a nearby bench as the Arsonist made his way toward Rhys, who now stood victorious over the dead pale fiends.

"Hand it over," the Arsonist said.

"What? No, I'm not handing the sword over to you," Rhys replied.

"It's my father's weapon," the Arsonist replied.

"It's our father's weapon, and he specifically wanted Bregan to find me and show it to me so that I could be the one to have it," Rhys replied.

"How do we know that he wasn't referring to me and not you? I bet he doesn't even know you exist. He spent most of his time with me while you and Farbris were off doing Deliverance knows what," the Arsonist replied.

"He knows I exist," Rhys replied.

"Sure, he does," the Arsonist replied.

"I'm keeping the sword. If you're so convinced that it was meant to go to you, then tell me, why did he let it sit inside this cathedral and rot inside a coffin while you slept in the nearby cellar all this time?" Rhys replied.

The Arsonist had no response. His hands tightened into fists as he turned to the now sitting Farbris. Rhys smirked as he sheathed the sword and took a seat in the aisle across from Farbris.

"Well, what is it that you wish to know?" Farbris asked.

The Arsonist approached Farbris, and as he neared his face with his own, he removed his dark hood and porcelain mask. The dark brown eyes of Farbris met the red eyes of the Arsonist, but the stare was broken as he felt the Arsonist place the mask in his lap.

"Why are you giving me this?" he asked.

"You know this mask," the Arsonist replied.

"I have no idea what you're talking about," he replied.

The Arsonist slammed his fist against the small wooden corner pillar of the church bench, breaking it off and sending it flying toward the nearby entryway. Rhys gripped his sheathed sword with wide eyes and if he would need to use it soon. "Stop lying and tell the truth," the Arsonist said.

"Alright, fine, just calm down," Farbris replied.

The Arsonist stood still in an aggressive stance with a crazy calm in his red eyes. They were framed with the shadowy circles of exhaustion. Farbris took a deep breath and looked down at the porcelain mask.

"This mask belonged to your mother, my sister," Farbris said.
"What happened to her, and where is she?" the Arsonist replied.
"It doesn't matter anymore."
"It does to me. I spent my entire childhood searching for that woman."

A tear dropped down from Farbris' left eye and landed on the porcelain mask, "she used to make these whenever we would stay at the lake house. She hated that damn place, and working on a small project like this would relieve her of the anxiety of it all," he said.

"Well, it's all I have left of her. I found it down in the cellar after my father abandoned me to continue his hunt for Zersten," the Arsonist replied.

"It pains me to hear all of this, and I find it strange that this mask was left behind here. I will say that this mask is incomplete, the ones I remember her making in our youth were colorful and bright, and the porcelain masks are just the base foundations that she would paint over."

The Arsonist reached down and snapped the mask away from the hands of Farbris. "Well, some things are better left unfinished, I suppose," he said.

Rhys stood up and approached them with the sword sheathed and in hand, "Uncle, what are we?" he asked, sharing the same concerned look on his face that the Arsonist had.

As they stared down at the nervous-looking Farbris, he closed his eyes and winced. "You're twins," he said.

"Why don't I believe you?" Rhys asked.

"Because he's a liar, and you have to ring the truth out of his fat neck to get anywhere with him, he knows more than he is leading us on to believe," the Arsonist said.

Farbris flicked his tongue against his bottom teeth as he stood up and began to take small paces back and forth in front of the bench, "Your mother was cursed by an awful man named Zersten during her pregnancy, and when it finally came time to give birth she delivered an only son," he said.

The Arsonist and Rhys both crossed their arms, but as the Arsonist noticed Rhys copying him, he decided to uncross his arms and let them hang a long side his waist.

"Go on," Rhys said.

"Marathair, my sister, was quite concerned, as was the father, Alarick," Farbris said, taking a deep breath before continuing, "during my time as a scholar, I had discovered the anti-curse ritual of separation, and so when the cursed child was brought to me by Alarick I performed a dark and evil sacrament to separate the curse from the child's flesh."

The eyes of both the Arsonist and Rhys were now the size of craters. The Arsonist's knees and hands shook uncontrollably with worry as he sat down on the bench near Farbris.

"I underestimated the potency of the curse and thus was unable to expel it from existence entirely, and so I held two baby boys in my arms and delivered them both to the parents." Tear strands ran down the old cheeks of Farbris as he let out a hoarse cough before continuing, "Alarick, your father, was confused and not thrilled by the idea but was willing to raise them both until his comrade and loyal friend Nielas appointed him to deal with the cursed child by ending their life. With the capture of my sister Marathair, I was then tasked with taking the child that was not cursed. When Alarick was done with the deed, he would meet with us eventually, and we would figure out a way to get my sister back, but that day obviously never came, and he never carried out the deed that he was appointed," Farbris said.

"How unfortunate," the Arsonist said, tightly gripping the knees of his pants.

"That's not what he means," Rhys said.

The Arsonist stood up and put the mask back on his face as he threw his hood back over his head and made his way toward the cathedral entrance. "Well, that's how it sounds. What a shame that the cursed bastard was spared by his father and had to go on to be a living curse in human form. I've heard enough. Feel free to keep the damn sword. I've got a friend to bury," he said.

Rhys and Farbris sat on a bench next to one another as the Arsonist slammed the cathedral door behind him. Rhys grabbed his uncle and hugged him tightly, "you did the right thing by telling us. I hope that your soul feels lighter after relinquishing such a heavy burden to bear."

Farbris was trying to speak, but it kept coming out incoherently. He finally gave up and sobbed away into his nephew's shoulder.

"I guess it sort of explains why I've had such a strange connection to him through those nightmares recently," Rhys replied.

"I've never quite understood how or why you were having those. There's something strange about that connection," Farbris replied.

"Perhaps in time, I will discover the meaning and finally understand," Rhys replied. His entire left shoulder was damp from the sobbing face of his uncle. His grey eyes grew heavy inside the dark cathedral as he stared up into the light. It was beaming down upon him from the stained-glass windows above.

Chapter Twenty-Eight

Thaniel awoke to the repetition of the horse's movement coming to a halt. A pair of hands pulled his once-shut eyelids open, revealing a dark red iris.

"Damn, he's one of us," the voice behind the hand said.

"Is he maddening yet?" another voice asked.

"No, not yet. At least not from the looks of it."

As the fingers released his eyelids, they snapped shut before reopening. Thaniel groaned as he tried to muster the strength to lean up and look around. A handful of very well-dressed men and women surrounded him. A young-looking woman was now holding the reins to his horse and leading it slowly past the men. They all had white hair, pale skin, and red eyes. Thaniel's heart sank to grief. He had been captured. The fear of being eaten alive had subdued his thoughts, and he could not think of anything else.

"He must be really hungry. We should bring him home with us," the girl said.

"Lord Argentwald already has plenty of mouths to feed," a man said.

"The Western Glades will soon be a red field of plenty, and those in the Argentwald court will never know hunger again," she replied.

Thaniel was confused by all that was going on as he was too afraid and too tired to remember the significance of the name Argentwald. All he could think of was the ominous landscape that surrounded the Argentwald Manor outside the Brooding Bridge.

"Fine, we will let Lord Argentwald decide what to do with him. Just don't let him near any of the cattle. I don't need him going berserk and killing any of the future blood casks," the man replied.

The girl leading Thaniel's horse reins looked back at him often as they marched on. Her fanged smile did not ease Thaniel's mind, and as he was slouching forward on his horse, sick with fatigue, he could not help but smell smoke in the air. He could not look around to see where it could be coming from, much like the screams of men, women, and children that came from the distance behind him.

He was in the front of the caravan, and it appeared to be marching out of the smoldering ruins of Amberwood Village. He could not look behind him to confirm it, but he knew it to be true in his heart. The entire village had been set ablaze, and the surviving residents were lined up and chained to one another with shackles around their wrists before being lined up in one long marching row. They were protected and led by the pale-skinned men and women as if they were a shepherd overseeing a flock of sheep.

As they marched north toward the Argentwald Manor, Thaniel was fading in and out of consciousness. He knew that something was different about himself now, but he had no way of checking to see for himself, but he realized that his eyes must be red and that the same sickness that plagued his captors must have infected him as well. The bite on his shoulder from the battle at Fort Quiver no longer burned. He couldn't even physically tell if it was still there or not.

The long hours of journeying from the ashes of Amberwood Village to the gloomy dead flower meadows that covered the grounds of Argentwald Manor felt like minutes for the half-conscious Thaniel. The girl holding his horse's reins led him to the large stable behind the Manor. Two pale men followed closely behind them while the others continued to herd the shackled villagers into a passage on the left side of the Manor.

As they descended the stairs into the Manor, their cries disappeared. All Thaniel could hear was the sound of the cold restless wind brushing against the tops of trees that loomed overhead. The two red-eyed men removed him from the horse as the woman led the horse into the stables to join the other horses. Each of the men took one of Thaniel's arms into their own before dragging him back toward the front of the cellar as his boots dug into the mud, leaving a trail in their wake.

Argentwald Manor was a somber-looking citadel that once beheld the beauty unmatched by any architecture in all the Realms of Light. Its ominous landscape was a sign of the times, and its towering stature was no longer a sight of glory. It was now a dreadful estate, protected from the surrounding woodland glades by a thick recurring fog that always came rolling in from the nearby river beneath the Brooding Bridge.

The people of Prosperwood had always forbade anyone from going near its glade. They believed that it was haunted with madness and anger. Thaniel knew very little of its history and significance, but he knew that he would soon find out what was so terrifying about this place and its newfound residency.

As the wide and heavy brown wooden doors with black finish creaked open to the front of the manor, the two men dragged Thaniel in and dropped him to the ground where his face met the black and white marble square floor.

"He's one of us, see to it that he gets properly shackled and fed, we will be back soon to bring him before Lord Argentwald," one of the men said.

Three young brown-haired women in rags came hurrying over toward Thaniel. As the two men walked away, Thaniel noticed that one of them was carrying his bow. One of the girls ran off to fetch a bucket of water as the other two girls grabbed each of his feet and began dragging him away by his boots.

Thaniel could see dozens of beautiful paintings along the walls that seemed to go up above him forever. The manor was much more beautiful inside than it appeared to be from the outside. Chandeliers and cackling laughter were all Thaniel could think about as these two small girls dragged him away into a room where they pulled him up onto an old wooden chair. The third girl returned with a bucket of water and a worn brown rag. She dipped the rag into the bucket to get it wet and then began to wipe the dirt and dried blood off of Thaniels face. As she finished wiping down his face, one of the other girls stood behind him and pulled his head back.

Thaniel was frightened, but his weakness made him incapable of resistance. The girl with the wet rag placed it back in the bucket and proceeded to open his mouth and hold it there in that position. Thaniel began to shake, and with all the strength in his

The Arsonist

body, he tried to clench his mouth shut and resist the girls. In the corner of his right eye, he could see the third girl approaching him with a small knife. Thaniel couldn't help but try and speak, to beg them for his life.

The girl with the knife cut open her left hand and gripped it tightly as she approached Thaniel. She held her bleeding clenched fist over his mouth and opened the clenched fist to let the blood drip from the wound and down onto his tongue. Thaniel began to squirm and panic, but his terror was short-lived and quickly replaced by satisfaction. A hunger and thirst that he did not realize he had not felt like it was being simultaneously quenched and satisfied.

His terrified eyes closed shut in ecstasy as he drank from the wound. His senses began to hum with alertness, and his body started feeling stronger than it ever did before.

The girls giggled as they released him, allowing him to lean forward in the wooden chair. His red eyes gazed at the three young girls. With a blood-soaked smile, he revealed his fangs to them. He did not thank them. He couldn't, he was conflicted, and the girls knew it.

Thaniel couldn't believe that he was consuming the blood of another human being, but the feeling it gave him was something he could not deny or describe. The emptiness that he felt inside of himself was now filled. Ashe rose to his feet, the two pale-skinned men from earlier had barged in to retrieve him. Iron shackles were quickly placed upon his wrists, and the two pale men began to drag him away by a connected chain.

"Where are you taking me? What do you want from me?" Thaniel asked. He was surprised that his ability to speak had returned to him along with his strength and awareness.

"To meet your gracious host, the lord of the west, Lord Argentwald."

Thaniel was confused but followed a long submissively. He did not attempt to resist the pulling of his shackle chain.

As the two pale-skinned men dragged him from behind, they passed through dozens of rooms filled with tapestries, maps, goblets, lavish furniture, and golden-trimmed bookshelves. Each room was crowded with men and women whose red eyes gleamed from behind their wine glasses as they lounged on pillows lying all over the marble floor. Their wolf-like eyes observed Thaniel with curiosity.

As he looked around, he would make eye contact with them. Feelings of extreme discomfort set upon both his body and mind as it felt like they were tracing the outline of his body with their grim stares.

When they finally arrived outside the metal doors that led to the royal chamber, the two men removed the chain and shackles from Thaniel's wrists before opening the doors and leading him into the dark chamber. Inside was only one source of light, an enormous chandelier that hung lower than the average one and had jeweled casings holding tall lit candles.

Several of these jeweled candle casings filled the three floating rings of the chandelier. Thaniel's eyes strained to see in the dimly lit chamber as he nervously rubbed the flesh of his wrists that had been rubbed raw by the shackles. The crowded chamber was narrow and rectangular. Aside from the narrow path from the gates to the throne, there were large pillows everywhere where many red-eyed guests lounged about with wine glasses in their hands.

Straight ahead of Thaniel, past the chandelier light, and against the northern wall, sat a tall throne. A middle-aged man lay across the cushioned armrests of the throne. He kicked his legs up on one while his back lay flat atop the other.

His head was lying back, allowing his white hair to fall low enough to touch the marble floor below. The metal doors closed behind Thaniel. The man on the throne looked over to notice Thaniel standing before him. He adjusted his slouching posture and sat up like a true noble on a throne.

"Welcome to my court," the man on the throne said.

"This is a lovely home you have here," Thaniel said.

The cackling laughter of the pale men and women lying on the pillows surrounding Thaniel was overwhelming, and it startled him.

"Home?" the man on the throne asked. He stood up from the throne with one hand gripping the sheathed dagger on his waist and the other holding an enormous chalice. The man took a deep sip from his chalice before setting it down on a nearby table and wiping his face.

"This is no mere home. It is the capital of the new world, a world I started to build long ago, and I will rule over that world from this citadel as the Moran's in the East did long ago before my time," he said.

"Forgive me, for I mean no disrespect. I guess I am not well versed in Western history nor its royal bloodlines," Thaniel replied.

"Oh, but I think you are. Thaniel son of Renson."

Thaniel was stifled by the man's words. He tried to create a facial expression that looked confused, as if he had no idea what the man was talking about.

"I'm sorry, but you must have me confused for somebody else," Thaniel said.

The man quickly unsheathed his dagger and stabbed it aggressively into the table, knocking his chalice onto the ground. The surrounding guests jumped back with fear into their pillow beds.

"Enough. do not take me for some fool, boy. I knew who you were the moment you entered my domain, and my men brought me that damn bow of yours," he said.

The spilled chalice on the floor had left a crimson puddle at the feet of the man, who was now angrily staring Thaniel down. A woman leaned forward from her pillow bed and began to lick the crimson liquid off the marble floor. The man looked down at her in disgust and kicked her face away from the puddle, "I've told you before, you are guests here, and guests do not eat off the floor like dogs. If you want to feed like an animal, then you will be cast out into the wild. Just like the rest of the maddening ones," he said.

The kicked woman whimpered and covered her bleeding face as she stood up and ran to the metal doors to the chamber. They opened up, allowing her to flee out of the space, and then they closed behind her. The man cast his gaze back upon Thaniel. "So, as you were. Please continue. But this time I advise that you correct your deceitful introduction, young man," the man said.

"Alright, yes, I am Thaniel, son of Renson."

The man walked back to his throne and sank into it as he gave his full attention to Thaniel, "and why are you here, Thaniel, son of Renson?" he asked.

"I am still trying to figure that out, my lord. I was brought here before you for reasons that were not revealed to me."

"My men claim they found you unconscious on your horse wandering outside Amberwood Village. Is this true?"

"I believe so, my lord, although I am not certain. My memory is kind of a mess right now. I was restless during my capture."

"Your capture?" the man asked, laughing as he motioned a girl in rags to bring him another chalice. "My boy, if you were captured, you would not be standing here before me in my chamber. You were rescued by my people."

"If I am no captive, then why am I here? Why did you shackle me and drag me into this hall of decadence? Why not set me free and let me be on my way?"

"Hold your tongue, boy, for I may confuse it for having ownership of you, and then I will be forced to liberate you from its tyranny by removing it from your mouth. You may not be my captive, but you are not my equal. You were brought here because I needed to see with my own eyes that the only son of Renson Cadere is now one of us."

"Well, you have seen me now. What else is it that you want from me?"

"I wonder, do you think your father will welcome you back with open arms when he sees your newfound complexion?" he asked, grabbing the new chalice off the silver platter the girl in rags held in front of him.

"If I provided him a sufficient explanation of how I contracted this illness, then he may take pity upon me."

The man choked up on the crimson liquid in his chalice and wiped the drippings off his chin, "illness? I have heard this rhetoric before. Always does it flee the lips of the ignorant, what you see as curse and ailment I see as strength and opportunity."

"Pardon me my lord but who are you? I have given you a proper introduction and explained myself but I do not believe you have done the same," Thaniel said, gulping as the dimly lit room became disturbingly silent.

"I am Lord Argentwald. What else do you wish to inquire from me?" he replied, sitting his chalice down on the armrest and standing up from his throne.

"Forgive me. I was only hoping to know your full name," Thaniel said, feeling anxious and not knowing what to do. He decided to drop to his knees in hopes that the court of this chamber would take pity on his vulnerable situation.

"Stand up. We do not kneel here. This is not some silly ranger indoctrinating ceremony."

Thaniel quickly rose to his feet to see Lord Argentwald, who now stood close and in front of him.

"Tell me, how long have you had this illness, or sickness or whatever it is you perceive it to be," Lord Argentwald said.

"Less than a week, I suppose," Thaniel replied.

"Is there any reason that I should let you live? You are no use to me in your current state, and after the siege of Prosperwood, your father will not be in a situation to bargain with me for your life."

Thaniel now understood everything he had heard during the march from Amberwood to the manor. The court was planning to attack Prosperwood, and he needed to do something to stop it. He knew that he would have to abandon his vows and improvise to survive in this climate, "my loyalty does not lie with my father. Truth be told, I was merely wishing to return to him so that I could claim vengeance for the position he has put me in," Thaniel said.

"You lie," Lord Argentwald replied.

Croaking voices from the surrounding fiends lying on pillows started whispering the word 'liar' under their breath repeatedly.

"I do not lie, my lord," Thaniel replied.

"Very well then, if you wish to have vengeance, you shall have it, but you will swear fealty to me and this court first."

"Of course, whatever it is you would have me do, whatever it is you wish, I am at your command. My only request is that you let me wield my bow."

"Slow down there, boy. Let's not get too ahead of ourselves now. Words are meaningless in this world. I need to see action before I can trust you."

"Fine. Tell me what you would have me do, and it shall be done."

Lord Argentwald grinned wickedly at Thaniel as he clapped his hands to motion the girl in rags from earlier to come hither. The girl made her way to them and stood before Thaniel with a vacant glass eye stare. Her long brown hair was tangled up like a rat's nest, and her brown eyes were darkened by the sleep-deprived shadow cast beneath them.

"Drink from her fountain of life," Lord Argentwald said.

Thaniel looked at the girl with questionable thoughts in his mind. He noticed she held no knife, so he was confused about what he must do to drink from her, "do I have to cut her hand, or will she do it herself?" he asked.

The chamber boomed with cackling laughter once again as men and women on pillows laughed and fell on top of one another while spilling their wine glasses all over the place. Lord Argentwald tried to cover his face to not disrespect Thaniel with his uncontrollable laughter. Thaniel stood before them with a frustrated look on his face, and confusion in his eyes.

"You must collapse the veins yourself. You must take her life to conserve your own. Life is a substance that can only be transferred from one vessel to the next," Lord Argentwald said.

Lord Argentwald walked away to dig the dagger out of the table. "I can see that you're conflicted, so I'm going to make this easy on you, either dig your fangs into her pretty little neck and take her life for your own to prove yourself to us, or take this dagger and slit your neck from ear to ear so that you may rid yourself of this terrible illness," he said, handing the dagger to Thaniel.

Thaniel held the dagger in his hands. He looked upon it with a boiling internal anger, knowing that he couldn't use it to kill Lord Argentwald. He knew that even if he did, the court would rip him to shreds soon after. He needed to find his father and warn him of what was coming to Prosperwood. He knew there was only one way to do that, and it would require him to survive this horrible ordeal.

He dropped the dagger to the floor and charged the girl in rags. He sunk his teeth into her neck and ripped her red life from her. In her final gasp of breath, she whispered faintly into his ear, "Thank you for saving me." Thaniel ignored her gratitude and continued to feast upon her remains to earn the trust and confidence of the court that surrounded him.

"My, oh my, do we have a wild one in our midst? Are you sure you're not maddening on us now, boy?" Lord Argentwald said. He pulled Thaniel off the girls in rags and handed him a handkerchief to clean himself off with. The court responded to Lord Argentwald's grim humor with more cackling laughter.

"About my bow," Thaniel said.

"Yes, yes. You will have your bow back, but I will warn you now that if I see one of those bright arrows go flying anywhere near this Manor, I will have your head put on a spike outside the Brooding Bridge."

"Thank you, my lord."

"We have one last final matter of business to conduct. Kiss the hand that feeds you," Lord Argentwald said, extending his jewel ring-covered hand out to Thaniel.

Thaniel swallowed the sigh of frustration he felt climbing up the insides of his chest and gave into self-degradation by kissing the ringed hand that lay before him.

"Welcome to Argentwald Manor," Lord Argentwald said.

Chapter Twenty-Nine

Without uttering a single word, the Arsonist crept down into the cellar to pick up his fallen comrade Glacier. The limp body was carried carefully outside and placed into a freshly dug grave in the ground that Vred helped make for the wolf.

Down inside the cellar, Lylah, Celosia, Viti, Fargo, and Bregan ate elk while Rhys and Farbris slept on the bed. The sun was set high in the sky, but Vred couldn't notice due to the grey winter clouds hiding its light. The Arsonist and Vred buried Glacier in his grave and laid him to rest underneath an overcast sky. Bregan eventually came out from the cellar to pay his respects to the wolf he hardly knew. He hugged the Arsonist, and the two sat and picked at the grass surrounding the fresh grave. Vred made his way down to pick through the scraps of elk in hopes of making a stew concoction with them.

"He was my best friend, and I didn't deserve his loyalty," the Arsonist said.

"What makes you say that?" Bregan asked.

"Look at where it got him."

"Yeah, but he gave his life to save you, you were his master, and he loved you enough to risk his own life to preserve yours." The Arsonist sat quietly brooding behind his porcelain mask. Bregan patted him on the back and stood up to make his way down to the cellar to prepare for bed. The Arsonist put his hand onto the grave and let the tears run down his cheeks behind the mask.

"You deserved better than this old friend, and mark my words, our paths will cross again someday, I just know it," the Arsonist said.

Down below in the cellar, Vred picked through the scraps while Celosia observed him with curiosity. "So what's a big guy like yourself going to do now?" she asked.

"What do you mean?" Vred replied.

"Like, you're not part of a crew anymore, and everything here is going to Deliverance in a handbasket, so are you going to head back east now?" she asked.

"No, I am a sellsword, always have been and always will be," he replied.

"Okay then, whatever that means," she replied.

He grabbed a handful of elk meat scraps, dropped them in a bowl of water, and then went outside of the cellar to see Fargo waiting beside a freshly built fire.

"Have you ever made stew before?" Fargo asked.

"It's all I used to make back on the pumpkin farm," Vred replied. He poured the water and meat into a kettle hanging above the fire.

Lylah and Viti dug through containers in the cellar, looking for anything of potential use. All they could find was moldy cloth and rope.

"Any luck?" Celosia asked.

"Not unless you want to hang yourself with a moldy rope," Viti replied.

Celosia chuckled and then put her hand on Lylah's shoulder. Lylah placed her hand on Celosia's hand and looked back at her with a smile.

"I might just hang myself if I have to spend more than another night in this cellar," Celosia said.

"I'm pretty sure we're heading out tomorrow morning. The boys found something extraordinary in the cathedral," Lylah replied.

"Yeah, so I heard something about a sword?"

"Aye, a very powerful weapon that could help turn the tide against the foe that swept across the Weeping Grove."

"Well, I wish them the best of luck with that."

Lylah removed her hand from Celosia's and pulled away from her. "What do you mean?" she asked.

"I figured our business here was done, and we'd be heading somewhere safe and away from danger," Celosia replied.

"These people are our friends, and they are going to need our help."

"What are we going to do? We're barely even apprentice-level druids, and besides that, weren't you the one that was contemplating leaving in the first place?"

"We have our wits, and our presence alone is enough to improve their morale. I guess the true words of someone I care about forced me to have a change of heart. My perspective on the situation has changed."

"Nobody was there for our morale when we almost got burnt alive in a tree back at the grove," Celosia replied. She turned away from Lylah and headed out of the cellar to join Vred and Fargo at the fire.

Lylah clenched her jaw in frustration and continued digging through the old crates with Viti. The loud snoring coming from Farbris made it impossible for Bregan to fall asleep next to him. Rhys awoke from the loud snoring and began to laugh as he turned to see Bregan staring at his father with dismay.

"He sounds like a damn bear," Rhys said.

"I can't possibly sleep with this. Father, you need to wake up," Bregan said.

"I've been awake," Farbris replied.

"No, you have been snoring for the last hour," Bregan replied.

"I was just resting my eyes," Farbris replied.

Rhys laughed as he picked up the sword and went over to Lylah and Viti to see what they were up to. "Find anything useful?" he asked.

"If one more person asks me that, I'm going to punch them in the throat," Lylah replied.

Viti stood behind Lylah and tried to make hand gestures that would motion Rhys to disengage from the conversation with Lylah.

"Is everything alright?" Rhys asked.

Viti sighed and dropped his arms in defeat.

"No, nothing is alright, we have no supplies, and I have no idea what the blazes we're still doing here. You have your sword, and that's great, but what are we doing now?"

"I'm sure the Arsonist has a plan."

"The Arsonist? He's an arsehole. To Deliverance with that man."

Viti sensing the tension rising in both Lylah and Rhys' conversation, decided to remove himself from the situation and head outside as well. He was intercepted by the Arsonist, who was walking down the steps into the cellar.

"He's not that bad once you get to know him," Rhys said.

"I don't think I want to get to know him, the only thing he's got going for him is that beautiful girl who risked her life to save us, and she's probably dead now," Lylah said.

The Arsonist was now standing behind Lylah with Viti. Although his face was concealed by his mask, both Rhys and Viti could tell his expression was disgusted.

"Well, what do you think we should do then?" the Arsonist asked.

Lylah jumped toward Rhys in fear, startled by the Arsonist's voice. "Don't creep up behind me like that," she said.

"Sorry, my ears were burning, and I thought that you might want to know what my plan is," he replied.

"That would be nice," Rhys said.

"I think we need to head to Prosperwood tomorrow at sunrise."

"Why Prosperwood? I don't want to go back to that damned place," Rhys replied.

The Arsonist tried to hold back his anger. He needed to keep his composure in front of his disagreeable peers, "it is the perfect place for us to load up on supplies and possibly go our separate ways," he said.

"Separate ways?" Lylah asked.

"Yes, separate ways. We can get food, shelter, and fresh supplies, and then everyone can head off from whence they came," the Arsonist replied.

Rhys shook his head in disgust and made his way near a crate to take a seat.

"I take it that you don't like this plan?" the Arsonist asked.

"No, not at all," Rhys replied.

"Well, it's the best I've got right now," the Arsonist replied.

"I think it's a good plan," Viti said.

Lylah and Viti took seats on nearby crates alongside Rhys while the Arsonist stood before them with his arms folded.

"I've got sixteen rounds left for my hand cannon and five vials left for my gauntlet. Vred and Fargo also have weapons, and now Rhys has a sword. S,o we're heavily armed for the journey to Prosperwood," the Arsonist said.

Lylah, Viti, and Rhys stared at him quietly, looking unimpressed.

"I don't know what you people want from me, speak and lead or be silent and follow," the Arsonist said.

"We should be taking the fight to those damn things out there," Rhys replied.

"Are you mad, Rhys? We won't last a day out there with the current state of our resources. I've been dealing with the ferals almost my entire life. Trust me when I say that they are far more cunning than the savage appearance leads you to believe," he replied.

"Fine, I am somewhat convinced, I suppose."

"Good, you're finally coming to your senses."

"No, I just want you to be happy, brother. I know you must be going through a difficult time, so I am going to avoid making it more difficult for you," Rhys said.

"Do not ever call me that again," the Arsonist replied.

An awkward but silent tension could be felt in the cellar, and even Farbris and Bregan could overhear the conversation from over on the bed.

"Prosperwood is a great idea, Bregan's mother is staying with a friend there, and I promised her I would return him to her," Farbris said.

"It's settled then. We'll head to Prosperwood first thing in the morning. Everyone should get some rest," Viti said.

"I'll head outside and tell the others," Lylah said.

"I'll stand watch on the steps of the cellar door tonight since I seem to be the most rested at the moment," Rhys said.

"How honorable of you," the Arsonist replied.

Rhys ignored the smug comment and began to push a large crate near the base of the steps so that he had something to sit on while he stood watch. He sat down and dug up the Compendium of Living Weapons out of his pack so that he would have something to read throughout the night. Lylah got Vred, Celosia, and Fargo to all to come back inside for the night.

Everyone made a space in the cellar their own as they settled down for the evening. That night, everyone but Rhys would sleep and get rest, and the Arsonist would occasionally wake up and check on Rhys to make sure he was not dozing off. Rhys began to wake everyone up immediately after seeing the rising sun's light shining through the crack in the cellar door.

Everyone carried anything they could find of value and headed outside to the front of the cathedral space. The Arsonist shut the door to the cellar behind him for what felt like might be the last time and then followed behind everyone as they made their way into the Amberwood forest.

Chapter Thirty

After being accepted into the Argentwald court, Thaniel agreed to go on a personal tour led by Lord Argentwald. On this tour, Thaniel discovered all of the horrors within Argentwald Manor, as well as all of its beauties. He saw what became of the Amberwood Village peasants in what Lord Argentwald called the distillery deep within the manor's basement. Members of the court referred to it as life's vineyard or the crimson winery.

Lord Argentwald also showed Thaniel the great armory he had assembled within the left sector of the manor. Thaniel watched in awe as dozens of pale-skinned soldiers armed themselves in chainmail with crossbows, spears, daggers, axes, and swords. Lord Argentwald made it very clear to Thaniel that the court would invade Prosperwood within the coming days and that they would take control of the west by force.

Screams echoed through the hallway floors as both Lord Argentwald and Thaniel returned to the central chamber where the tour had started. The chamber was still occupied by about a dozen red-eyed guests that had not assembled in the armory to prepare for war. Thaniel could see how full the chamber was the moment he stepped inside it behind Lord Argentwald, but he couldn't help but feel the manor itself was cold and empty despite its large populace.

"If you want your bow back, you will need to retrieve it from Oliver. He should be down in the old cistern dealing with the cattle remains," Lord Argentwald said.

Thaniel could feel his blood-fed stomach turn at the idea of a cistern filled with dead bodies. "If he's busy, I wouldn't want to disturb him. Perhaps I will just get some rest or go for a walk to admire the lovely art that your citadel has to offer for admiration," he replied.

"I'm sure he's not terribly busy. He's just dumping the husks into the old well," Lord Argentwald replied, laughing as a new girl in rags poured blood from a decanter into his chalice.

"Alright, well, I appreciate the information. I will see if I can find my way to the cistern to find this Oliver fellow," Thaniel replied. The metal doors to the chamber closed behind him as he exited the space. As he made his way down the hallway, he passed a room with the door wide open.

"You're going to be the one to kill the Arsonist this time," a man's voice said from the room, "or I'm going to tell Lord Argentwald of your treachery, and you know what he does to traitors."

Thaniel came to a sudden halt after hearing the mention of the Arsonist. He knew that name. It was the criminal he had been sent to hunt down by his father. The elusive Arsonist had always seemed to get away from the rangers that were sent after him.

"I understand, and if I had not been intercepted by that damn beast that's been roaming the glade for years now, I would have finished the job," a woman's voice replied.

"How are you so sure that he'll be at Prosperwood when we begin the assault anyways?" the man asked.

"Because I know him, and that's why I was the one you recruited for the task, remember?" she replied.

Thaniel decided to step back and peer into the room where the conversation was being had.

"Can I help you?" the man asked.

"I heard you mention the Arsonist, I know him, and I have been hunting him for quite some time," Thaniel replied.

"Well, you're obviously not good at it then. Who are you anyway?"

"My name's Thaniel. I'm new here."

"I see. Well, my name is Victoyos. Perhaps you can accompany Miss Seranda here to the armory. She still needs to pick out the weapon that she's going to use to kill the Arsonist," he said.

Seranda pulled her face away from the man. She made her way past Thaniel and out of the room. The man grinned at Thaniel and motioned him to follow her, and so he did.

"Hey, wait up. I'm coming with you. I need to get my bow back from Oliver in the cistern," Thaniel said.

"I don't need your company," Seranda replied.

Thaniel ignored her statement and continued to follow her down the marble steps to the armory, "I was actually hoping you could help me find the cistern," he said.

"Sounds like somebody didn't pay attention on their royal tour," Seranda replied.

"You knew about the tour?" Thaniel asked.

"Of course I did. What, did you think you were special? He gives every new member of the court that same silly tour of his," Seranda replied.

"I see," he replied.

"No, you don't see. Otherwise, you would know where the cistern is, and you would stop following me," she replied.

"That's not what I meant," he replied.

Seranda pushed the metal doors to the armory chamber open and made her way to the table that had a mound of sheathed daggers on it.

"You like short blades, huh? More the close quarters type?" Thaniel asked.

"I like daggers. They give you more control with the proper footwork," Seranda replied.

"Yeah, it helps on long journeys too if you're conditioned properly because then they end up feeling light as a sewing needle," he replied.

"I've never held a sewing needle before," she replied.

Thaniel suddenly realized his mistake. His pale face began to feel warm with nervousness as he anxiously started fidgeting with one of the sheathed daggers on the table.

"I didn't mean it like—."

"Just stop talking," Seranda replied. She grabbed two letter openers that she knew would be easy to conceal in her waist-gripping black and grey corset dress that she wore. She strapped the one with the ebony hilt to her waistband and put the one with the ivory hilt down into her long brown leather boot.

"So why is that man having you kill the Arsonist?" Thaniel asked.

"Who? Victoyos? He's too scared to do it himself, and he knows that the Arsonist and I have a certain history together," Seranda replied.

"What kind of history?" Thaniel asked.

"That's none of your damn business," she replied.

Thaniel felt like he was walking on eggshells at this point. He decided to keep his lips sealed shut for the rest of his time spent with her in the armory.

As Seranda finished loading up on equipment in the armory, she noticed Thaniel sitting on a stool and dozing off into nothingness. She approached him and snapped her fingers in front of his face to catch his attention.

"Do you want me to take you to the cistern or not?" Seranda asked.

"You'll take me?" Thaniel replied.

"Only because it's on the way to where I need to go next, not because I feel sorry for you," she replied.

"Understood," he replied.

They walked in complete silence to the other side of the manor where the passage to the cistern lay. It was once an old cellar that the Argentwalds had put in to store their clean water. Due to the current population inhabiting the manor, the water had no longer become a necessary resource, so the cistern became somewhat of a tomb over the years.

"I still don't understand why all of us have white hair now. My hair used to be as dark as night and my eyes as blue as the sapphires in Lord Argentwald's chalice, but now I just look like everyone else around me," Thaniel said.

"It's part of the burden of the gift, they say, but if you ask me, I think it's just a way of this world reminding us that we're cursed and different, we will never be what we once were, we are forever stuck within this pale guise of death until we've bled the Realms of Light dry and become the vile creatures that we truly are," Seranda replied, opening the wooden door to the stone stairway that led to the cistern below.

"So those things out there, those savage-looking cannibals, were once like us?" Thaniel asked, following Seranda down the winding stairs.

"Aye, they are ferals now," Seranda replied.

"Ferals? Everyone else in the court calls them the maddening," he replied.

Seranda stumbled a bit and caught herself as she looked back at Thaniel with concerned eyes, "right. My mistake. I don't know why I said that. They are the maddening, and ferals is just some idea that crawled into this silly head of mine," she said.

"No, it's quite alright. I don't honestly care what they are called. I think feral sounds more fitting anyways," he replied.

Seranda felt a sense of relief washing over her mind as she continued down the stairs with Thaniel following closely behind her.

As the two made it to the base of the stairs, they knew they were now in the cistern by the sound of their boots stepping in the foul-smelling waters.

"Well, here we are. The lovely cistern of Argentwald Manor," Seranda said.

"I have never smelled a place so foul before in my entire life," Thaniel replied.

Seranda and Thaniel's nostrils were invaded by the putrid smell of stagnant water and rotting flesh that had worked together to create the foulest-smelling odor ever known. Thaniel could feel his mouth begin to water and tingle as he prepared to spew into the water below.

"Disgusting, you better not do that on me. Look the other way if you're going to do that again or grow a stronger stomach," Seranda said.

Thaniel wiped the vomit residue and drool off his chin before proceeding to follow Seranda, "I'm sorry, I just can't believe something could smell so repugnant," he said.

Seranda ignored his apology and continued to move ahead through the filthy waters, "Oliver, are you here?' she asked.

"Aye, I'm here," Oliver replied. He was in the process of dragging bloated rotten corpses from what was known as the dump pit. It was a hole in the distillery that would drop all the dried-up or dead humans that could no longer be drained of their blood. He was grabbing them by their decaying heels and dragging them through the water to the bone pile against the sewer drain of the cistern while kicking away nearby rats in the process.

"Why aren't these people given proper burials?" Thaniel asked.

"Does a cow or chicken get a proper burial after it has been consumed?" Seranda replied.

Thaniel looked away in disgust as he attempted to cover his mouth and nose with the collar of his tunic.

"Oliver, Lord Argentwald has informed this man that you have his bow, and he would like you to return it to him," Seranda said.

Oliver flicked his tongue against the inside of his cheek as he wiped his wet hands off with the bottom layer of his tunic. "What happened to the spoils of war rule? I found the bow, so it's mine now," he said.

"You dare defy Lord Argentwald?" Seranda asked.

"Defy? He's the one that's going back on his word," Oliver replied.

"The bow is very important to me. It's a family heirloom, sir," Thaniel said.

Oliver made eye contact with Thaniel and proceeded to look him up and down with a sarcastic smirk on his face, "shall I have the Eastern Vale Symphony march over here and play you a sad song with the smallest instruments they can find?" he asked.

"No, I don't believe that will be necessary," Thaniel replied.

"Don't be an arse," Seranda said.

"Piss off. You have a lot of nerve coming down here and trying to strong-arm me into giving up what is rightfully mine, especially since your neck was this close away from the cutting block," Oliver replied, making a small gap of space with his index finger and thumb while scowling at Seranda.

"Fine. I'll just tell Lord Argentwald that you refused to obey, and we'll see whose neck ends up on the cutting block tomorrow," Seranda replied.

"You can be a real cold bitch. You know that?" Oliver replied.

"So I've been told, now, where is the bow?" she asked, adjusting the dagger on her waistband so that it could be revealed. She gripped the hilt of it tightly with her right hand to let Oliver know she meant business.

"I left it in my quarters by the alchemy lab," Oliver said. He turned away to continue his laborious task of moving bodies from one side of the cistern to the other. Thaniel waved goodbye to him, but Oliver shook his head with frustration as he grabbed the heels of a nearby corpse.

The Arsonist

Seranda and Thaniel quickly hurried out of the cistern to escape its awful atmosphere and began to make their way down the hall toward the alchemy lab. When they arrived at the lab, they found it vacant and not currently in use.

"Everyone must be gathering at the armory to prepare for the war," Thaniel said.

"Most likely, although I do know that the chemists here have a family that lives in hiding within Prosperwood, and it's possible that Lord Argentwald dispatched them to contact their family and prepare them to create a diversion inside, thus distracting their outer guard defenses," Seranda replied.

"That's bloody brilliant," Thaniel said.

"Poor choice of words," she replied.

Thaniel felt embarrassed and swallowed the lump in his throat. Seranda began to browse the shelves of colorful vials in hopes of finding what was on her mind.

"I take it that you're looking for a particular vial?" Thaniel asked.

"Aye, that is why I agreed to take you to the cistern, I needed to come here, and it just so happened to work out because your bow is in one of the rooms in this hallway," she replied.

Seranda's ruby-red eyes lit up her white face as she discovered the vial she was looking for.

"Is that the one you were looking for?" Thaniel asked.

"Yes," Seranda replied. Her excitement could be seen through the shaking of her hands that held the vial and concealed her massive grin. The liquid inside the vial appeared to be thick and its color was that of a dark amber shade. Seranda held it up in front of her face and in front of a nearby lit candle so that she could read the label better. The cork cap to the vial had the letters

"N-L" etched into the visible top to indicate that it was not lethal.

"What is it?" Thaniel asked.

"Tondro root extract," she replied.

"Never heard of it," he replied.

"That's because it's an Argentwald family secret," she replied.

"What purpose does it serve?" he asked.

"It's a non-lethal paralysis poison. We use it on the cattle here to help keep them alive when we start bleeding them dry," she replied.

"How does it help them?" he asked.

"It slows their heart rate and stops them from bleeding out as we slowly cut or peel them," she replied.

"That's terrible. Are they alive and aware during the whole process?" he asked.

"I don't know. I mean, how would I?" she asked.

"That's a fair point. It just seems like a fate worse than death to inflict upon someone. I mean, we may be sick or gifted, or whatever. But we're still humans, so why do this to each other?" Thaniel replied, shrugging his shoulders in disappointment.

Seranda's facial expression began to show signs of frustration that matched the annoying headache she could feel gathering in her skull. She grabbed a new empty vial, one that was marked for lethal concoctions. She started pouring the Tondro root extract into the new vial.

"You ask too many questions. You have to drink the blood of the living to survive. Just try to act like you don't have a conscience for a minute while I check this out on the logs," she said.

"The court keeps a ledger for tracking the checking out of vials from the lab?" Thaniel asked.

Seranda turned to glare at Thaniel, who immediately lowered his head in embarrassment and shame, "I'm sorry," he said.

Seranda shook her head as she grabbed the nearby quill and dipped it in ink to sign off on taking the poison out of the lab, "now, let's go get that bow of yours," she said.

As they prepared to leave the lab, they were startled by Victoyos leaning on the doorway frame while playing with the string of Thaniel's bow. "That poison better be lethal and for the Arsonist or so help me I—," Victoyos began.

Seranda handed him the vial to show the lethal marking. "The Arsonist is as good as dead," she said.

Victoyos handed her back the vial of poison after reading the marked label. "Good, here is the bow. I was told by Lord Argentwald to make sure that our new court member Thaniel has it before I send him away," he said, holding the bow out toward Thaniel, allowing him to take it.

"Send me away?" Thaniel asked.

"Yes, you will be going with Edith and Philip to the border between Prosperwood and Cyanakin Hold to keep eyes on the rangers as they assemble and prepare to defend Prosperwood from our invasion," Victoyos replied.

"I see. Well, I better get some rest and prepare to move out immediately," Thaniel replied.

"Yes, see to it that you are properly well-fed before you leave. Our master does not embrace failure as much as your past ranger comrades might have, we have already tasted victory with the sacking of Amberwood Village, and we can't afford to lose this war for Prosperwood," Victoyos replied.

Thaniel nodded, and with his bow in hand. He made his way out of the lab and toward the main hall to drink from the blood chalices and get some rest on one of the many pillow beds. Seranda attempted to follow but was blocked by the arms of Victoyos, who was now doing everything he could to block the entrance to the lab.

"Lord Argentwald suspects something, and as his most loyal subject and cunning warrior, I feel obligated to tell him of your treachery. Perhaps if you spent a night in my bed, I would be willing to continue to keep your traitorous acts a secret," Victoyos said.

"I would rather sleep with the rats down in the cistern," Seranda replied.

"That could be arranged," he replied.

Seranda moved her hand near the hilt of the sheathed dagger on her waist as if prepared to draw the blade from the scabbard. Victoyos watched as she moved her hand closer to the blade and began to laugh as he stepped back out from the laboratory entrance and into the hall.

"You won't be able to protect him forever, and if you fail to eliminate him this time, I will kill you both myself," he said.

Seranda remained silent as her vicious-looking red eyes peered into his.

"Good luck," Victoyos said. His lips curled into a wicked grin as he proceeded to walk down the hall and toward his bedroom.

A single cold tear fell from the left eye of Seranda, and as it ran down her cheek, she wiped it away before it could fall to the floor. She took a deep breath, and with the poison in her hand, she made her way out of the lab and toward the entry gates to the Argentwald Manor.

Chapter Thirty-One

As the Arsonist, Rhys, and the rest of the companions arrived inside Prosperwood, they were amazed by how filthy and calm the city was despite the circumstances of everything that had happened in the surrounding forests.

"So here we are, wondrous and pleasant Prosperwood," the Arsonist said.

"Home sweet home," Farbris said.

Rhys pulled the Arsonist aside to have a word with him in private as the others ran off to the nearest pub to purchase a couple of flagons, along with a chicken platter.

"So if we're all going our separate ways. Then where does that make you end up?" Rhys asked.

The Arsonist smiled unnoticeably from behind his mask as he pointed past Rhys' right ear and up toward the sky. Rhys turned to see what he was pointing at to see a very large balloon striped with yellow, blue, and red colors. It sat tied to a basket and grounded to the top of a wooden tower as it swayed back and forth in the wind like the top of a tall tree.

"What in the blazes is that?" Rhys asked.

"That's what we're getting on," the Arsonist replied.

"We? Oh no, I am deathly afraid of heights, and that thing does not look stable at all," Rhys replied.

"Suit yourself. I'm sure Farbris will come along with me," the Arsonist replied.

"Where do you plan to take that thing?" Rhys asked.

"Down south and beyond the Southern Abyss," the Arsonist replied.

"And what do you hope to find down there?" Rhys asked.

"The other night while I was outside, I overheard Fargo and Vred mention something about Alarick, my father, heading with their old crew down to the Southern Wastes in search of an old enemy," the Arsonist replied.

"Old enemy?" Rhys asked.

"Aye, an old enemy named Zersten, he is to blame for all the tragedy in this world," the Arsonist replied.

"Never heard of him," Rhys replied.

"Of course, you haven't. You're the sheltered one, remember?" the Arsonist replied.

Rhys was not amused by the Arsonist's unkind words and decided to make his way toward the pub to meet the others. Once inside, he took a seat next to Farbris, whose forehead was resting flat on the wooden table.

"Are you alright, uncle?" Rhys asked.

"Aye, I just need to smoke my pipe again, or I might kill someone," Farbris replied. Rhys and Bregan laughed as they shook their heads and took sips from their cups.

"Is the Arsonist already going his separate way? I don't see him joining us and the others," Lylah asked, tapping Rhys on his shoulder to get his attention.

"He's a wanted man. I'm sure he is just laying low for now and trying not to draw any attention to himself," Rhys replied.

"The man has an unforgettable mask strapped to his damn face. How can he not draw attention to himself?" Fargo asked.

"He's the Arsonist. He is more cunning than any of us," Viti said, nudging Fargo with his elbow. He started to make mocking gestures with his hands at Fargo, who laughed in between coughs as he slammed his mug on the table.

"He's not an Arsonist. He's just an arse," Celosia said.

Lylah looked at Celosia with disappointment before storming out of the pub.

"Uh oh, looks like you're in the doghouse now," Fargo said.

Celosia nudged Fargo hard enough to make him spill his mead onto his lap.

"Great, now I look like I pissed myself," Fargo said.

"Be glad that its mead and not the real thing, next time you make a silly jest at me and my friend, you might just release the real thing as I break your nose," Celosia replied.

"Friend, huh? Since when do friends snuggle up and hold hands?" Viti asked.

"What do you mean, lad? We do it every night," Fargo said, placing his hand mead-soaked hand on top of Viti's hand. Viti pulled his hand away in disgust. He squinted his eyes in confusion at Fargo, who was laughing hysterically.

"What's the matter? Afraid of playing for both teams?" Fargo asked.

Viti shook his head as he stood up from the table to get another ale.

Celosia stood up with blushing cheeks and hurried out of the pub after Lylah.

"Someone is in a cheerful mood today," Bregan said.

"Aye, I get to finally drink again and eat a normal meal in a normal place like I'm a normal human being," Fargo replied.

"Normal? I don't see anything normal about you," Rhys said.

Fargo and Rhys' faces met one another from across the table with complete seriousness in their eyes. Fargo started to smirk, which led Rhys to burst out laughing, thus breaking the uncomfortable silence. Viti returned with an ale mug in each hand.

"You're good at busting my balls, lad," Fargo said.

"Not as good as Viti is apparently," Rhys replied.

Viti's face was dazed with bewilderment as he squinted in confusion, "that doesn't even make any sense," he said.

Both Rhys and Fargo started to laugh so hard that Fargo fell backward out of his chair. Farbris continued to sink his forehead into the wooden table as both Viti and Bregan shook their heads in uncomfortable disgust.

***

Celosia finally caught up to Lylah in a nearby alleyway down the street from the pub.

"Where are you going?" Celosia asked.

"I just need to be alone, so I can hear myself think," Lylah replied.

"What do you need to think about?" Celosia asked.

Lylah pushed her face into her cupped hands before looking up at the night sky and letting out a long, drawn-out sigh, "you're distracting me with conflicting feelings. I can't be around someone with an attitude all the time, I need to think clearly, so maybe the Arsonist was right. Maybe we should just go our separate ways," she said.

Celosia slowly grew closer to Lylah, and her lips began to tremble as she got within touching distance, "you don't mean that," she said.

"What if I do?" Lylah asked.

"You're just distancing yourself from the whole thing because you're afraid of getting hurt," Celosia said, holding Lylah's hands and peering deep into the depths of her eyes.

"What if I am?" Lylah asked.

"It's going to be okay. You don't have to go north and face your father alone, and you don't have to worry about me. I can take care of myself. I saved your arse back at the grove, remember?" Celosia replied.

"What are you even talking about? I held my own," Lylah replied.

"I sat there with you at the bank of the lake and watched over you, remember?" Celosia replied.

Lylah smirked with blushing red strawberry cheeks as Celosia came close to her face. They embraced one another in the moonlit alleyway to the sound of laughter booming from the nearby pub.

***

The Arsonist moved with stealth from the palisade gate entryway to the tower that grounded the giant colorful balloon. He moved cautiously, walking in shadows to avoid any guards from detecting him as he feared they would recognize his appearance with or without his mask intact. He slyly proceeded to the top of the stairway with his flintlock pistol in hand.

Nobody was guarding the balloon. As he approached the balloon to inspect it, a fair-skinned woman with light brown hair and eyes stood up unexpectedly from within its basket. "Can I help you, sir?" she asked.

"Are you Lady Winter?" the Arsonist asked.

The woman began to laugh so hard she couldn't breathe for a moment. She let out a cough and held up her index finger to ask the Arsonist to give her a moment.

"What's so funny?" the Arsonist asked.

"You think I'm Lady Winter?" she asked.

"Well, isn't that who this was gifted to?" The Arsonist asked, flinging his unarmed hand about while motioning to the balloon.

"Aye, you're right about that, but I am not the gift receiver. I am the captain of this ship," she replied.

"I see. Well, what is your name then?" the Arsonist asked.

As he held his unarmed hand out in front of him, he couldn't help but notice the woman blankly staring at him, "you tell me your name first, and put that hand cannon away," she said.

"You know what this is?" he asked, placing the pistol back in its waistband holster.

"Aye, I do," she replied.

"My name is the Arsonist, and yes, I am a wanted man, but I would assure you that anything you have heard is not true," he said.

"Oh? The Arsonist? The man who bedded a dozen girls at once and made them all squeal in ecstasy? Well, if you insist that everything I've heard is false, then I guess I won't believe that legend," she replied.

The Arsonist nervously laughed while trying to make eye contact with her, "well, that part might be true," he said.

"Yeah, right, I was making it up. You're that dumb arse that keeps buying junk from my cousins. I see that you finally invested in something worth investing in, though. That hand cannon is pretty nice, isn't it?" she replied.

The Arsonist was surprised by her statement, but his expression remained concealed. His eyes widened in fear as he saw her reach down and pull out a similar-looking hand cannon.

"I have one myself. Care to see?" she asked.

"I have enough experience with my own that I don't think that will be necessary," he replied.

The woman was now pointing her hand cannon directly at the Arsonist, who began to slowly back step in nervous fear.

"Then I suggest you step back down those stairs behind you and go back to where you came from. You're not stealing this hot air balloon," she replied.

The Arsonist regained his composure and came to a standstill as he opened his arms and hands to her, "What if I hired you to fly it and take me and some friends somewhere?" he asked.

"I can't take more than five people, depending on their body weight, of course, and—," she stopped.

The woman lowered her pistol and placed her hands on her

waist, "I'm not taking you anywhere, but nice try," she said.

"It's very important. The fate of the West could be involved," he replied.

"Sure, now scurry along Arsonist. I'm sure you've got places to burn and people to save," she replied.

"You never told me your name," he said, clenching his fists in frustrated defeat.

"The name's Gabby," she said, with her hands still pressed against her waist. A big sly smirk on her face was the last thing the Arsonist saw before turning to head back down the stairs.

As the Arsonist went down the stairs, his mind began to race. He was trying to think of a way to steal the hot air balloon. His primary concern was how he would fly it, as he and his companions had no experience with such a device. He knew he was going to need Gabby's help, but she was unconvinced by the Arsonist's words.

As he reached the bottom of the tower, he found a nearby stack of barrels and crates to hide behind. It was here that he would await the sunrise and attempt to devise a plan.

***

At the pub, Rhys and the others continued to drink themselves into a drunken slumber. Farbris managed to steal some pipe tobacco from a drunk patron and take a few drags from his pipe outside, thus calming his throbbing headache and anxious nerves.

His relaxing experience was interrupted by the sound of Bregan calling his name from the entrance to the pub.

"Father, I do not wish to sleep here. Where is Mother currently staying?" he asked.

Farbris deep inhaled smoke from his pipe before proceeding to blow large smoke rings toward the full moon in the sky before responding to his nearby son, "Faelina is staying near the symphony hall on Livinworth Street," he said.

"She's not Faelina. She is my mother," Bregan replied.

Farbris let out a dramatic sigh and furrowed his brow, "oh, for light's sake, you know what I meant," he said.

Bregan ran up to Farbris to hug him before making his way toward Livinworth Street. Farbris felt his son's body press in, soft and warm. This was the love he had been waiting for. He inwardly thanked Deliverance and hugged all the tighter. Seeing the sight of Bregan in Prosperwood again brought joy to Farbris.

Bregan took off down the street as Farbris took another deep drag from his pipe that he would soon release into another large smoke ring. He suddenly remembered his terrible encounter with the Argentwald court at the Glade Belt with Rhys and the Arsonist. He recalled that the blood tax had not been paid in full. He feared for what was to come as a consequence. He began to choke on the smoke in his lungs as he gasped for air and tipped his pipe upside down to dump out the leftover tobacco before hurrying back into the pub to find Rhys.

Chapter Thirty-Two

Argentwald Manor, Thaniel followed closely behind the heavily armored Edith and Philip. The three of them left the ominous glade of Argentwald Manor and quickly made it to the glade belt before heading northwest toward Cyanakin Hold.

As Edith and Philip dismounted from their horses and grabbed their crossbows, they ran up near a grass knoll that would give them a perfect line of sight of the coming and going forces of the Cyanakin rangers. Thaniel noticed their sudden vulnerability and looked around to ensure that they were not followed before releasing an arrow into each of their backs. The light arrows impact exploded their bodies into ash almost immediately.

As Thaniel looked up from his bow, he noticed a large cavalry force approaching the gate. His grip on the bow tightened with rage as he muttered the name 'Hyde' under his breath before darting into the roadside brush to get a closer look.

Thaniel wanted to aim his bow at Hyde and end him before he could finish dismounting, but he could not afford to draw that kind of attention to himself. He needed to get inside somehow and find his father so he could warn him of what was coming to Prosperwood. The fortress was heavily guarded, so he knew there was no way he could slip past the guards and make his way through.

He regretted eliminating Edith and Philip the way he did, for he now realized he could have used their bodies to create a minor diversion. There was only one way he was getting in that fort, so he tore a long piece of cloth off his cloak and wrapped it around his face to make a scarf to cover the bottom half of his face below his nose. He flipped his hood over his head and slowly began to walk toward the front gate.

"Hold, do not take one more step, or we'll shoot," a guard said.

"I am Thaniel Cadere. I bring word from Fort Quiver. I need to speak with my father, your commander," he said, holding up the bow he knew the guards would recognize to confirm his identity.

"Very well, we're glad to see you're still alive, sir," the guard replied.

As the gate opened, Thaniel quickly made his way through and into the fortress courtyard while keeping his head facing the ground and avoiding any eye contact with the rangers.

"Look, Thaniel lives, and he has Arrowguard," a ranger said.

Snow began to fall lightly upon the stronghold, and after seeing a flake land on his boot, Thaniel held his leather-gloved hand out in front of him to catch another large snowflake. His admiration of nature's beauty was interrupted by the noise of his father's piano playing from his chamber up above. As Thaniel made his way up the stone steps, he could hear the piano noise ended abruptly.

He made his way down the hall, where he could listen to both the voice of his father and Hyde speaking behind a closed wooden door.

"We were greatly outnumbered at Amberwood Village. The fiends had already infiltrated the town while we were crossing through the woods, preparing for a skirmish. We had not been aware that they were feeding on our wounded and sleeping in the middle of the night until they decided to set fire to the village," Hyde said.

"What of Fort Quiver?" Renson asked.

"During the battle for Amberwood, a messenger arrived from Fort Quiver reporting that they had requested reinforcements, and so I ordered my forces to abandon Amberwood Village and move out to Fort Quiver, and when we arrived at the rear wall the Fort was already gone, none appeared to have survived," Hyde replied.

Thaniel's red eyes glowed in the cold dark hallway outside Renson's chamber as he continued to eavesdrop on the deceit that Hyde was spewing out. Renson remained seated at his piano in silence, a dark rage had taken hold of his heart, and Hyde could see it.

"Mavis and I looked everywhere for the bow, sir, and we tried to take back the fort, but it was over-run. That was when we returned to Amberwood to find it completely emptied. We couldn't even find any corpses to bury," Hyde said.

Renson looked up from his piano with trembling eyes and lips to see Hyde and Mavis standing before him in the candle-lit space between the piano and the door to the hall.

"Is this true, Mavis?" Renson asked.

"Yes, my lord, I'm afraid so," she replied.

Thaniel couldn't believe that his friends were lying, and before he could muster up the courage to barge in and confront Hyde and Mavis for their treachery, he hesitated at the sound of his father's whimper.

"My lord, I am so sorry for your loss, but what should we do now?" Mavis asked.

Renson's sadness and rage had combined into an unstable tantrum. His blue eyes suddenly became bloodshot, and his hands began to shake as the nails extended outwards into claws. Veins in his neck became large and exposed as the buttons to his tunic popped off, revealing a muscular chest that quickly became buried under a thick black coat of fur. Hyde and Mavis couldn't believe what was happening before their eyes.

"What is happening to him?" Mavis asked.

"He's turning into some kind of beast. We need to leave, go, get help," Hyde said.

Renson's human facial features became unrecognizable as they shifted into ones more wolf-like in appearance. Before Mavis and Hyde could make a move for the door, Renson unleashed a furious howl that pierced their ears. As Renson's transformation was nearly complete, he pushed forward with all his might hurling the piano into Mavis. She died immediately as the piano crushed her body against the stone wall behind where she and Hyde were standing.

Thaniel could not wait any longer. He opened the wooden door to see Mavis crushed between the wall and the piano and Hyde cowering in fear beside it as a tall wolf-like creature covered in black hair towered over them both.

Hyde turned to see Thaniel standing in the open doorway and hurled himself through the entrance. He began to sprint down the hall toward the stairs. The wolf-like creature lunged at Thaniel with unbelievable speed before picking him up by his neck.

Thaniel dropped the bow at the beast's feet as the beast lifted him from the ground. His hood swung back behind his head, and the scarf that once covered his face had now fallen below his chin. Drool dripped down from the foul beast's fanged mouth, and hot hair exhaled from its wet nostrils into Thaniel's fear-stricken face as it sniffed him and looked upon his pale flesh.

The beast looked down below its hind legs to see the bow. As it did, it released its clutch on Thaniel's throat, allowing him to fall to the ground. The beast acted as if it suddenly remembered or recognized the bow and its wielder as it started back-stepping away from Thaniel and into the dark corner of the chamber.

Thaniel gasped for air as he rubbed the sore skin of his throat. The beast had now lowered itself to the ground, where it now moved on all fours. It slowly approached Thaniel and got close enough to where their two faces were in front of one another.

"Father?" Thaniel asked.

The Beast took one last deep sniff of Thaniel before moving past him on all fours and heading out into the hallway. With incredible speed, it moved up to the ceiling of the hallway and followed it down the stairs with cat-like movements.

Thaniel fell to the floor on his back. He was shocked at what he had just seen. The thoughts of his mother's mangled corpse that he found on the glade belt road as a child came rushing back to him. He remembered that summer morning, the smell of the trees in the air, the sounds of the birds chirping, the dew on the white flowers that crowded the road itself, and the taste of honey that he ate from a wooden jar as he pretended to be a ranger on the road with his small wooden sword.

He was there again, in the memory, as a small child looking down upon his mother's body, but this time he understood her fate. Nobody but his father was able to recognize her body that day. He claimed it was because of the dress remnants, but when his father first saw the body, she was naked as the grave keeper washed her body and prepared it for a proper burial. It never made sense to Thaniel, and he lived with the discovery and loss of his mother his entire life, never knowing what took her from him and what kind of creature could have inflicted such a brutal death.

The answer was now in both his heart and mind, and although he felt a certain peace resolving a burden that had suddenly become a lot lighter for him to bear, he couldn't help but feel anger toward his father. He knew now that his father was the one who murdered his mother, and he demanded answers but knew that the only way he would get them was if he pursued the beast his father had become.

Thaniel heard from down the stairs as he carefully made his way down the hallway with his bow in hand. As Thaniel made his way down the stairs and into the empty barracks chamber, he pulled back the string of his bow. The glowing light arrow it conjured emitted the only light that could be seen as he slowly made his way through the chamber and out into the courtyard.

The snow had begun to stick to the ground outside. The shredded bodies of many rangers littered the courtyard grass. Thaniel couldn't believe how quickly the beast managed to slaughter his brethren. He strongly wished to look for Hyde in hopes that he would find him alive. That way, he could put an arrow in his throat and claim the vengeance that he so deeply wanted, but he knew that the beast that now consumed his father was now more important.

Thaniel paid no attention to rangers that scurried out of the fort and into the woods. As he went through the courtyard and toward the gate, he noticed large wolf-like paw prints in the cold and wet dirt. A nearby ranger lay on the ground in front of the gate. He was still barely breathing despite his chest being badly wounded. Thaniel approached him and looked down upon him to see his brown eyes widening as he coughed up blood.

"End my suffering," the ranger said.

"May Deliverance watch over you now, brother," Thaniel said, releasing the arrow he had been holding back into the ranger to end his pain. Thaniel mounted his dark horse outside and made haste as he followed the track marks of the beast into the nearby forest that separated Cyanakin Hold from Prosperwood village.

The track marks disappeared below a large tree that loomed high over the western palisade wall of Prosperwood. Thaniel's heart sank as he discovered where the tracks ended and where they were heading. With his left hand on the reins of the horse and his right hand gripping his bow, he motioned the horse to turn around. Together they darted into the dark snowy amber colored forest and back to the glade belt road that would lead them to the gates of Prosperwood.

Chapter Thirty-Three

Celosia and Lylah were snuggling up on a stone bench on the far northern street of Prosperwood known as Feathered Road. Its name came from the pigeons that occupied its path due to all the benches where residents would sit and feed them breadcrumbs.

The bench faced north and had a clear line of sight of the Prosperwood Ferry that came back and forth ever so often from across the deep and dark waters of the Swollen Strand River. The two women could clearly see the Ferry slowly coming in closer to the Prosperwood dock. They both were surprised to see so many people on the Ferry coming across from the northern shore. The wooden ferry was large in size, but this group of people onboard was larger, and they were packed in tightly, standing hip to hip.

"Once they land and empty out, we could always buy a pass and board it, and then we could head north together and find your father," Celosia said.

"I'm not leaving the others, especially without telling them," Lylah replied.

"What's with you and these people? The arse, sorry, the Arsonist, even said that we would get here and then go our separate ways, so why not do just that? Celosia replied, rolling her eyes as if they were marbles rolling away from her nose.

"I can't explain it. Ever since I touched that monolith at the grove, I can't help but feel that I need to do something important, and these men seem to be doing something important. I feel like I

need their help as much as they probably need mine," Lylah replied.
Celosia lifted her hand off Lylah's shoulder and removed her arm from around the back of Lylah's neck before standing up to look at her face to face.

"No, you don't, you don't need them, and they don't need you, but I do," Celosia said.

"You were fine before you met me, and you will continue to be just as fine with or without me," Lylah replied.

"That's not true, I willingly pursued druidism at the grove so that I could find purpose in my life, and although that experience was taken from me by those albino cannibals out there, I left that place on a rowboat with my newfound purpose. You," Celosia said, with eyes swollen from tears.

Lylah didn't know what to say, and as she looked away from Celosia, she noticed the ferry was now entering the docking station at the shore. One man sat mounted on a grey horse in the very front of the ferry while the others behind him stood crowded and heavily armed. Lylah recognized the horse. She recognized the banners the men in the far back were holding up. It was the Proditore Tower banner, and when she looked closely, she realized the light-haired man on the horse was her father, Nielas.

"Are you even listening to me?" Celosia asked.

With a crazy calm in her eyes, Lylah lifted her right hand and pointed straight ahead to the ferry. Celosia turned around to see a large group of heavily armed men and women marching slowly behind Nielas.

"What in the—," Celosia stopped.

"That's my father," Lylah replied.

The two stood up and began to run back toward the pub to tell the others what they saw.

θθθ

Back at the pub, Farbris stormed into the drinking hall to find Rhys passed out and drooling on the sticky wooden table they had all occupied the night before.

"Rhys, wake up. It's important," Farbris said.

Rhys mumbled incoherent nonsense before opening his eyes and rubbing them, "Uncle? What is it?" he asked.

"Remember those bloodsucking fiends we met on the glade belt road some nights ago?" Farbris asked.

"Aye, I do," Rhys replied.

"We never paid the blood tax, and I have a feeling that Lord Argentwald is not pleased. We need to get out of here before something terrible happens," Farbris replied.

"I think you're overreacting, uncle, they would have done something immediately, and there's no way they can break through the defenses here, and even if they did, I'm sure we could take them. I have Lightfang, and we have the Arsonist," Rhys replied.

Farbris abruptly grabbed his nephew by his robe collar with a worried look, "listen to me. These are not the savages you hacked and slashed your way through back at the cathedral. These are cunning, well-trained, and somewhat intelligent beings. They are sadistic as well as merciless," he said.

Rhys pushed his uncle's hands away and looked at him with concern, "what do you want to do then?" Rhys asked.

"I'm not sure, but I am not leaving your aunt or my son here to die. We need to get them and board that balloon vessel with the Arsonist before nightfall," Farbris replied.

"Very well, do you know where Bregan is?" Rhys asked.

"Aye, I am a bloody fool and let him run off to his mother's friend's house alone, I should have gone with him, but I wasn't thinking clearly. It has been a long journey for me these last few days," Farbris replied. Rhys gently patted his uncle on the back, who had started to weep as he took a big sip from Rhys' half- empty mug of ale. Farbris wiped the ale off his chin and then looked sharply at Rhys.

"Let's get going then, shall we?' Fabris asked.

"I don't know where the Arsonist is, but we need to find him before we attempt to start boarding the balloon vessel," Rhys replied.

"Aye, what about the others?" Farbris asked.

Before Rhys could reply, he saw Celosia and Lylah barge in through the front doors to the pub.

"My father and a large force of troops have just arrived in Prosperwood," Lylah said.

"Why is that important for us to know?" Rhys asked.

"Because he might be able to help us, you know, turn the tide on these savages that are overrunning these lands," Lylah replied.

Celosia aggressively tugged on Lylah's arm to get her attention. "How can you be so sure of that? The way you described him in the past made him sound like a complete arse," Celosia said.

"Why else would he be here?" Lylah asked.

The Arsonist

"I'm sorry dear, who is your father again?" Farbris asked.

"Nielas, Nielas Proditore," she replied.

Farbris' eyes widened in disbelief as he covered his bearded mouth with his left hand. "This is getting worse by the moment," he said.

"What? Why would you say that?" Lylah asked.

"Your father and I do not have a good history, and if he discovers Rhys, or worst of all, the Arsonist, he will not be the kind father you may have previously known," Farbris replied.

Lylah looked at Farbris with confusion as Celosia continued to tug on her arm fiercely.

"Lylah, what do you want to do?" Celosia asked.

Lylah was at a loss for words. She didn't know what to say.

"I'll tell you what I think we should do," Rhys said.

"Nobody asked you," Celosia replied.

"Fine then, suit yourself," Rhys replied.

Lylah's silent trance broke as she looked at Rhys with emotional intensity growing on her face, "what do you think we should do?" she asked.

"I think Farbris here should head upstairs and wake our traveling companions, and you two should come with me to search for Bregan," Rhys said.

"You remember where Sabrina lives?" Farbris asked.

"Aye, I used to pass her house every day on the way to the Frederick family house to tutor their youngest," Rhys replied. Farbris nodded in compliance as he turned to hurry up the nearby stairs to the bedrooms where Viti, Vred, and Fargo were sleeping.

"Let's get going then," Celosia said.

As Farbris entered the large room upstairs, he noticed how crowded with beds it was. Many patrons were sound asleep in the dimly lit bedroom of the pub, including the three he sought,

"Fargo, I need you to wake up," he said.

Fargo lunged forward with a knife in his hand, bringing it close to Farbris' bearded neck. He quickly dropped the knife upon realizing who it was standing above him, "what is the meaning of this?" he asked.

"Prosperwood is in grave danger. We need to move, wake the others, and meet me downstairs," Farbris replied.

***

Rhys, Celosia, and Lylah made their way toward Sabrina's house to find Bregan, but when they finally arrived, they found Bregan asleep, lying against the door to the small shack of the house.

"Bregan?" Rhys asked.

"Cousin?" Bregan said, rubbing his eyes as he sat up before them

"Your father told us to come get you and your mother. Why are you out here?" Rhys replied.

"I came here looking for her as well, but nobody is home," Bregan replied.

Celosia anxiously kicked at the ground with her feet as Lylah kneeled by Bregan and put her hand on his knee. "Do you know where she is?" Lylah asked.

Bregan looked over to his left. He lifted his right hand and pointed toward a large building, "I think she went there. The whole nice part of town appears to be emptying out and heading there. I saw many well-dressed men in top hats with canes making their way over there a couple of minutes ago," he said.

Rhys' heart felt as if it had just stopped as he turned to look at the large building that stood in the distance, "the symphony concert," he said.

Celosia pushed her lips to the side as she squinted her eyes in confusion. "The what?" she asked.

"It's a large concert being put on by Dorian. He's a piece of shit that hails from the East," Rhys replied.

Lylah and Celosia smirked as Rhys cast his eyes down to the ground below and shook his head in frustration. "I bet she is there too," he said.

Lylah raised her left eyebrow in curiosity as she smiled, "Somebody else that you don't want to see?" she asked.

"Aye, Lady Winter," Rhys replied.

"You're still on about her?" Bregan asked.

Bregan and Lylah joined each other in light laughter as Rhys turned away from them, "I'm not going in there. I can't," he said.

"I'll go then," Bregan replied.

Celosia noticed a large group of dark hooded silhouettes moving from out behind a large house and disappearing behind the large symphony hall. She nudged Rhys and pointed straight ahead to them, "who are they?" she asked.

"That's a good question. I have no idea. Maybe they're the performers," Rhys replied.

As Bregan stood up to brush off his pants, he noticed something jump into the air off the thatch roof of one of the small houses in the distance before landing on top of another thatched roof, "the better question is, what in light's name is that?" he asked.

Lylah, Celosia, and Rhys turned to see what appeared to be the large wolf-like creature that chased them through Amberwood.

"It can't be," Celosia said.

"It has to be. Nothing else in this realm moves like that," Lylah replied.

"We need to get back to the pub. We need to find the Arsonist and make way for the balloon vessel," Rhys said, pulling Bregan closer.

"We're not leaving without my mother. Now let me go so I can go get her," Bregan replied.

"I can't do that, not with that thing leaping around town," Rhys replied.

Celosia let out a long, drawn-out sigh before grabbing the hands of Lylah and pulling her in for a kiss. As she pulled away from Lylah's face, she smiled with sadness in her eyes. "I'll go to this concert building thing and find her, but I have no idea what she looks like," Celosia said.

Lylah was breathing heavily but her face remained calm as Celosia let go of her hands. "You go find your father. Maybe he and that little army of his can take care of that damn beast," Celosia said.

Rhys swallowed his pride and gripped the hilt of his sword as he nodded at Celosia, "I will go with you if Lylah will take Bregan safely back to the pub. He needs to be with his father," he said.

Lylah nodded as she attempted to dry her wet eyes with the sleeve of her tunic, "come on, Bregan, we need to move quickly before it sees us."

Bregan hugged Rhys and followed Lylah as she moved with stealth into the shadows cast by the nearby tall houses.

"Let's go," Celosia said.

Rhys followed her as they made haste toward the symphony hall building.

Chapter Thirty-Four

Bowmen and torches lined the palisade walls. The heavily guarded watchtowers made up each corner of the square-shaped village perimeter. Thaniel arrived at the sealed wooden gates on his dark horse. Two guards in front unsheathed their swords as they aggressively approached him. Thaniel was confused that they were coming toward him with such a threatening presence.

"He's one of them. Kill him," one of the guards said.

Thaniel had forgotten that his pale skin, white hair, and red eyes were a visible indicator to the people that he was one of the wretched members of the Argentwald court.

Before both of the guards could strike him down with their swords, a handful of crossbow bolts came soaring in from behind them, striking them in the back and leaving them dead on their stomachs. Thaniel looked to his right to see about a dozen familiar faces of the Argentwald court charging toward the gate armed with swords and crossbows.

"That was a good diversion," Victoyos said, dismounting from a familiar looking horse.

"The horse that I owe my life to," Thaniel said.

"Here, take it," Victoyos said, handing the reins to Thaniel with one hand as he unsheathed his sword with the other.

The Arsonist

Members of the court poured into Prosperwood as they breached the gate, shooting their crossbows at the guards that lined the palisade walls. Thaniel rode the horse past them without firing a single shot at the Prosperwood guards that attempted to pursue him. He needed to find and put down the beast that was his father.

As he rode past the pub, he passed an old man smoking a pipe and looking at him with strange curiosity. Thaniel paid no attention to them as he continued to gallop through the filthy streets. A group of guards came running past the pub continuing their chase on foot after Thaniel.

***

Outside the pub, the old man, Farbris, nearly dropped his pipe as he saw Thaniel ride by on his horse. "I know that horse," he said.

Viti, Vred, and Fargo joined Farbris outside as the guards chased after Thaniel on the horse.

"Those idjits will never catch that horse," Viti said.

Vred and Fargo walked a few feet away to see where the guards chasing Thaniel had come from. As they turned the corner, they noticed a large force pouring through the destroyed wooden gate.

"We're in trouble," Fargo said.

"Aye, we best find the Arsonist and get out of here," Vred said.

Farbris and Viti joined them to see the violence that was taking place at the front of the village.

***

Thaniel continued to ride and flee from the guards until he noticed a large dark silhouette leaping impossible heights beneath the setting sunlight. He couldn't tell if it was the beast or if his mind was playing tricks on him.

Through the falling snow, he could see the silhouette land on the roof of the left watchtower. As the shouting of guards nearing behind him grew louder, he motioned the horse to keep moving as they hurried along.

"Get him!" one of the guards shouted.

The guards in the watchtower could see Thaniel coming toward them, but before they could take aim at him with their crossbows, one of them was grabbed by the face and pulled out of the window and up the roof. The silhouette became a clear figure to Thaniel.

As he approached the base of the tower, the decapitated limp body of a guard fell from the roof above and landed down at the hooves of Thaniel's horse. He looked up in disgust to see that the silhouette was the beast he was pursuing.

He dismounted from his horse and made his way to the door, which he quickly opened before hurrying up the wooden stairs. He didn't look back to notice that the horse had taken off down the road, thus abandoning him inside the tower at the stairway.

The guards pursuing Thaniel on foot noticed that his horse had taken off without its rider, and they discovered the decapitated corpse of one of their comrades outside the tower's door. They hurried in after Thaniel, who was now nearing the top of the stairs.

As he made it to the top of the tower, he noticed a guard gripping the bleeding stump of where his right hand had once been. The guard looked up from his wound to see Thaniel standing in the entryway. Thaniel ignored the guard and darted to one of the nearby windows to see if the beast was still nearby.

The guard bolted into Thaniel with all his body weight, and together they fell out of the high tower window and down below. They fell until their bodies both hit the thatch roof of a nearby house which imploded as their bodies made contact with it.

Thaniel had landed on the hay covered cot of whoever lived in the house, and the guard had met the dirt floor. The guard did not survive the fall, but Thaniel did. This was due to the bow on his back transforming into a shield and breaking his fall moments before impact. Thaniel lay in the collapsed wooden cot but couldn't move. He struggled to breathe. He felt as if the wind had been knocked out of him by the guard that had crashed into him at the top of the tower.

As the dust in the air from his crash cleared, he could see through the hole in the roof that the guards were looking down at him from the watchtower window. He could also see the beast prowling atop the tower and preparing to grab another one of them. Thaniel tried to open his mouth to yell and warn them, but the words wouldn't come out. The guards' screams were all Thaniel could hear as he struggled to stand up, but as their screams went silent, he looked up once more to see that they were gone. He could no longer see them in the windows of the watchtower, only the beast.

"Damn you," Thaniel said.

Hunger overwhelmed Thaniel's senses as the smell of fresh blood filled the space around him. The fallen guard that had previously charged him out of the window was teeming with it.

Thaniel could hear his own heartbeat racing as his red pupils dilated. His hands shook uncontrollably as a surge of fatigue entered his entire body. He quickly gave in and began to use his combined hands as a cup to scoop up and drink from the pool of life that was leaving the lifeless body of the fallen guard.

As Thaniel quenched his thirst, he could hear the stampeding sound of a hundred marching footsteps passing the door to the house he was in. As he approached the crack in the wooden door to peer outside, he saw a large battalion of troops with Proditore tower banners marching past the tower. He saw the recognizable and unmistakable light hair that covered the back of his uncle Nielas' head.

He couldn't believe his own eyes. He hurried back over to look up and out of the hole in the roof to see that the beast atop the watchtower was now gone. He picked his shield up off the dirt floor. As it transformed into a bow, he pulled his scarf over his blood-stained mouth and brought his dark hood over his head. Thaniel waited to open the wooden door until the battalion of soldiers turned and passed out of sight. Once they were no longer visible, he looked to see that his dark horse companion was missing. He cursed the dark steed before making his way on foot down the road that the familiar horseshoe tracks led down.

Chapter Thirty-Five

The Arsonist stood halfway up the wooden stairs that led up to the hot air balloon, where Gabby slept on the wooden basket floor with a bedroll and lantern. He looked out into the city to see that which he could not believe, a war had broken out in the front gate, and although the guards of Prosperwood were fighting valiantly, they were quickly losing ground.

He knew he had little to no chance fighting off the fiends that were pouring into the village. The decision to escape became clear to him when he noticed the familiar faces of Bregan and Lylah sneaking alongside the walls of a nearby tanners' shack. He couldn't bring himself to abandon his newfound friends to share the same fate as those that were slaughtered at the front gates. He hustled down the stairs and toward Lylah and Bregan.

"Oh, for light's sake," Lylah said, grabbing her chest with her left hand while holding Bregan's shoulder with her right.

"Did I startle you?" the Arsonist asked.

Bregan laughed as he pulled away from Lylah and approached the Arsonist.

"Yes, please, for light's sake, don't do that again," Lylah said.

"I'm sorry," the Arsonist replied.

"It's okay. We need to get to the pub. You should come with us," she said.

"Stay behind me but stay close," the Arsonist said, pulling his pistol out.

The two front watch towers exploded into flames as

The Arsonist

Argentwald's court members celebrated with cackling laughter. They paraded through the poorer districts of Prosperwood, shooting their crossbows and killing the paupers at will.

The Arsonist, Bregan, and Lylah made their way past an open alleyway. The screaming charge of an Argentwald court member could be heard coming at them from the alleyway. Each of her shining swords gleamed in the moonlight as she neared Bregan. Bregan moved back into Lylah to dodge the incoming attack as the red-eyed woman went berserk. She fell forward and separated the Arsonist from Lylah and Bregan.

Before the Arsonist could aim at the fiend and open fire, Lylah pushed Bregan out of the way and grabbed the woman by both her wrists. Lylah shoved the woman against the wall and kneed her in the crotch while tightly gripping their wrists. The woman let go of the swords she held as she tried to snap her fang at Lylah's neck.

Bregan picked up one of the swords by the hilt before plunging it into the woman's stomach. Her red eyes went still as she slowly slid down the wall. The Arsonist's impressed facial expression could not be seen behind his mask, but he nodded at Bregan to acknowledge his deed. Lylah's mouth and eyes were wide open with shock.

"We need to move. Come on," Lylah said.

The three hurried down the street until they came to the pub where they saw no sight of their companions.

"Where did they all go?" Bregan asked.

"We're up here," Viti said.

The three looked up behind them to see Viti, Fargo, Vred, and Farbris sitting atop a small house across the street from the pub.

"What in the blazes are you doing up there?" Lylah asked.

"We were trying to hide from those fiends that are attacking the city," Fargo replied.

Vred helped lower Farbris off the roof before jumping down to join him.

"I told Rhys this was coming," Farbris said.

"We'll have plenty of time to say I told you so later. We need to get to the symphony hall and regroup," Lylah said.

"There's no time for that. We need to get to the air balloon quickly. This place will be overrun within the next hour," the Arsonist said.

Lylah grabbed the Arsonist by the sleeve of his coat and turned him around so that she could see him, "we are not leaving Rhys and

Celosia here to die," she said.

The Arsonist pulled away from her and looked at Fargo and Viti as they jumped down from the roof, "I hate to say this, but maybe we should split up then. We have to secure the air balloon and hold down the tower that it's attached to. It's too close to the front gate district and will surely be overrun if we all make our way to wherever it is that Rhys and Celosia have run off to," he said.

"They're at the symphony hall. They were looking for Bregan's mother," Lylah said.

"Very well, I will go and—," The Arsonist stopped as Lylah cut him off.

"No, I will go back and get them. You infiltrated the air balloon already and will be of more use there. Besides, you're heavily armed and can help hold down the tower."

"Alright," the Arsonist replied.

"Fargo, how good is your aim?" Lylah asked.

"The best in the West, my lady," he replied.

"Good, you're coming with me," she replied.

"I'm coming too," Farbris said.

The Arsonist's gauntlet-protected hand grabbed Farbris' left shoulder tightly. "No, you're staying here with me, old man," he said.

Farbris gasped and shook his head before letting out a sigh, "fine," he said.

Bregan crossed his arms as he stood beside Lylah, "I want to go too," he said.

"No, I forbid it," Farbris replied.

"Too bad," Bregan said.

Farbris' brown eyes lit up with anger, "don't even think about it," he said.

Lylah shook the curly head of hair on Bregan's head before bringing her face down to his, "listen to your father and stay here. I'll have Viti come with me instead," she said.

"If Viti is coming, then I surely am as well," Bregan said, looking at Viti, who looked away to avoid making eye contact with him.

Fargo handed Viti a long knife and nodded at him before giving him a pat on the back.

"Viti?" Bregan said.

"I'm sorry, Bregan. You're too young for this sort of thing," Viti said.

"I'll help hold down the air balloon. Good luck, friends," Vred said.

Bregan frowned in disbelief as Farbris grabbed his arm and motioned him to follow. Lylah, Fargo, and Viti took off into the dark village as Vred, Farbris, and Bregan made their way to the air balloon tower with the Arsonist.

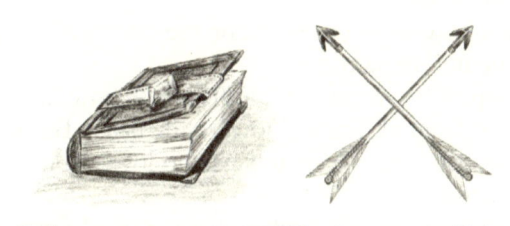

Chapter Thirty-Six

Smoke engulfed the evening sky as it continuously rose in the poorer districts of Prosperwood. Although the smoke was blowing north to the wealthier part of town where the symphony hall was located, the outbreak of violence at the city gates was not impacting those already seated inside the symphony hall. As Celosia and Rhys approached the lavish doors to the building, they were stopped by a well-dressed man with a very large, waxed mustache.

"I'm sorry, but I'm afraid you're too late. The show has already begun," the man said.

"The city is on fire. The show is about to end," Rhys said.

"It's probably just the house of some poor pauper bastard who dropped a lantern on their bed," the man replied.

Celosia balled up her fist and swung directly into the man's face. He grabbed his bleeding nose with both his hands. "Help!" he cried. "This bitch just assaulted me!"

Rhys unsheathed his sword as he saw an armed guard open the door and come rushing toward him, "what did you do that for?" Rhys asked.

"We don't have time for this," Celosia replied.

The guard was charging while wielding a large wooden club. Before he could reach Celosia and Rhys, he was tackled by a large wolf-like beast.

"Run," Rhys said.

Celosia darted for the doors and entered the building, but before Rhys could catch up to her, he was separated from her by the beast. It stood on its hind legs before him. The man with the large, waxed mustache, and bleeding nose was crawling away toward the door to get away.

"Close the doors and just go," Rhys said.

Celosia closed the doors behind her leaving the man and Rhys outside with the beast.

The man began to yell as he hit on the door with his bloody hands. "Let me in!" he said.

Rhys gripped his sword's hilt tightly with both hands. He pointed it out in front of him and toward the beast. Before the beast could lunge toward him, it leaped back and lowered itself to dodge an incoming arrow.

Rhys quickly turned his neck to see a hooded figure standing behind him with a bow drawn. The beast grabbed the man with the large, waxed mustache and hurled him toward Rhys, knocking him to the ground. As his sword went flying across the dirt and out of his reach, the beast began to charge toward him.

The hooded figure let loose another arrow of pure light toward the beast but missed again as the beast leaped diagonally to its left, landing on the side of the roof of a nearby house. It let loose a vicious piercing howl before proceeding to climb up the roof and away from them.

The hooded figure kneeled next to Rhys and the man with the bloody nose. "Are you alright?" he asked

Rhys pushed the unconscious man with the bloody nose off of him so that he could stand up. He noticed the hooded figure's red eyes and flinched back on the ground. He quickly crawled toward the sword to grab it.

"Why are you frightened? I mean you no harm," the hooded figure said.

"Who are you?" Rhys asked.

"My name's Thaniel. I am a ranger of the West," he replied.

"Ranger?"

"Aye, a ranger, but I am sick now."

"You're not sick. You're cursed. I know those eyes when I see them," Rhys said, gripping his sword and pointing it fiercely at Thaniel.

"I promise you that I mean you no harm. I mean, I just saved you from that beast," Thaniel said.

Rhys suddenly felt as if Thaniel spoke the truth. He looked at the man's eyes and thought of his brother.

He lowered his sword but kept his hands tightly gripping it. "You're right, and I thank you for my rescue," he said.

"We need to follow it and kill it," Thaniel replied.

"I've encountered it before. It was hunting my companions and me in the glades not long ago. I assure you that its reflexes are too swift. You have to catch it by surprise with a physical force that is close and personal. It will react too quickly for us to kill it from afar," Rhys replied.

Thaniel kicked a nearby rock as he started to think.

"I would love to help you hunt that beast. Trust me, I really would. That thing and I have some unfriendly history between us, but I need to get inside this building to find someone important to me," Rhys said.

Thaniel nodded, but before he turned away, he noticed the sword that Rhys was holding.

"Is that what I think it is?" he asked.

Rhys looked down at the sword and then back at Thaniel, where he finally noticed the bow he was wielding. It was Arrowguard.

"This is unbelievable," Rhys said.

"Is that Lightfang?" Thaniel asked.

"Aye, and you wield Arrowguard," Rhys replied.

"We have the perfect weapons to put that beast down. Come on, I saw a girl run in there, and she was with you, right?" Thaniel replied.

"Yes, but what is your point?" Rhys replied.

"Let her find that important person of yours, and you come with me to put that beast down, you and I, just like our weapons previous owners used to put down many foes before our time," Thaniel replied.

"Our fathers?" Rhys asked.

Thaniel's covered face bore confusion that quickly transformed into realization as he looked more closely at Rhys' white hair,

"You are Nielas' son?" he asked.

"No? I am the son of Alarick," Rhys replied.

Thaniel's eyes widened with happy surprise, "Alarick? I can't believe it," he said.

"Aye, to tell you the truth, neither can I," Rhys replied.

"That makes us cousins, then. I am the son of Renson Cadere," Rhys couldn't believe his words as his eyes widened in happy surprise, as well. "This is an incredible discovery, but I really need to go. You should come with me," he said.

"Fine, I will help you find this friend, but then you are going to use that sword of yours to help me slay this beast," Thaniel replied.

Rhys nodded at Thaniel before attempting to open the doors to the symphony hall, but he couldn't. The doors refused to push open as if something was blocking them from the inside. "What is the meaning of this? Celosia, open the door!" he said.

He continued to pound on the door with his fist but received no response. The snow continued to fall and stick to the ground in Prosperwood as a cold breeze blew past Thaniel and Rhys.

"Maybe she didn't want to be followed," Thaniel said.

"I guess not. I wonder if there is another way in," Rhys replied.

"I'm not sure, to be honest, we can go check around back, or I can try to blow this doorway open with Arrowguard," Thaniel said.

"That might draw too much attention to us. I did see some hooded figures heading in from the back entrance where the stage performers enter," Rhys replied.

"That sounds like trouble worth investigating. Let's go," Thaniel said.

The two men hustled to the back of the hall to find a locked door. Rhys kicked it in anger and yelled for someone to open it.

Thaniel motioned him to stand back as he fired an arrow into the door handles, allowing Rhys to open the doors. The two hurried into the darkness of the hallway. They could hear the sounds of violins and cellos slowing down to a perfect close. The brief silence that followed them came to a swift end as over a hundred patrons rose to their feet in a round of applause. They began to clap as the curtain lowered on stage.

"The second act will begin soon," a man said.

The symphony hall was a massive and remarkable space filled with gold, wood, and delicate architecture that was unique and decadent in design. The hall could house up to two hundred seated patrons, and the stage that lay before them was a polished wooden floor. It laid atop a stone platform. It was shielded from the audience view by a dark purple curtain. The stone platform was lowered below the stage where the musicians would load up onto it from down below, and then they would be raised up before the crowd as the purple curtain lifted.

As Rhys and Thaniel entered the lower backstage where the platform was lowered, they encountered a handful of black hooded figures wielding large swords.

"Lord Argentwald's knights," Thaniel said.

Rhys furrowed his brow in confusion, for he had never seen anything like them before. "Knights? Those still exist?" Rhys asked.

"Only in a black-blooded court like Argentwald's," Thaniel replied.

The blacked hooded knights charged and joined combat with Thaniel and Rhys, whose living weapons came to their defense. Thaniel could see Lord Argentwald and a handful of other familiar court members smirking back at him while standing beside the seated symphony musicians that appeared to be dead. They were all standing on the stone stage as it was slowly raised up and out of Thaniel's line of sight.

Chapter Thirty-Seven

As Fargo, Viti, and Lylah approached the symphony hall, they attempted to open the front doors, which they quickly discovered were locked. Viti got a running start and then ran to throw all his body weight into the doors. Fargo pulled an arrow back after seeing the blood on the ground and the nearby unconscious man with a large mustache.

"This doesn't look good," Fargo said.

Viti stood up and gripped his shoulder as he winced in pain before running back to repeat the process. This time he was joined by Fargo, who ran into the doors with him. As they crashed into the wooden doors, they felt whatever was barring their entry behind the doors give way. As the doors burst open, Fargo and Viti let out painful groans as Lylah helped each of them to their feet.

They ascended the winding stairs to the seating area quickly. They could hear the crowd's roaring excitement as the purple curtain concealing the stage rose. When Lylah arrived at the top of the stairs, she caught her breath and looked down to see the dark room dimly lit as the purple curtain finished its rise, thus exposing the candle-lit stage.

As the stage became more visible to the audience, they let out screams of fear and gasps of disbelief as Lord Argentwald bowed triumphantly before them. Behind him, a handful of members from his court dug their fangs into the dead symphony musicians' slit throats.

Dorian was alive without a slit throat, but his hands were bound behind his back, and his mouth was gagged by a piece of leather tied around his head. He stood alongside Lord Argentwald, who held him by the back of his neck with his left hand while wielding a long sharp dagger in his right hand. The seated crowd began to stand up in a crazy panic and shuffle about while trying to flee the now unstable setting.

"Ladies and gentlemen, I am Lord Argentwald. The ruler these lands, and the collector of a blood tax, that you have failed to pay."

As the audience tried to flee to the only exit, they were cut off by more than a dozen black hooded figures wielding swords. Lylah noticed the brown skin of Celosia as she was dragged onto the stage by her hair.

"A tax that you will pay tonight, but before I can do that, I shall give you the second act of tonight's entertainment," Lord Argentwald said, leaning down to pick up a violin before cutting Dorian's hands-free from the rope bond that they were in. He handed the violin to Dorian and motioned him to play it.

As this was happening, Lylah got the attention of Fargo and pointed to Celosia, who was being dragged across the stage. Fargo drew back an arrow before taking aim on the hooded figure that was dragging her across the stage. Dorian began to cry as he dropped the violin to the ground and removed the gag that denied him the ability to speak.

"Everyone, run for your lives!" Dorian cried.

Lord Argentwald closed his eyes in disappointment as he swiftly dug his dagger into Dorian's throat before pushing him down to the ground with the dagger still inside his throat.

"I regret to inform you that the concert is now over. The taxation of your veins shall commence," he said. His mad and exciting laughter was interrupted by an arrow from Fargo's bow that flew through the air and pierced the forehead of the nearby hooded knight dragging Celosia by her hair.

Lord Argentwald's wolf-like red eyes pierced the crowd as he signaled his knights to finish what they came to do. One by one, the knights brought their swords down upon the fighting crowd, cleaving them down as they swarmed the stage, trying to climb onto it in an effort to escape the impending doom that was the hooded knights.

Fargo drew back another arrow and aimed at a knight that was cleaving the crowd. As the arrow pierced the knight's back, it reached back reactively to pull it out. It turned around to see Fargo preparing to draw back another arrow.

"We have to do something," Viti said.

Cackling laughter was coming from below the stairs behind them as Fargo fired another arrow into the hooded knight bringing him down to his knees. Lylah watched in fear as Lord Argentwald attempted to force Celosia to stand up on the stage. He laughed as he dodged her kicking legs and grabbed her by her throat with his white-gloved hands.

He picked her up and turned her around with force to face the crowd. Celosia tried to bite Lord Argentwald's hands to release his grip. It was no use, and it only frustrated Lord Argentwald. He sighed as he used his hands to snap her neck, killing her, before sinking his teeth into her neck.

Fargo was now taking aim at him with a drawn arrow. Before Fargo could let loose the arrow, he was stabbed from behind. The sword went through his back and out his stomach as he let loose the arrow. It went flying upward into the ceiling above the audience.

Lylah screamed at the sight of Celosia's death on stage, but before one of the red-eyed fiends could attack her, they were intercepted by Viti. Lylah watched as Viti tackled the fiend coming up the stairs and plunged his dagger into their chest. One of the remaining red-eyed fiends removed their sword from Fargo's body before charging Lylah, who barely dodged the attack as the blade severed some of her long blonde hair.

Viti charged at the fiend that attacked Lylah and stabbed his knife into its back continuously until it stopped moving.

"Look out," Lylah said.

Viti turned to move but was paralyzed with pain as a sword was brought down upon his lower left leg, severing it from his body. Viti let out a horrifying scream as he plunged his knife into the knee of the attacking fiend. It backhanded Viti with its gauntlet-covered hand knocking him back and into unconsciousness.

Before the fiend could plunge its sword into Viti's chest, it was tackled by Lylah, who had tightly wrapped her hands around the man's skinny neck. She began to strangle him with a mad look in her eyes. As he eventually stopped breathing, she let go. She looked over at Viti, who was unconscious and losing a lot of blood. She cried as she put her hand on his chest.

"I'm so sorry," she said.

Lylah picked up Fargo's bow and grabbed an arrow from the

quiver. As she stood up to aim at the stage, she became overwhelmed with rage. Lord Argentwald was gone, and Celosia's lifeless body remained with the dead musicians on stage.

The black-hooded knights continued to cleave the fighting members of the audience down with their swords while others surrendered to them, sensing the inevitability of their demise. Lylah knew that there was no way she could kill all the knights and save the audience. She ran down the stairs with a bow and arrow in hand. Tears flooded her eyes, blurring her vision as she tripped on her way down the stairs.

As she made it to the exit and fell to the dirt floor, she saw the plated feet of a dozen soldiers behind the grey hooves of an armored horse. As she looked up with swollen tear-drenched eyes, she saw the worried face of her father, Nielas.

She stood up and dropped the bow and arrow in silence as tears ran down her dirty white cheeks. Her father, Nielas, motioned two of his men to seize her. They approached her and got a hold of her arms without any resistance. They brought her to Nielas' horse, where they helped lift her onto it. As she sat on the horse behind her father, holding onto him, he motioned his horse and battalion to turn and head toward the gate district. As they moved out, she looked back toward the symphony doors to see Bregan crouching and waving from behind a crate near the doors. She shook her head at him and looked forward to avoid drawing any attention to Bregan. As he stood up to run away toward the hot air balloon tower, he felt a hand grab his shoulder.

Chapter Thirty-Eight

Rhys gripped the shoulder of Bregan, who lunged back and let out a frightened voice cracking scream. Rhys placed his left index finger pointed up in front of his lips. He was motioning to Bregan to be silent.

"It's okay, Bregan, it's Rhys. It's your cousin."

Thaniel nervously waved with closed eyes so that Bregan wouldn't see his red pupils.

"Who is this?" Bregan asked.

"This is a new friend I made, his name is Thaniel, and I owe him my life," Rhys said.

Bregan rolled his shoulders and scowled at Rhys as he stood up and eyeballed Thaniel, "I don't like being sneaked up on," he said.

"I know you don't, but I had no choice. We have to be quiet and get back to the air balloon. Let's move," Rhys said.

As the three prepared to move out, they were startled by an unexpected hand clapping behind them.

"I really didn't think that you would betray us," Lord Argentwald said, clapping his white-gloved hands together slowly. As the clapping ceased, he signaled a dozen red-eyed fiends to begin sprinting toward Thaniel, Rhys, and Bregan.

"Run," Thaniel said, letting loose an arrow, bringing down one of the red-eyed fiends. Rhys and Bregan began to sprint as Thaniel fired arrows into the incoming red-eyed fiends.

"I'll meet you at the air balloon tower," Thaniel said.

"Bring me his head. It will be a nice addition to the skulls that line the Brooding Bridge," Lord Argentwald said. He turned back to the door of the symphony hall as he motioned for more members of his court to join the fray against Thaniel.

Rhys looked back to see a cloud of ash before Thaniel as he swiftly let loose arrow after arrow into the crowd of red eyes.

"I'm so tired," Bregan said.

"I know, I am too. We have to keep moving, don't stop, okay?" Rhys replied.

Bregan nodded as they both continued to sprint down the dirt road with heavy breath entering and leaving their lungs. Thaniel started to run back toward Rhys and Bregan while looking back and releasing an arrow into the incoming pale-skinned faces that neared him.

"Kill him already," one of the court members said.

Thaniel turned right and away from the direction that Rhys and Bregan were heading so that they would follow him instead of them. As he ran, he noticed the familiar long white hair and seductive face of Seranda crossing the street in the distance. His heart sank as he noticed her. He knew that he wouldn't be able to bring himself to release an arrow in her direction. He made another turn down an alley to avoid her.

She looked over to see the crowd of her pale-skinned comrades rushing into the alleyway but saw no sign of Thaniel. As Thaniel sprinted down the alleyway, he could hear the court members gaining on him. He turned to fire an arrow into them, and as he did, he tripped on a root growing out of the ground and fell onto his stomach, dropping his bow.

As the court members caught up to him, he grabbed the bow, and before a blade could reach his chest, he pulled the bow in front of him as it abruptly transformed into a shield. Multiple blades fell upon the shield as Thaniel held it with his right hand and used his left to drag his body weight back.

"There's no room to get around. This alley is too small," one of the court members said.

"Then crawl over this damn shield of his," another member said.

Thaniel struggled to stand up on his feet, and as one of the member's bodies fell on top of his shield in an attempt to crawl over it, Thaniel felt himself become surrounded and overwhelmed by the members of the court.

"Look out behind us," one of the court members said.

Thaniel looked up to see the foaming mouth of a fiend looking down at him from above the shield. As the fiend went to lower its sword into Thaniel's face, it was pierced through the chest by a spear-like blade. The fiend dropped its sword and collapsed on top of the shield as Thaniel pushed it off and stood up with the shield handle gripped by both hands.

He looked down the alley to see Rhys standing at the end with Lightfang transformed into a spear. He looked down at the snowy ground of the alleyway to see that Rhys had skewered all of fiends from behind.

"I guess you can say we're even now," Thaniel said breathlessly.

"Aye, now come on, we've got to move," Rhys replied.

Thaniel rushed down the alley after Rhys as he saw him take off, running back toward the road he was on previously with Bregan.

As Thaniel caught up to Rhys, they both turned the corner to find Bregan sitting and panting against a wall. Rhys looked down the road to the tower where the hot air balloon was grounded. As he gazed down the filthy road that stretched out before him, he could see the whole village of Prosperwood burning as smoke filled the air. Memories of his home that he shared with his uncle Farbris filled his mind as Thaniel tried to get his attention.

"Where are we going now?" Thaniel asked.

Rhys pointed to the colorful hot air balloon that danced with the winter winds in the distance.

Chapter Thirty-Nine

Vred stood watch at the bottom of the stairs that led up to the tower where the hot air balloon basket sat. The Arsonist was at the top, pointing out and showing Gabby the violence and fire spreading through the entire village. The recent events had convinced her to come around, despite the suggested maximum weight concerns she had. She began to make preparations for them to depart from Prosperwood.

Farbris made his way down the stairs to check on Vred and Bregan. As he arrived at the bottom, he only found Vred, who was fixated on a small battle happening down the street.

"Where is my son?" Farbris asked.

The words of Farbris startled Vred, who leaped back with his sword in his hand.

"He said he had to go to the bathroom, and he didn't want to do it near me, so I let him go behind the building over there," Vred said.

"You let my teenage son go to the bathroom by himself. In the middle of this chaos?" Farbris replied.

"I wasn't going to follow him and watch him do it," Vred said, confused by the question as if Farbris had just answered it himself.

"Well, how long has he been gone?" Farbris replied.

"Ten minutes, give or take?" Vred replied.

Farbris' eyes lit up like fireworks in a dark brown sky. "Ten minutes give or take?" he said.

"Aye, is that not normal?" Vred replied.

"To take a piss? Aye, it is," Farbris replied.

"I had no idea it was that one," Vred replied.

Both the men took turns huffing and shaking their heads in confusing disappointment with one another. As the Arsonist arrived down stairs, he noticed the tension between them, "Is everything alright?" he asked.

"No, Bregan is gone," Farbris replied.

"Vred, where did he go?" the Arsonist asked.

"He told me he was going to the bathroom real quick, and then he never came back," Vred replied. He leaned against the tower's wooden frame and cupped his hands against his face before dragging them out and stretching his cheeks downward, "I'm so sorry Farbris. I had no idea that he would just take off like that," he said.

"Wait until you have your own kids someday. You'll learn pretty quickly," Farbris replied.

"Well, Gabby says we should be good to go within the next twenty to thirty minutes. I really hope the others arrive soon because she doesn't plan to stick around much longer than that estimated departure time," the Arsonist said.

Vred watched as the skirmish down the road ended in red-eyed fiend victory, "I hope she doesn't draw any attention to us. I'd like to keep my blade dry before we leave if possible," he said.

The Arsonist placed his hand on Vred's shoulder and patted him gently, "I hope so, too," he said.

Farbris went up the stairs to see if Gabby required any assistance.

"Is he going to be alright?" Vred asked.

"Yes, he's just a worried father, that's all," the Arsonist replied.

A subtle and slight shaking in the ground caught the attention of both Vred and the Arsonist as they looked down the road to see a large battalion of soldiers marching behind a grey armored horse.

"Who are they?" Vred asked.

"Judging by their banners, I'd say they're a northern army," the Arsonist replied.

"Friend or foe?" Vred asked.

"If I had to guess, I'd say neither, if that makes any sense," the Arsonist replied.

"Not really, but if they're not a friend of yours, then they're a foe of mine," Vred replied.

The Arsonist smiled from behind his mask as he made his way back up the stairs.

***

Located on the other side of the northern battalion was a pile of debris made up of old broken-down crates and barrels. Crouching behind it were Rhys, Bregan, and Thaniel. The three young men squatted behind the rubble as they watched the battalion moving through the filthy dirt road.

"How are we going to get to the tower? I have a feeling that these soldiers aren't friendly and will kill us on sight," Bregan said.

"I know them. That man on the horse is my uncle Nielas, I can speak with him, and he will grant us safe passage," Thaniel said.

"Well, go up and have a word with him then, and we'll wait back here," Rhys said. Thaniel swallowed the lump in his throat and nodded his head as he built up his inner confidence.

"Alright, you two hang back here and wait for me to signal you to come forth," Thaniel said.

As Thaniel departed from the tall rubble pile and made his way up toward the back of the battalion, Bregan used this moment to tap on Rhys' shoulder to get his attention.

"What is it?' Rhys asked.

"I have a bad feeling about all of this. I think we should go around and take a slight detour. If those soldiers end up being hostile, we might be too far for their arrows to hit us," Bregan replied.

"I think we're better off waiting here until the coast is clear," Rhys said.

Bregan shook his head in disagreement as he leaned back against an old potato crate. As Thaniel got closer, he caught a glimpse of the blonde hair and curvy body that belonged to his cousin Lylah. She was holding onto his uncle Nielas on the grey horse.

"Lylah, Uncle Nielas, it's me, Thaniel."

Before Lylah could turn around to see and say something, a row of guards with spears and crossbows now blocked her vision and was focusing their attention on Thaniel, who stood still with his hands up in the air.

"Drop the weapon," one of the guards said.

Thaniel slowly lowered his torso toward the ground as he gently let go of the bow from his hands and onto the dirt below.

"I'm the nephew of your captain," Thaniel said.

Nielas motioned his horse to break ranks and head to the rear line. He wanted to investigate what the commotion was all about. As he arrived in the far back line, he noticed the hooded and mouth-covered Thaniel standing still with his hands up in the air declaring his state of surrender. He noticed the shining metal of Arrowguard at Thaniel's feet. Nielas' grey eyes gleamed like moonlight struggling to shine through smoke. "Where did you find this bow?" he asked.

"Uncle, it's me. It's your nephew Thaniel."

"I have no nephew, at least not one with red eyes like yours. You're lucky that I don't have you executed right now. I will spare your blood-sucking life this once for bringing me this bow. Now flee this scene before I have you skewered by one of my spearmen," Nielas replied.

Thaniel was shocked at what Nielas was saying to him, and he froze in fear as he watched a heavily armed soldier wielding a crossbow approach him to pick up the bow. Lylah did not recognize the man who claimed to be her cousin, but she recognized his voice.

"Your mercy will not be forgotten," Thaniel said.

The soldier retrieved the bow and brought it to Nielas as the rear force returned to its standard marching ranks. Nielas, now wielding the bow in his right hand while managing his horse reins with the left, motioned his horse to move forward in an effort to return to the front line of his battalion.

"Father, I think he was telling the truth," Lylah said.

"Whether he or not does not matter. Did you not see his eyes? He is gone," Nielas replied.

Lylah nodded in agreement but felt a sinking feeling in her heart as her brain registered the cold truth in Nielas' words.

Thaniel lowered his hands as the battalion continued to move forward. He could feel Rhys motioning to him from back at the debris pile. As Thaniel turned to walk back to the debris pile in defeat, his covered face looked troubled as he neared Rhys.

"Where did Bregan go?" Thaniel asked.

"What do you mean?" Rhys replied.

They both looked around and noticed he was gone. Rhys' heart began to race as he looked around in a crazed panic, "Bregan!" he called.

Rhys got no reply no matter how many times he shouted, asking for the whereabouts of his cousin Bregan. Thaniel motioned Rhys to follow him around the nearby curving road as it would cut through the village houses and be a slight detour toward the tower where the hot air balloon was grounded.

As they raced through the winding maze of an alleyway, they could suddenly hear the cackling laughter and heavy footsteps coming from somewhere near the alleyway exit point. As they arrived at the end of the alleyway, Thaniel slowly peeked his head out. Around the corner he could see a large group of black hooded and pale-skinned men and women coming from the street to the left of the wooden tower where the hot air balloon was grounded.

The battalion was slowly marching from the southern part of the street that the alleyway poured out into. The tower they needed to get to was in the middle of the two incoming forces, and Thaniel knew that they were about to be in the middle of a messy skirmish if they didn't move quickly.

The tower was still far away, but as Thaniel looked closely, he could see Bregan running down the street toward it. Rhys peeked his head around to see Bregan. Immediately after seeing him, he took off out of the alleyway toward him.

"Bregan!" Rhys cried.

Bregan looked back to see Rhys but continued running toward the wooden tower in the distance.

Thaniel hesitated to peek out at the fear of being fired upon by the incoming battalion. After mustering up enough courage, he darted toward the direction of Rhys and Bregan. He was immediately intercepted by Oliver, and a handful of other pale-skinned men.

"Where are you going? You're going to miss the grand finale," Oliver said.

"I was just looking for my horse," Thaniel replied.

"You won't need it. We're about to start shackling prisoners and marching them out to the Manor. Dripping them dry will be a delight," Oliver replied.

Thaniel nodded in agreement as he fell into ranks with the other red-eyed men and women that were heavily armed.

"Hey, what happened to your bow?" Oliver asked.

"It was on my horse, and when I got knocked off of it by a guard, it went riding wild into the street with it," Thaniel replied.

"Ah, I see. Well, here, have this sword," Oliver replied. He unsheathed one of the many swords he had tied to his back and handed it to Thaniel, who quickly accepted it with a tight grip on the ebony hilt.

"You're not so bad after all, ranger," Oliver said.

"Thanks, I guess," Thaniel replied.

The red-eyed fiends came to a halt as they turned the corner and saw the battalion marching toward them. Nielas motioned his men to also come to a halt and asked Lylah to dismount off his grey horse.

As the battalion stopped their march, Nielas left behind Lylah and proceeded to ride ahead. Lord Argentwald broke through the dark hooded ranks on horseback and proceeded ahead to meet Nielas on the road between both armies. Thaniel adjusted his scarf in hopes that Lord Argentwald and anyone else that knew of his treachery would not notice him in the formation.

***

As Bregan came running down the street, Vred could see him with Rhys trailing far behind him. He hurried up the stairs to let the Arsonist and Farbris know. The Arsonist could already see them on the road in the distance before Vred arrived to notify him, but as the Arsonist gazed down the road at Rhys and Bregan, his heart grew heavy.

His porcelain mask was now concealing a somber look of hopelessness as he watched the black fur-covered body of the wolf creature leaping from thatch roof to roof as it pursued Bregan like a looming cloud of death.

"Do you see that? Is that what I think it is?" Farbris asked.

The Arsonist could not hesitate any longer. He looked down the side of the tower to see a thatch roof only six feet below the platform he was standing on. He looked around to see all of the house's thatch roofs that were not very far apart. He knew he could intercept the wolf creature faster if he traveled similarly to the way it was. He began to remove the heavy metal flamethrower gauntlets from his hands as he knew they would offset his balance and weigh him down. They each made a loud thud sound as they hit the wooden deck at his feet.

The Arsonist turned to look at Vred as he removed his large belt that carried the flintlock rounds and flamethrower gauntlet fuel vials.

"Vred, make sure Gabby is ready to go. We are departing as soon as they get up these stairs," the Arsonist said.

Vred nodded but struggled to say anything in return as he picked up the gauntlets and belt and carried them into the balloon basket. The Arsonist leaped over the wooden railing of the tower and down onto the thatch roof below. He looked ahead and began to sprint and jump from thatch roof to roof with his flintlock pistol in his right hand.

***

Rhys, who was far behind Bregan, looked upward to his left to see the wolf creature leaping from roof to roof with its hunting gaze cast down on Bregan.

"Bregan, stop," Rhys said.

Bregan came to a swift halt as he turned around to see what Rhys was yelling about. The Arsonist was moving with incredible momentum in the distance as he leaped from rooftop to rooftop, heading in the wolf creature's direction. The wolf-like creature's blood-red eyes could not see the Arsonist approaching them since they were fixated on Bregan down below.

As the Arsonist got close enough to open fire on the beast, he came to a halt three roofs away from the creature and aimed at it with his pistol. The beast leaped off the roof toward Bregan as the Arsonist pulled the trigger.

"Come here!" Rhys yelled.

Before Bregan could decide to run to Rhys, the creature tackled him. Its wolf-like claws had dug into Bregan's spine and chest as it collided with him with all of its body weight.

"No!" Rhys wailed. The piercing scream released from his lungs could not match the outcry that came from Farbris, who was at the top of the wooden tower on the other side of the street.

The Arsonist couldn't even bring himself to blink; he was furious. The beast began to dig its fangs into the body to feast upon its fresh kill, and as it did, Rhys began to charge toward it with his sword drawn. The beast noticed the incoming attack and leaped over Rhys, whose momentum betrayed him as he stumbled over Bregan's body and fell to the ground.

As the wolf landed on the ground, it turned around to see Rhys lying on the floor. He had cut open his knee on the road and was gripping it as he let out a painful cry. The beast let out a fierce howl, and as it fixed its vicious gaze upon Rhys, it looked up to see the Arsonist standing behind him.

The Arsonist dug his hand into his pocket to grab one extra round he had brought. He quickly reloaded the pistol before aiming it at the beast. The beast's charge was stopped by the sounds of cackling laughter and taunting battle cries coming from behind it.

The beast turned its neck to look back and see both the dark hooded fiends and heavy armored northern battalion marching toward them.

"Can you walk?" the Arsonist asked.

"Yes, it just really hurts," Rhys replied.

The Arsonist handed the pistol to Rhys, whose grey eyes squinted in confusion. "Take this. You might need it. I loaded one round into it. If you get intercepted, it might be best to take your own life with it," he said.

"Why are you giving me this?" Rhys asked.

The Arsonist helped Rhys stand up. Then he reached down to pick up Lightfang lying in the snow nearby. "Because I'm taking this," he said.

Rhys started to laugh, but his transient happiness was interrupted by an abrupt cough that forcefully arrived in his throat.

"I'm going to buy you some time. This bastard and I have some unfinished business to settle between us," the Arsonist said.

"I'll see you back at the balloon," Rhys replied.

The Arsonist did not respond as he gripped the sword with both hands and pointed it out in front of him. The wolf-like creature turned its attention away from the incoming crowd and back toward the Arsonist as it snarled. Rhys shoved the pistol down into the waistband of his pants before picking up Bregan. As he limped toward the hot air balloon in the distance, he could see Vred holding his uncle, whose angry sobbing cries deafened all nearby ears.

Lylah stood in front of the heavily armed battalion and could see the back of the hairy black wolf creature standing before the Arsonist on its hind legs. Thaniel stood in the middle of the red-eyed fiends and could barely see the beast. Nielas rode in front of the two armed groups while Lord Argentwald rode alongside him on a similar-looking grey horse. The body of armed people came to a uniformed halt as they approached the wolf-like creature from behind.

The Arsonist could see the army behind the wolf creature, but he did not care. As the creature lowered itself to the ground, it began to growl and creep forward on all fours. The Arsonist continued to grip the sword in front of him with both hands. He remained calm as the distance between him and the beast shrank. He took a deep breath behind his porcelain mask, and then with the sword raised above his head with both hands, he charged forward toward the beast. As the beast charged forward to meet him, it lunged into the air to avoid the sword from being brought down to meet its fur-covered flesh.

The Arsonist suddenly lost control of his body. He leaned back and pushed the sword above his head with both hands as he dug his heels into the snow. As he slid with the snow underneath the wolf, the sword's blade extended outward like a spear and sliced through the leaping wolf that had lunged itself overhead.

As he collapsed on the ground on his back, he watched the wolf fly above his head in two halves. He exhaled deeply and stood up while still gripping the sword.

The Arsonist looked down upon the beast that he had just sliced in two and felt a surge of relief wash over his mind. The triumph escalated when he heard the voice of a familiar woman calling his real name from behind him. As he turned around to confirm where the familiar voice was coming from, he felt a dagger enter his chest.

Seranda let go of the dagger and stepped back away from him. The Arsonist couldn't believe it. His fiery red eyes widened in disbelief as he stood expressionless, speechless, and confused. He slowly blinked behind his mask as he looked down at the dagger sticking out of his chest.

He could feel his body begin to shut down as he let go of the sword and fell back into the snowy cobblestone road. His eyes closed behind his porcelain mask as he softly exhaled and faded away.

Chapter Forty

Lylah and Thaniel could not believe what they were seeing as they stood conflicted in their respective crowds with both awe and sadness. Seranda kneeled next to the body of the Arsonist while Nielas and Lord Argentwald approached her on horseback.

"You did well tonight, Seranda," Lord Argentwald said.

"Thank you, my lord," she replied, wiping the lone tear from her cheek as she stood up and smiled at him.

"Do not be so sad, child. I will not punish you for your past treacheries. You have redeemed yourself tonight and shall remain safely in my court."

"Thank you."

Lord Argentwald leaned down from his horse with his ringed fingers extended to Seranda. She kissed the large ring on his middle finger before walking away to sit on a crate outside one of the nearby houses. Nielas dismounted from his horse and walked over to the Arsonist's body to examine him. He recognized the porcelain mask immediately. Memories of both Marathair and Alarick began to flood his mind.

"Is something wrong?" Lord Argentwald asked.

Nielas returned to reality at the sound of Lord Argentwald's voice, "yes, I'm fine," he said, picking up the sword and scabbard, "It would seem that I now have everything that I came here for."

"Good, now, I expect you to get on that ferry and head back across the river to that frigid wasteland you call home. Never return here again without Zersten's approval," Lord Argentwald replied.

Nielas nodded his head in compliance as he mounted his horse, "I don't plan to return, and I appreciate your willingness to work together through these harsh times," he said.

"Yes, and as Zersten appreciates your cooperation, I too appreciate your ability to recognize a great ruler of the West when you see one," Lord Argentwald replied.

"Of course," Nielas replied, joining his battalion. He had Lylah rejoin him on his horse as they moved as a unit out north toward the docks where the ferry was. Lord Argentwald noticed Rhys limping up the wooden stairs in the distance and ordered his red-eyed fiends behind him to move forward to the tower and destroy the red, yellow, and blue color striped balloon that floated above it.

Thaniel, realizing that now was his moment to slip away while they were all distracted, fell back into the ranks before falling out into a nearby alleyway. Seranda watched intensely as the court brushed past her.

"I didn't think you had it in you," Victoyos said. He chuckled as he unsheathed his blade and fell into the crowd of bloodthirsty fiends that began to rush toward the wooden tower in the distance. Seranda wept as she stood up and walked toward the body of the Arsonist. As she kneeled beside him, she grabbed and held his hand.

***

Vred rushed down from the top of the stairs to help Rhys carry Bregan's body up to the balloon basket. As he helped carry Bregan and Rhys up the stairs, they met Farbris and Gabby in the basket.

"Gabby, we need to go. They're coming," Vred said.

Gabby closed the wooden door to the basket behind them as she blasted the burner flame into the envelope mouth. Within seconds the balloon lifted off the ground and started slowly soaring away. She now stood behind the helm, and as she steered it away from the Argentwald Manor that lay east, everyone in the basket could feel things slowly turning right. The hot-air balloon was navigated by a helm-connected mechanism, and it was very slow at turning despite its moderate traveling speed.

"What if they hit the balloon with a crossbow bolt?" Vred

asked.

"Let's hope that doesn't happen," Gabby replied. She laughed as Vred crouched low in the basket with his hands on his head. Her light brown eyes flickered with excitement behind the dark-tinted lenses of the goggles she was now wearing.

"I'm usually not one for praying, but in this case, I might just make an exception," Vred said.

Rhys hugged Farbris, who wailed as he held the lifeless remains of his son Bregan. The sun had risen, and its light spread across the crisp winter sky. When the red-eyed fiends finally arrived atop the wooden tower, the hot air balloon was already high in the clouds.

"They look like ants from here," Gabby said.

Rhys refused to look over the edge down at the amber leaf-colored trees due to his crippling fear of heights. Farbris endlessly wept over the loss of his son as Vred calmly sat beside Rhys, whose eyes were closed in quiet contemplation.

"So, where are we headed now?" Vred asked.

"Where do you want to go?" Gabby asked.

Rhys' grey eyes slowly opened to see Farbris, Vred, and Gabby looking at him while patiently awaiting a response, "take us to the Southern Wastes," he said.

"Aye," Gabby replied.

The hot air balloon steadily floated high above the snow-covered glades of the West as sunlight peered out from behind its red, yellow, and blue stripes. Rhys sat on the floor leaning against the willow cane-weaved wall while holding the flintlock pistol and flamethrower gauntlets on his lap. As he studied them carefully, he pondered the Arsonist's actions. He knew the losses that he and his uncle had suffered were great, but he couldn't help but feel the light of Deliverance pulling them South.

Tyler Kirk

Book 2 coming soon...